Copyright
Cover Design by AprilVolition

Chapter 1

When the hunters first rolled into town, Nix was wearing a nine-year-old named Callie.

She was a cute little thing with flaxen pigtails and pink Minnie Mouse barrettes. Middle class, white-collar family, very low-key. The kid loved to play with porcelain dolls, and she went with her mommy and her aunt to church every Sunday—or she used to, anyway. Nix didn't have the patience for shit like that, and her cover wasn't so important that she couldn't risk blowing it once in a while. Or so she'd thought.

In hindsight, stabbing Aunty Ida in the gut with gardening shears might have been what caught the attention of those hunters in the first place. But the woman was such an obnoxious old bitch, Nix could hardly be blamed for that little slip up. Kid was better off this way.

Nix watched the hunters drive up to the Sonora police station in their rusted piece-of-shit Ford. When they got out, they were surprisingly clean cut and well dressed. Like they were fooling anybody. She could see the gun rack in the back of their vehicle—this was *California*, not Texas. They stood out, even in the middle of nowhere.

Nix had been in the game a long time, she knew what to look for. Unfortunately, chances were good that they did too.

Callie's mother came up behind the swing and gave her daughter a gentle push, lifting Nix up just high enough that she could get a clear view over the bushes on every upswing.

There were three of them. A weathered old man led a twenty-something boy into the station. The boy's suit was ash gray, the man's a charred black. They were no doubt impersonating some high-end law enforcement. Feds, probably. Nix scoffed.

A girl was sitting in the cab of the truck, waiting, her head bent over something in her lap. Still too young to pass as a federal agent. The old guy might be a problem—weren't they always?—but all in all, the lot of them didn't look particularly competent.

Nix could almost make out their license plate from here, if she could just—

The swing stilled with a weary screech and Nix looked up to see Callie's mother with her hands on the steel chains, holding Nix in place.

"Time to go, Callie," Mother Dearest said.

The woman never missed an opportunity to get in Nix's way. "I'm busy," Nix told her. "Leave me alone."

Mother's pencil-drawn eyebrows rose and her mouth opened, lips red and spotted pink where the lipstick had worn away. In her most grating voice, Mother started in on her usual lecture, saying, "Excuse me? Now, I know things have been rough lately, but that attitude of yours, young lady, isn't—"

Nix's patience dried up like the woman's prematurely wrinkled face. Mother had behaved for a while, but Nix could tell she was about to start pushing at those boundaries again. If Nix didn't discipline her, she'd never learn.

"Listen, you stupid bitch, back off or I'll do to you what I did to Aunty Ida." Nix was aware that the syrupy-sweet little girl voice wasn't lending her threats any credibility, but that didn't make her any less serious.

Children chattered around them, crawling over the slides and monkey bars, soaking up the bright sunshine. A gust of wind swept through the playground, carrying their giggles and shouts, distorting the noise. No one tried to sit near Nix.

Mother gawked stupidly. "Wha—what did you just...?"

Nix rolled Callie's baby blues. If the hunters were here for her, she'd deal with them when the time came. Otherwise, she'd just have to stay under the radar until the storm passed. No sense in losing a perfectly good setup if it wasn't necessary. So long as this year's archnemesis didn't catch wind of her location, Nix was in the clear—honestly, drive one Mercedes off a cliff and you never hear the end of it.

Ah, well.

Nix jumped off the swing in a fit of exuberance. "Mommy! Mommy! Can we get ice cream? Please please please?"

It was enough to distract the woman temporarily. And Nix *did* love ice cream. Being nine really had its benefits. Kids had always been her favorite style. They usually came with a fleet of servants at their beck and call, and ample resources—secondhand, but still. And best of all, whenever she got caught with blood on her hands, adults would dote all over her with their concerned and earnest expressions. They'd give her crayons and ask, "Oh honey, are you all right? Did someone hurt you? Now, just tell the nice officers what the scary man looked like, okay?"

The adults were almost as adorably naive as the kids. And this one, little Callie, she was Nix's new favorite. The others always screamed and cried and kicked up a fuss inside their heads. But Callie? Nix opened up Aunty Ida in the sunroom over iced tea and oatmeal cookies, and Callie complained that she was missing her cartoons.

Kid was a natural, a real charmer. Nix didn't want to give her up so soon, but with these idiots in town...well, she could always kill them, she supposed. That would have to be enough reassurance for the time being.

The old guy turned before the door to the station closed, his gaze meeting hers across the road. He held her eyes and Nix held his. Then he looked away and the moment passed.

Nix took Mother's trembling hand and smiled up at her.

Chapter 2

The hunters moved fast.

Less than a day passed before they were knocking on Callie's front door and suddenly the girl from the truck was standing in the doorway of the kitchen, ten short steps away.

Immediately, Nix was ready to fight, to flee, to do whatever needed to be done. She dropped the red crayon in Callie's hand, letting it roll off the table and to the cracking linoleum floor, waiting for the hunter to make the first move.

Far from the guns-blazing entrance Nix was expecting, the girl simply walked up to the table with a friendly smile and stooped to retrieve the fallen crayon. The swinging door whooshed closed behind her.

"What are you drawing?" the girl asked, all good humor and ease.

"Who are *you*?" Nix countered in Callie's sugar-coated voice.

The girl chuckled, like this was cute and funny and there was no potential for a battle to the death between them in the next thirty seconds. "My name's Rachel," she said. "You're Callie, right?"

Nix nodded as Rachel pulled out a chair next to her and sat in it without invitation.

Sunlight slipped through the blinds and splayed over the blue countertop where fourteen fresh apple pies were cooling on wire racks, some stacked on top of each other, some balanced precariously on the stove, and a solitary one set in an opened cupboard for lack of anywhere better to place it. Nix liked apple pie.

Mother liked being alive. They had a mutually beneficial arrangement going on and were both quite happy with it. Nix wouldn't let these hunters ruin things for them.

Nix scrutinized the girl and considered the likelihood that this was all some elaborate trap, a ruse, and Nix was momentarily offended at their assessment of her intelligence. But Rachel wasn't forcing holy water down her throat or whipping a bible out, so it seemed more likely that *they* were the stupid ones here.

Nix could hear voices in the other room, just barely rising above the din from the construction site down the street. Two men and Callie's mother chatted in hushed tones in the living room. Nix was surrounded. By idiots, apparently, but surrounded nonetheless.

Rachel pointed one ragged nail at the sheet of paper on the table and said, "I heard about what happened to your aunt. That must have been really scary."

Nix glanced down at the paper. For the first time, she noticed the streaks of red crayon blood and the corresponding pool of crimson. A stick-figure woman lay in the center. Her dress had blue and yellow flowers on it and she wasn't wearing any shoes. It was cheerful and lovingly crafted with clean lines and pretty colors and no real attempt at depth or realism. More Picasso than Rembrandt. Mother would love it—there was definite fridge potential here.

Nix caught the hunter's green eyes and flipped the paper over. Her lighthearted Sunday-morning dalliance with Callie's art set was starting to look like a bad decision.

Rachel put her hand on Callie's and squeezed a little. After a tense moment of confusion, Nix discreetly pulled away and tucked Callie's hands into her lap. Some people had no concept of personal space.

"It's okay," Rachel said. "I saw some scary things when I was little, too, and I used to draw them sometimes. It can help to put the pictures in your head on paper. Makes them a tiny bit less scary that way, don't you think?" She turned the paper back over and pursed her lips. "Your mom said you were there when it happened. Do you remember seeing anything strange before your aunt fell down?"

Nix shook Callie's head. Something about this girl was oddly familiar, but Nix couldn't quite place her. The voices in the other room were still whispering, conspiring. The more they found out about Ida's little accident, the more likely Callie would pop up as a prime suspect. It was only a matter of time now that these hunters had caught her scent. Though she was confident by this point that Mother Dearest was no tattletale, humans could be unpredictable when they were driven by fear.

"You sure?" Rachel looked pensive, like she was contemplating some clever child-therapy methods of extracting information. Any moment now, she'd be pulling out dolls and initiating a miniature reenactment. Nix hated it when they brought out the dolls. There was always the awkward *'Where did the bad man hurt you?'* questioning period, when in reality it was quite the other way around.

Nix could run, but she liked it here. Here was safe; an oasis in a dangerous and bloodthirsty desert. And she wasn't about to concede her territory to a bunch of rednecks with Chuck Norris complexes. She would just have to find a way to get rid of them.

Nix's first impulse had Callie's hands twitching for the blunt craft scissors before she quelled it. Callie gave a cute little sigh of disappointment deep inside her own head, which Nix ignored. As unimpressive as they seemed, there was still something about these hunters that gave Nix pause. She had a feeling about them, and not a good one.

She wondered how much they already knew, who they'd shared their suspicions with, how many degrees of separation they had from the enemies still gunning for her head on a pike. Conundrums. This time, Nix let Callie's sigh into daylight.

Then it occurred to her that there *was* one surefire way to find out.

Nix grinned inwardly while her borrowed face frowned and she worried Callie's bottom lip between her teeth. "Can I tell you a secret?" Nix stage-whispered.

Rachel's eyes lit up. "Of course."

"Promise you won't tell my mom?"

"Promise," Rachel agreed. A second's hesitation on Nix's part had her crossing her chest solemnly and adding, "Cross my heart and hope to die."

Nix leaned close to breathe into her ear, "When I'm done with you, you'll wish I'd just stabbed you with gardening shears like Aunty Ida."

Rachel gasped, but that only made it easier to slide in.

Nix was already pulling her on, slipping under that creamy, smooth skin and behind those vivid, green eyes. She squirmed around until she'd found a good fit, until the angles and curves were snug like a well-tailored suit. It wasn't a perfect fit—it never was—but it was close enough.

She felt Rachel's heart thundering in her ribcage, and it was *her* heart. She felt Rachel's dark curls tickling against her neck, and they were *her* curls. Rachel's lungs expanded in a long inhale, sucking in the apple-pie air, and they were Nix's lungs now.

Nix smirked and Rachel's lips quirked up at the corners. She stood, body pulling and bending and stretching at Nix's command like one of Callie's marionette dolls.

Nix blew a kiss to her sweet little hostess, now slumped in her chair and fast asleep.

"Be a good girl," she told Callie. "I'll be home soon."

Chapter 3

The old guy's name was Daniel Whipsaw, but Rachel knew him as 'Danny'—or 'Pops' when she was feeling especially fond of the man. He looked at Nix, at Rachel, across the checkered table in Ember's Diner for a long moment, his eyes unreadable.

Nix restrained from fidgeting under his scrutiny while Rachel screamed and screamed and *screamed* inside her head.

Finally, Danny said, "Ice cream for lunch?"

Nix hesitated, then nodded and plastered on a convincing smile while shoveling another scoop of chocolate vanilla swirl into Rachel's mouth.

"Yeah," the boy, Elliot, said. "Thought you were on a health kick, Rach."

A little chill ran up Rachel's spine when Elliot said her name. He smiled at her affectionately and nudged her foot with his own under the table.

She shrugged Rachel's shoulders and licked the ice cream from her lips while watching Elliot watch her. "Nothing wrong with indulging once in a while, right?"

Elliot smiled awkwardly, silent.

Danny grunted noncommittally, stabbing his fork into a piece of meat. His cell phone buzzed and he pulled it out, glancing at the screen with a nod and setting the phone on the table. "So, the kid?" he asked.

Nix stilled, realizing he was probably talking about Callie, and Rachel's little undercover FBI-intern thing she was doing back at the house. "What about the kid?"

His voice was impatient as he clarified, "What did you find out?"

"Oh," Nix said, sloshing melted ice cream around in her bowl with a spoon, "nothing."

"Nothing?" Danny repeated.

"Yep, nothing." Both hunters were staring at her now, so Nix added by way of explanation, "She was pretty traumatized by the whole thing, obviously. Real upset about it. I couldn't get much out of her, but she didn't remember seeing anything...*strange*—and I *did* ask. Maybe it was just an accident, after all. Like the papers said."

"*Pfft*," Danny scoffed. "Accident. Like hell that was an accident." Another slice of bacon saw the business-end of his fork. The phone buzzed again and the name *Joan* flashed on the screen. Danny checked it, continuing distractedly, "Four bodies are what I'd call a *pattern*. There's definitely something going on in this town."

Four? Nix mentally reviewed her current body count, but nope, she'd only been here a short while and Ida was the first fucker to push little Callie too far. No, really. She'd been careful this time around. She had the whole low-profile thing down to an art most days, but staying in one place for too long made the insects come out of the woodwork.

Nix offered a vague sound of agreement. Her body count coming up short suggested that something else was indeed going on in this town. She hadn't noticed any breach of her territory, so it couldn't be one of her kind. Whatever it was, there was no way in hell Nix was taking the fall for it. That would just be unfair.

Elliot threw her a conspiratorial glance and smirked while cutting up his food into bite-sized squares. He turned to Danny and commented good-naturedly, "You think something is happening in every town, Pops."

Another noncommittal grunt. Danny was a man of few words, it seemed. He shoveled food into his mouth like they were facing a famine, while absently fingering the silver pendant around his neck.

Nix didn't recognize the symbol, but even from across the table she could feel its power. It had the markings of a protective charm, probably an anti-possession amulet. It would figure. Hunters were so paranoid about that.

She had heard of Daniel Whipsaw in passing; whispers here and there from friends and enemies alike. He was known for keeping company with a hunter named Rousoe, a man whose collection of supernaturally enhanced weapons was much sought after in certain circles.

Whipsaw, though, he was something of a celebrity himself. Admittedly, a celebrity that Nix had barely heard of before she started rummaging through Rachel's memories, but legend had it that he once slaughtered an entire nest of vamps in Illinois with nothing but a broken machete and a git-'er-done attitude. The only werewolf to ever escape his grasp had limped to safety with a broken leg and one eye gouged out, and now they called the poor bastard *Lucky*.

Daniel was a tank with the strength of three men, an expertly trained former navy seal, and a heartless son of a bitch with more killer instinct than your average rabid bear, Rachel instructed Nix, having moved on from rage to threats.

"He's exorcised worse shit than you, bitch!" Rachel hissed, furious at Nix's amusement.

And to think that Nix was having lunch with him, completely and utterly under his radar.

In person, he wasn't as intimidating as Nix would have expected. Particularly not with Rachel's memories fluttering about in her head: Pops teaching her how to ride a pink two-wheeler, showing her how to fieldstrip her weapons, patching up her scraped knees. The man was all soft and squishy on the inside, regardless of

Rachel's protests to the contrary.

There were memories of Elliot in there as well. Lots of them. The boy had just returned from a two-year stint in the army, and he looked like it, too. His hair was still short and cut with military precision, and judging by his posture, Nix was fairly certain there was a stick up his ass.

None of these hunters were related but there was no doubt they were family. Like a patchwork quilt. Daddy, big brother, little sister, it was fucking adorable. Nix was going to have fun with this.

Nix leaned back and dropped her spoon into the bowl with a note of finality that a bowl of ice cream didn't really deserve.

It was no secret that Nix had a certain fondness for humans. In fact, she kind of loved them. She loved them in the way she would love a stray dog with three legs, or the runt in a litter of abandoned kittens. They were just so damn cute and helpless, how could she not? So when she put them out of their—or more frequently, *her*—misery, it was a kindness, really.

And with these hunters, Nix was feeling especially kind.

Chapter 4

It was an hour later when Nix was finally alone, dropped off at a cheap motel on the outskirts of Jamestown to continue 'researching' while the boys went on their merry way in the truck to do the fun work.

It was here that Nix was able to pay attention to her host for the first time, on the condition that the girl shut the ever-loving-fuck up for five minutes and stop with the shouting. Eventually she would run out of steam and calm down, but Nix generally didn't care to keep her hosts gagged or sedated. She liked the company, so sue her.

"Hello, Rachel."

An instant of shock, the silence almost as deafening as the shouting, and then Rachel cursed Nix in English, Italian, German, and Latin. Rachel wasn't even fluent in German or Italian, but she knew enough to throw around some *very* dirty words. She even tried to sneak in some obscure exorcism chant, but in her current position, that was just laughable.

"They're going to notice," Rachel prattled, once she'd finished repeating 'cast thee out' in frankly terrible Latin. *"And then they're going to kill you. You have no idea who you're messing with here."*

Nix pulled Rachel's hair free of its ponytail and fluffed it up a bit in the mirror. "Don't be trite," Nix told her. "That's what they always say. Blah, blah, 'my friends are going to rip you apart,' and so on. Gets old after a while. You know, you have such nice hair. It's perplexing that you don't do anything with it."

"They won't let you get away with this."

Nix stared at her new face in the mirror, assessing its features, wondering if it was a lack of knowledge of modern beauty norms on Rachel's part that kept her from fully realizing her own potential or if she simply didn't give a fuck. Didn't she know how to play the part? "And with a bit of makeup and a new wardrobe, you might even pass for pretty. I bet your boy Elliot would notice you then." The girl had a fair complexion, thick eyelashes, full lips. Lips like that had a whole world of potential.

Rachel bristled at the turns Nix's imagination took, the girl starting to pick up on the images Nix was spoon-feeding her. *"You wouldn't dare."*

Nix tugged Rachel's shirt up and whipped out the Swiss Army knife that Rachel kept in her pocket. Rachel panicked for a moment, but Nix shrugged off her concern. "Take it easy. This'll only hurt for a second."

With careful, practiced movements, Nix carved a few tiny sigils into the skin along the girl's ribcage, just enough to ensure that no passing archdemons could recognize her in this body. 'Safety first' was Nix's motto. She swiped at the blood and pulled the shirt back down when she finished.

Rachel was less than impressed.

Nix smirked at her reflection and winked. "You and me, kid. We're going to have a lot of fun together. I can tell already."

§

Nix slid Danny's key into the lock on the motel room door separating Rachel and Elliot's room from his, until she heard the telltale click she was waiting for. He probably hadn't even noticed she'd lifted it yet, so there was no harm in a little trespassing. Rachel, however, protested at the intrusion, a pit of anxiety forming in her stomach because she worried Pops might be mad at her and that was apparently The Worst Thing Ever.

"*He'll know you went in here. We're not supposed to go in. He'll know.*"

"Like he knew I was in *you?*" Nix asked playfully, giving Rachel a mental poke.

That shut the girl up nice and quick.

Nix eased the door open and stepped inside. The curtains were pulled tightly shut, leaving the room dark despite the January sun shining cheerfully outside.

Nix tiptoed carefully across the carpet and toward the front door where the light switch was located. She had to be mindful of any potential traps. Paranoid hunters had a way of making everybody else just as paranoid as they were, usually by doing stupid shit like constructing elaborate booby traps all over the damn place.

Nix's paranoia turned out to be baseless, and she made it to the door without meeting any hazard greater than stirred-up dust bunnies. When she flicked on the switch, the room flooded with fluorescent light, making Rachel's eyes water.

The room had the same worn burgundy carpet as Rachel's, with the same flyspecked yellow wallpaper and oak veneer desk set. An ancient television was screwed to the wall in one corner.

Lining the far wall, above the bed, was a collage straight out of a stalker's training manual. Road maps stretched on for ages, tacked into the drywall, each map layered over the next. A piece of red yarn was tangled in the mess, looping and spiking from map to map, plotting out some as-yet-undiscovered constellation.

Rachel was silent.

An assortment of tiny pins were jammed in here and there for good measure, and Nix had to admire how skillful Danny's impression of a neurotic crazy person was. This, she assumed, was what hunters these days considered investigative research.

She knelt on the bed to take a better look. The tacks seemed randomly placed, marking out towns and roads in red and yellow, which was probably their attempt at color-coding this abomination, but Nix had no idea what she was looking at. A plot of past hunts, maybe? Future hunts? A single red tack was stuck in the center of Sonora, California.

Nix moved along the wall, following the red string as it bounced around from town to town in no apparent pattern. It skipped over Sonora. Whether this was a good thing or a bad thing, she didn't know. A bit higher up on the wall were cutouts of newspaper articles—including one of Ida and several others reporting on recent deaths in the area, all in the span of three weeks and two towns. Aside from Ida, the other three 'victims' were men—the manly lumberjack kind of men, all of whom had met accidental and *unlikely* deaths.

In Jamestown, a hammer fell twelve stories and lodged itself straight into the eye socket of the first guy—Tuolumne County's coroner ruled it death by traumatic brain injury. A very inventive death if Nix had ever heard of one, and Nix was pretty inventive about these things herself.

The second guy from Jamestown got his intestines torn up from the inside, started coughing up blood in a local restaurant and keeled over before anyone could figure out what was wrong with him. What was wrong, according to the article, were the twenty-seven drywall screws embedded in various locations along his digestive tract. The widow's lawsuit against the restaurant hit the press almost before her husband's death had. Classic.

The last man—from Sonora, and more of a business exec than the others had been, but still in the construction business—fell face-first down a flight of stairs. He crashed through a wooden railing and managed to get himself impaled on it. Took two hours for the firefighters and paramedics to saw him out, and by that point he was long gone. This last one lacked a certain creative element, but Nix supposed it got the job done.

Ida, naturally, had tripped on the carpet and landed on the pointy end of her gardening shears, poor old gal. Could've happened to anyone. Couldn't just leave those things lying around. But yeah, she could see how Danny might consider this spate of freak accidents to be a touch suspicious.

A book lay on the bedside table, something ancient and written in a variation of Italian. An old dialect, perhaps. Nix flipped it open and thumbed through the pages, mostly looking at the pictures and…oh. Yes, that was definitely a chapter on exorcisms. Fantastic.

It was a short chapter, and from what she could read of it, it was less of a how-to guide than a recounting of some old stories about creepy-crawly things getting yanked out of people's throats, so Nix considered this to be fairly harmless. They had some eccentric tastes in reading material, though.

"You know anything about this?" Nix asked.

"*Wouldn't tell you if I did,*" came Rachel's smartass response, as if she had any choice in the matter.

Nix skimmed through Rachel's thoughts but came back with nothing of value. There were dark places that Nix couldn't quite access, but Rachel couldn't either, so at the very least Nix was confident the girl was incapable of intentionally withholding information from her.

Nix ran Rachel's fingers over the frayed paper where a few pages had been torn out of the book. With a contemplative "*Hmm,*" she closed it and set it back down at exactly the same angle she'd found it in. Wouldn't want to draw any unnecessary attention. She was already playing with fire, after all.

Nix sighed, straightened the sheets, turned off the light, and returned to Rachel's room. She set the lock on the door behind her from Danny's side before closing it and pocketing his key to return the next time she saw him. For such a celebrated hunter, the man sure was an easy mark for pickpockets.

It wasn't the revelation she'd been hoping for and already Nix was starting to question the wisdom of taking this young hunter out for a joyride.

She couldn't exactly kill the girl or hop bodies now without raising suspicion. Rachel knew too much about her, like the fact that she existed at all, which by Nix's estimation was, indeed, *too much*. And unfortunately, that was about the only thing Rachel did know. There was a reason she was forced to wait in the truck while the other two traipsed about in the field. The girl was hopeless. Whatever the wall of maps meant, Danny hadn't felt the need to share it with his adopted daughter.

Rachel had a whole lot of theory and no practice, which was a pity, really. She had the potential. She had the drive. What she lacked was opportunity. All she had in her head were books, like a walking grimoire of ancient texts and shitty teen romance novels.

Nix had no interest in the gardening practices of fourteenth-century monks or the finer points of werewolf seductions, but she couldn't let her efforts so far go to waste. She'd keep looking until she found something, even if that meant riffling through the troubled mind of a nineteen-year-old girl with a fetish for monsters that sparkled and drove environmentally friendly cars.

Ever the optimist, Nix rummaged through Rachel's duffel, looking for a makeup bag that she was pretty sure didn't exist.

The girl had dozens of books, mounds of paper and notebooks and pencils with teeth marks in them. She pulled out one of the notebooks and found it full of scribbles, mostly lists of translations. Some sigils were scrawled across the front, nothing overly interesting, but still highly indicative of reading too many bullshit paranormal-investigation websites, because half of them were utterly useless, and the other half increased the fertility of Rachel's notebook.

What the girl needed was a life. A real life. One with makeup bags, preferably, and less anti-demon paraphernalia. This just wasn't a healthy way to live.

Nix groaned and abandoned her search. Pointless even trying, really. She'd just have to fix things herself.

Chapter 5

Nix wandered down an alley between Main and Willow, just a short distance from a local church. She hadn't spent a lot of time in Jamestown, but she knew enough to find her way around and some things just never varied from place to place. This was the last stop on her supply run.

She shifted the plastic bag of eye shadow and lipstick on her shoulder and dug around in Rachel's pockets, pulling out two twenties. Nix brushed off the lint, then handed them to a teenager in exchange for a little baggie of his mother's knockout pills. The pills were just for insurance. She couldn't have her new doll wandering off if she had to run a few errands in somebody else's skin.

Nix took out Rachel's phone to check the time—kids these days had no respect for the sanctity of timepieces. It would be another two hours until she expected the boys to return, maybe more. They probably wouldn't even notice she'd left the motel. Seemed like they just dragged the girl around with them anyway—dead weight they could afford to lose.

Apparently Nix thought that too loudly, because Rachel wandered off to pout and stomp around like a child in one of the quieter parts of her brain. In the absence of screaming and shouting, it seemed Rachel wasn't sure what else to do with herself. Callie had never been this much trouble. A few extra cookies, and Callie had *offered* to slice her mommy up for Nix.

Lost in nostalgia, Nix nearly walked right past Cirrik on her way back down Main Street.

A seemingly unprovoked rage stirred in her the moment she saw him, so she knew it had to be Cirrik in there. Nix had a sixth sense for fuckwits, and it never let her down when it came to their king. He was wearing a postal worker, and for some reason he appeared to be delivering the mail.

When their eyes met, he stopped in the middle of the sidewalk, his postal worker stalled in front of Nix's little hunter. A woman with a baby stroller inched around them with a pointed glower, muttering something untoward under her breath.

Cirrik stared at Nix for a moment with an intense but bewildered expression, then recognition dawned in his gaze. She should have known the sigils couldn't conceal her from him. Familiarity bred a contempt that couldn't be easily deceived by magic. "Nix," he greeted her, grinning. "Been awhile."

Nix forced a polite smile onto Rachel's lips and nobly restrained herself from eviscerating him in broad daylight in front of dozens of human witnesses. She'd have to find some stronger sigils next time. "I'd say. About a century, at last count."

He brought a finger to his postal worker's scruffy chin and squinted. "We were in Venice the last we met, were we not?"

Prick. Useless, no-good, son of a bitch. Nix crossed her arms. "Florence, actually," she corrected him.

His eyes sparkled in the sunlight like something out of Rachel's moronic romance novels, but when he smiled it was *his* smile, the one she remembered, and not his host's. "Ah, yes. Florence. Very romantic."

She was going to kill him. She was going to rip his stupid little mail-boy open and fill it with salt, and she'd do it far enough away from civilization that Cirrik would die like a baby bird on a hot sidewalk, writhing in agony as his fragile little soul extinguished from the lack of a host.

Her lips twitched, the half-hearted attempt at a smile faltering. "Romantic?" she said from between clenched teeth. Nix pointed out the very important fact that on their last meeting, "You tried to banish me, remember? I do."

He'd practically thrown her at some whackjob priest who had been staging attacks all around the area. Romantic. Nix scoffed. Romance didn't come in buckets of flaming holy oil. Her body had never recovered, poor thing.

The bastard winked at her. "But it *was* romantic, would you not say? I love the new outfit, by the way. Not your usual style, but it does suit you."

"Wish I could return the compliment." The postal worker's packaging left a lot to be desired. He was middle-aged, but scrawny and lanky, with sandy-blond hair and a permanent fake smile plastered on his face. Cirrik walked with an ease and confidence that was entirely out of place in that body.

He glanced down at himself with the briefest hint of self-consciousness in his stolen blue eyes. He brushed his hands down the front of his navy vest and raised his chin. "Yes, well. Desperate times, you know. Hard to manage in this economy. I...did not realize you had moved to this town. Last I heard, you were in the wind. Something about an archdemon and a certain stolen something? Or was it a certain *demolished* something? I can never keep it straight."

It was good to know the rumor mill was about as reliable as ever. A shopkeeper pushed past them with a broom and Nix lowered her voice but didn't move for him. "That was a *misunderstanding,* okay? And I haven't moved here," she said, not that it was any of his business. And what the hell was he even doing here, anyway?

She couldn't possibly have chosen a less popular locale. Cirrik showing up in the middle of nowhere like this, where she just happened to be hiding out, that couldn't be a coincidence. "I'm just passing through. Last *I* heard, you were halfway across the world with some two-bit hinoenma whore."

"Her name was Kuroko, and I do not appreciate your tone."

Nix smirked. "But you don't deny that she was a two-bit whore?"

"That is quite beside the point. And as it happens, certain events of late necessitated my relocation. It would seem that this strange little corner of the earth is now the place to be."

She pursed Rachel's lips, scuffing the toe of one sneaker against the concrete sidewalk. Cirrik had a bag slung over his shoulder that matched his outfit. It was filled to bursting with envelopes of all sizes and colors and the question just kept nagging at her, "You aren't *really* delivering mail, are you? Tell me you're not."

He stilled, leaving his postal worker's mouth partly ajar. His left eye twitched. "I'd...rather not discuss my work at this time."

It was always delightful to see the mighty fall. Nix snickered. "What, no anthrax scares? No ticking bombs in brown parcels?"

"If only. No, it is more of a long-term project. Building an arsenal, gathering intelligence, making preparations."

Arsenals. Intelligence. Preparations. That didn't sound like Cirrik at all. In spite of being a cowardly ass, he truly *was* a lover, not a fighter. Nix could give him that. His posture was tense, his tone anxious. She couldn't recall ever seeing him this edgy before. Something must have shaken him to get him worked up like this...or someone.

"So you're working for someone." She narrowed her eyes. "Who?"

He huffed as though the very suggestion was an affront to his character, but she could tell his heart wasn't in it. "I will have you know I'm working *with* someone. Multiple someones, as a matter of fact. These are dangerous times, Nix. Hunters nowadays are not the simpleminded pests that they were in bygone years."

She wondered if she should mention that she was currently riding one of those formerly simpleminded pests, but she didn't feel the need to share anything with Cirrik that she didn't have to. "You're scared of some hunters? Because I've met some of those nowadays hunters and they aren't all that sharp, I assure you."

"There are things that you do not know, Nix."

"So enlighten me," she said.

"The game has changed. There are rumors...."

Nix sighed. "Oh please. Rumors? Rumors are what have you trembling in your skinsack like a calf off to slaughter?"

He did have a flair for the dramatic. There was a time when she had liked that about him. With another huff, Cirrik said, "Our kind are dying Nix," as if this explained everything.

Her brow furrowed. She shifted the bag on her shoulder. "What do you mean *dying*?"

He waved his hands, nearly knocking a letter from his bag. "I mean they are being killed, butchered, ceasing to exist. *Real* death, my love. Not banishment, not some recycling process or a temporary removal of chess pieces from the board. It is worse than anything I have ever seen before, not since...well. My compatriots and I have formed a united front against this new enemy."

Nix raised one of Rachel's could-be-pretty-with-a-bit-of-plucking eyebrows. Bullshit.

Cirrik added as if in afterthought, like he already knew he was going to regret this but couldn't help himself, "You should...join us."

An olive branch, if she'd ever seen one, but the only thing those were good for was firewood, as far as Nix was concerned. "Yeah, well, I'm not much for *compatriots*, myself." This wasn't any of her concern, and she suspected he was blowing things way out of proportion. Nix was in enough shit as it was; she didn't need to get involved in anyone else's.

"Yes, I do recall that." Cirrik sighed. "I do not presume to hold sway over your decisions, Nix, but for your own safety you should at the very least consider my offer. There is strength in numbers."

To his credit, he did sound genuinely worried for her. She ought to kick him in the shins just for that. Though given Rachel's height advantage over Nix's usual bodies, maybe Nix would nail the fucker in the balls instead. "You, worried about *my* safety? I doubt that."

"I assure you, this new threat is very real and so is my concern." He paused and said, "If you decide to take me up on my offer, give me a call." Cirrik produced a small white card from his front pocket and handed it to her with a flourish.

Nix glanced at the information laid out in little bricks of text on one side of the card. Ye Olde English Font, the dumbed-down art of the monks filtered into pixels. Pretentious, as always. "John Smith, eh? How quaint." She tucked it into Rachel's jeans for propriety's sake. "Never took you for the cell-phone type. Always were such a luddite."

"Times change. One must adapt or perish." Cirrik's voice softened as he said, "I *have* missed you, Nix."

She bristled at the sincerity in his tone. "Fuck you, Cirrik."

His host's lips quirked up in an amused half-smile. "Well, all you had to do was ask, love. I seem to recall a number of occasions in which we both thoroughly enjoyed each other's company."

This was complete bullshit, the whole thing. She wasn't getting involved in any wars, real or imaginary. She had her own problems. And she certainly wasn't getting involved with *him*. Charming psychopath that he was, he wouldn't sway her ill opinion of him. At least, not significantly. But perhaps, just this once, she'd let him live. For old time's sake.

Nix edged away. "I have places to be. I'd appreciate it if this little rendezvous stayed between us. You know, archdemons and misunderstandings and whatnot. Can't be too careful."

"Certainly. Well, I won't keep you."

"How considerate of you," Nix said, already walking away. "Oh, and Cirrik?" she added, glancing back over her shoulder to catch his gaze. Nix hoped this would be the last she had to see of him for another century. Next time she wouldn't be so merciful. "Watch your back."

Cirrik beamed. "Naturally, my dear."

A block and a half away, Nix tossed his card into a trashcan.

Chapter 6

Nix admired the lackluster handiwork of the motel room's yellow wallpaper while trying to coax Rachel back out. Rachel was a particularly stubborn host. Nix just wanted to play. A little attention was all she was asking of the girl—and her body, silence, and cooperation, of course, but those were a given.

Being subject to Rachel's cold-shoulder, after exhausting all the avenues of investigation she could think of that didn't involve the other hunters, meant that Nix was *bored*. Terminally bored. Oh God, could boredom be fatal? This felt fatal.

"*God?*" Rachel said skeptically, a raised eyebrow of judgment implied in her tone, but hell, at least she was talking again.

"It's a figure of speech," Nix said defensively.

"*Just what kind of demon are you?*"

Nix shrugged, planting Rachel's feet on the table on top of a bunch of manila folders, and crossing her legs. She leaned back in the chair and stared at the ceiling for a change of scenery. "What were you expecting, the boogieman?"

"*There's no such thing.*"

Nix nearly fell out of her chair. "Are you kidding me? Of course there is. Damn, what are these hunters teaching their kids nowadays? What do you think happens to all the little children that get sucked under their beds at night and are never heard from again, stranger abductions?"

Rachel offered a tentative, "*Well, yeah. Don't tell me they get transported to some magical fairy world or something?*"

Nix scoffed. Foolish girl. "Of course not. They get eaten. Bones and all. Nothing left to find."

"*The boogieman's a carnivore?*" Rachel asked, a note of genuine interest in her voice, and for a moment it felt like they'd found some common ground. Nix was pretty sure this was what Oprah called a *bonding experience*.

Nix casually corrected, "The PC term is just *boogie*, actually. Gender neutral, and there's more than just the one. And yes, obviously they are carnivores. What would a vegetarian do with a kid? Didn't they teach you this in Sunday school or wherever?"

"*Never came up, no.*"

Nix heard the rumble of an engine that sounded like it was one speed bump away from being put out of its misery for good. She knew that engine. Nix sat up and slid her feet off the table.

The door opened and Elliot staggered in. He walked straight toward her, his jaw as tight as the line of his lips, and for a second Nix wondered if she'd been made. Rachel perked up at the prospect.

He set his bag on the floor then leaned into her and whispered, "*Please* tell me you found something. He's driving me crazy, Rach, I don't even—hey," he paused, leaning back and taking a good look at her, "are you wearing makeup? It, ah...looks nice." A light blush rose to his cheeks and colored the tips of his ears.

Nix smirked. *"Told you it would work."*

Rachel ignored her.

Danny entered the room, kicking the door closed behind him. Elliot straightened. Nix glanced between the two men.

Danny nodded at her in acknowledgment and said, "How'd the research go, darlin'? This a demon or ain't it?"

Nix froze.

Right. Research. Shit. Three hours and she had nothing whatsoever to show for it. Well, she had the makeup and the pills and there was that great little café on 5th with the croissants...but nothing that could help her *now*, which was the problem.

"I told you that they would notice. See? You're done for now."

"Do you want me to spin your head around and vomit all over the place?" Nix threatened, unimpressed at Rachel's snarky backtalk. "Because I will. I won't like it, but I will do it if you insist on being so uncooperative."

If she wanted a demon, Nix would show her a goddamned demon. Nix determined when Nix was done for, not sulky little hunters with no respect.

"Um, well...." Nix skimmed through the previously ignored manila folders on the table, covertly brushing off the dirt smudges from her shoes while looking for some thread of bullshit she could feed to them. She didn't have to stall for long before she realized with tremendous relief that she didn't have to feed them bullshit at all. "Oh!" Nix held up one of the coroner's reports triumphantly. It was so obvious, of course these hunters wouldn't have seen it. If the other bodies had the same...yes, they did. Excellent. "This isn't a demon at all. These are hex marks."

She pointed excitedly at the picture attached then spread the others out on the table for their perusal. On each body a bit of dirt was smeared somewhere on their person, barely noticeable unless you were looking for it, what with all the blood and guts and eye juices. Easy enough to overlook. Each body but Ida's, of course.

Danny leaned over her and frowned, not sharing her enthusiasm. "What is it I'm supposed to be seein' here?"

Nix huffed and grabbed a black marker, outlining the symbols on the business exec's autopsy photo to reveal the shape of a crude circle with an X through it on the back of one arm.

"A witch?" Elliot asked.

Nix shook her head at the poor, simpleminded pest. "Nah, not with these sigils." Nix passed him the photograph. "This is older; elemental. Probably a dryad. From the looks of it, a vengeful one." She pushed herself up from the table, set her hands on her hips, and grinned. "And I bet I know exactly where to find it, too."

Danny stared at her. "You do?"

Did she ever. "They just started tearing up the woods on the edge of town in Sonora, by the old Ellaport Bridge." The sound of jackhammers had shaken Callie's street for three weeks. Nix was ready to kill the noisy fuckers herself but it looked like some thoughtful tree-hugging monster beat her to the punch. "Some developer bought the land a couple years ago and just got approval to build a department store. It's the talk of the town. Timeline fits, too. And dryads do not take kindly to land developers, let me tell you."

"But the woman had no connections to any construction businesses, we already ruled that out," Danny said.

"So you—*we* must have missed something," Nix suggested, quite reasonably. "Maybe she was doing some accounting work under the table. She strikes me as the tax-evasion type. Either way, the rest makes sense and I'm sure that old lady was involved in it somehow. The creature shouldn't be far from the construction site—most likely, it'll be hanging around a very old tree. They love trees. Like, *really* love them. Bit of an unhealthy obsession, if you ask me."

"How do you know all of this?" Elliot asked, one eyebrow raised as he leaned back against the table. His eyes hadn't left her since he'd entered the room.

She shrugged. "You told me to research. I researched. That's why you brought me along, isn't it?"

Danny piped up with an eloquent, "But—"

"We'd better hurry," she said, "if you want to track it down tonight, before anybody else gets a hammer in the eye or whatever. They're most active just before dawn, and nearly impossible to find when they're napping." So long as she kept the men distracted, Nix figured she could gather some intel without them questioning her too much. She grabbed Rachel's jacket from the back of her chair and pulled it on. "Oh, and ditch the guns—only way to kill it is a wooden stake through the heart. Like a vampire...but messier."

She pushed past Elliot but Danny held a hand out to stop her. "Where do you think you're going?"

"Are you kidding? No way am I missing a dryad hunt. This is going to be great." She hadn't seen one since eighteenth-century Prague. The massacre had been legendary. Missing this now would be like missing out on front row seats to the *Olympiakoi Agones*.

"Whoa, hold up," Danny said. "This is gonna be dangerous, darlin'. I don't want you involved."

Nix smiled sweetly, a little impressed all of the sudden that Rachel put up with this every day without losing her sanity. "I'm not a little kid anymore, *Pops*," she reminded him. "I'm going to need to learn how to protect myself eventually, don't you think? Can't do that by hanging around libraries and reading books all the time. And if you want to find the thing, you're going to need me."

He stared at her, frown deepening the wrinkles around his mouth, until he looked away and said, in a very put-upon tone, "Fine. Just...don't do anything foolish, and if I tell you to do somethin', you do it. Understood?"

Nix saluted cheerfully, already feeling the boredom lift. "Yes, sir. Got it."

She followed Elliot out to the old truck. Behind her, Danny searched the pockets of his blue jeans, asking, "Hey, either of you seen where I put my room key?"

Chapter 7

The forest was utterly devoid of light. No stars, no moon, just miles and miles of deep dark nothing. Three flashlight beams bounced across the bridge, followed by three sets of footsteps crunching over dry gravel and California scrub.

Little creatures stirred in all that darkness—creatures that were probably watching them right now, following their procession with beady nocturnal eyes.

Something fluttered in the trees overhead as they made it across the bridge. A bird, maybe. A low hissing sound followed and the trees rustled, raining leaves down on them. Maybe not a bird.

Nix bounced on her toes, practical sneakers worn thin enough to feel the pebbles under her feet. Nix hadn't gone hunting for dangerous creatures in a dog's age. The good old excitement of the hunt was making Rachel's little heart go pitter-patter, and Nix had to admit that she enjoyed it.

Danny had carved out his role as leader of the pack and was wandering a few feet ahead of them into the forest. He walked with misplaced certainty; a confidence that was cute in its ignorance, but mostly just sad. Poor bastard had no idea what they were going after—not really. Nix dropped some details here and there on the way, but with ancient elemental creatures like dryads, well...it was necessary to learn from experience. Textbooks just didn't cut it.

As twigs snapped under their shoes and rocks were shifted out of place, it occurred to Nix that her time with these hunters may well be cut short. Dryads were so very messy, after all. Her work here could be done before it had really started. This shouldn't have been disappointing—what the hell did she care how they died?—and yet....

"Shh," Danny whispered as skittering sounds drifted toward them from deeper in the forest. He motioned for them to head right, and he started toward the left, where the noise was louder. "Don't go far."

Elliot touched her shoulder lightly and moved ahead of her. Nix rolled Rachel's eyes. Chivalry was dead for a reason. If it was the last thing she did with these hunters, she was determined to earn this girl some credibility, on principle alone. Not that Rachel would care. She'd already reverted to ignoring Nix, even after their quality bonding at the motel.

Elliot was clutching a 12 gauge shotgun like a lifeline, despite the fact that she had explicitly told him not to bother. Shotguns would be about as useful against a dryad as throwing a box of confetti at it. At best, it would be entirely unfazed. At worst, it would be *very* pissed off.

But hey, she'd warned them. Let them march off to their deaths like idiots—Nix didn't care. She followed Elliot, wandering into the woods until she could no longer hear Danny shuffling around.

Their flashlights were bright beacons in the darkness, screaming to their prey—or more aptly, their predator—that they were ripe for the picking. She'd warned them about that, too. At this point, evolution was quite warranted in knocking them off the map.

Elliot slowed, stopped. Nix nearly ran right into him.

"Did you see that?" he whispered, turning toward her.

Nix glanced around, then shrugged. Elliot's eyes locked on something over her shoulder and widened in realization.

Nix only had time to think, "*Aw, fuck,*" before something slammed into her side, and suddenly her new doll was airborne. She let it happen, for the sake of appearances, but she didn't like it one bit.

Gravity reasserted itself promptly and she crashed into the side of a tree with a winded *ooph*. Rachel's elbow took the brunt of the impact. Blood ran down her arm, a warm stream sliding beneath the sleeve of her jacket. She brought a hand to the wound and poked at it with curiosity, vaguely aware that Elliot was having a mini freak-out and was currently engaged in a doomed battle against a very annoyed dryad.

The shotgun blasted. Birds and creepy-crawlies scattered, the noise of their escape a resounding echo following the shot.

Nix glanced at Elliot as she brushed the leaves from her hair.

Surprise, surprise, the dryad was not even remotely bothered by Elliot's attack. Who could have predicted such a thing? Nix held Rachel's arm to her chest, the limb now numb and tingly in a way that was more peculiar than painful, not that it mattered much. It had been a while since she'd torn one of her dolls, but the pain did have a certain appeal in its finality. That was the thing about dolls; they broke so easily and fixed so poorly. A pity to have to replace Rachel so soon.

Elliot grunted and shouted, swiping at the towering dryad with his shotgun.

Nix leaned against the tree and watched. The creature had to be at least three feet taller than Elliot, not including the mossy spikes adorning its head. Elliot's odds were not good, but the little engine-that-could just kept on chugging.

"You're just going to stand there? Do something!" Rachel cried, acknowledging Nix's presence again, and oh, wasn't that convenient now that she wanted Nix's help.

It lashed at him with one long arm, its fingers thin and tapered, knocking the shotgun to the ground. Elliot followed quickly after.

Nix pursed her lips, evaluating the dryad's technique as it pierced Elliot's left shoulder and tore a startled shout from his throat.

Not a lot of finesse, but she supposed it was effective enough. Nix would have started with dismemberment, herself. Rip off one of those finely muscled arms and then start sliding it down Elliot's throat...yeah. Nix grinned, a little dizzy off the mix of adrenaline and endorphins pumping out of Rachel's squishy glands. God this was fun.

Elliot screamed at Rachel to run, but Nix was enjoying the show. He clambered to his knees, trying to get his feet back under him. The dryad snapped a branchlike limb against his chest the moment he succeeded, and it sent him stumbling backward and falling on his ass.

The slender creature really packed a punch, considering its normal preference for nonviolence. It being ticked about all its trees getting the ax was logical, Nix supposed, but she wasn't especially fond of dryads in the first place, and she certainly didn't feel sympathy for the ugly things. Nasty do-gooders, the lot of them.

Danny's voice shouted over the noise, and she could hear him plowing through the trees like a battering ram, snapping branches and stomping on roots.

He'd be too late.

Elliot was very much at the dryad's mercy. He thrashed around as it pinned him in place with black roots. Elliot got in the occasional kick that hit its mark, but that wasn't enough to loosen the dryad's grip and really only served to piss the woodland spirit off.

A particularly well-placed kick snapped off some tender new growth, pungent sap dripping down its ugly bark, and the dryad shrieked with rage, twisting its appendages into one sharp weapon and taking aim.

"Please," Rachel said, "*I'll be good, I swear, I—I'll help you find whatever it is you're looking for. Please, just save him!*"

Nix sighed. It wasn't as much fun when she wasn't the one doing the impaling, anyway. In a rare moment of pity—she really should be sainted for this—Nix grabbed a fallen branch, snapped it over her knee, and plunged the sharp end of it into the dryad's back with a strength that Rachel alone did not possess. It tore right through its misshapen, knotted spine and out the other side.

The dryad's shrill death keen pierced through the forest. The ground shook beneath them, like an aftershock from an earthquake, the forest screaming back.

Nix twisted the branch once for good measure. Green ooze poured out, thicker than the sap it bled, the dryad's life juices splattering over her canvas shoes. In Germany, four hundred years ago, they'd made love potions out of that shit. It was poisonous as all fuck, but your sweetie damn well never looked at anyone else.

It dropped to its knees—if they could be considered knees—in a burbling, swiftly decomposing mess. The hollow inside it emptied and the creature's ramshackle framework returned to the dirt. The sweet stench of rot filled the air and Nix choked, grimacing. Always so messy.

In the pile of dryad mulch, a single green acorn gleamed. Nix crushed it with her shoe.

Elliot was breathing hard, staring at her like *she* was the nine-foot tree monster with a mean streak. She looked back and caught sight of Danny standing there between the trees, gun half raised and mouth half open. He'd seen the show, too. Pity, she'd been doing well with the whole pathetic-damsel thing. As well as she could, anyway.

Nix walked over the mulched corpse toward Elliot.

She held out her hand.

When he didn't move, she wondered if her performance had been too revealing, if the hunters could see past Rachel's familiar face to what lay beneath.

Then Elliot reached for her hand and she was pulling him up.

Chapter 8

If they wondered where the new and improved Rachel had come from, Danny and Elliot didn't take the opportunity to ask. This wasn't the first time Nix had seen this degree of ineptitude on the part of her host's loved ones, the people who should have noticed when something was wrong but never did.

With teenagers, it was like humans expected them to act possessed these days. Mood swings and dramatic shifts in character were all seen as par for the course when hormones entered the equation, and even the occasional homicidal slip was brushed off as being a phase. Still, Nix had to wonder how they managed to miss the change in Rachel. Callie's mother had figured out something was wrong in only a few days, and that bitch was less perceptive than an extra-stupid rock.

As Nix pondered the matter, Rachel's beloved family didn't wonder anything at all. A unanimous decision was reached that helpless little Rachel impaling a dryad with a broken branch the size of a fence post was entirely unremarkable. C'est la vie.

The ride back was punctuated by bursts of good humor and manly understatements of pain. Elliot was bleeding all over the upholstery, which Danny insisted was Unacceptable with a capital U, as if the mess could possibly make the truck any shittier than it already was. Regardless, Elliot was exiled to the backseat with Rachel so that he could proceed to bleed all over *her* property instead.

"It's just that it's damn near impossible to get blood stains outta these seats, you know, son. Hard to explain to the cops if we get pulled over," Danny said, trying to sound gruff while shooting concerned glances at them through the rearview mirror. Upholstery aside, it was also the only way Danny could convince Elliot to lie down and rest during the trip back to the motel.

The amulet around Danny's neck winked at her in that mirror every time a car passed by, headlights glinting off the metal. The silver chain was like a barbed-wire fence and the pendant a *No Trespassing* sign, and oh, how Nix *wanted* to trespass. This would all be so much easier if she could just slip into *his* skin. His gaze caught hers, and Nix broke eye contact, looking down at the damsel of the hour.

"I know, Pops," Elliot replied, not looking at all put out by having to lie across her lap. There wasn't enough room for him to stretch out, so his knees were propped against the window, but he had yet to complain.

Nix absently brushed Rachel's fingers through Elliot's blond hair as they drove, and he leaned into her hand like a contented puppy. Rachel was positively tickled by his reaction to her touch, even though Nix was the one to initiate it.

The girl was giddy from the adrenaline while Elliot was drunk with it. A sleepy drunk, to be sure, but he was far more relaxed than Nix had seen him before. Nix liked him better this way, all bruised and bloody and inexplicably trusting. The boy's blood seeped warmly into the fabric of her jeans. It was oddly endearing.

Danny caught Nix's reflected gaze and said, "Hey, darlin', keep pressure on that wound, will you? No, the one on his shoulder, it's the deepest. Yes, like that. Good girl."

Elliot hissed between his teeth as she pressed down hard against the deep laceration on his shoulder. It made him prettier, and Nix sort of saw what had Rachel on pins and needles around him. Big brother was going to be cute once she got him screaming.

"It stopped bleeding already, Pops, I'm fine." He smiled at her and added, "Could have been a whole lot worse. How's the arm, Rach?"

"Can't feel a thing," she replied, still holding it against her chest for the sake of appearances.

Elliot shifted slightly, reaching up to rub the palm of his right hand over her left bicep for no apparent reason but to have an excuse to touch her. Rachel nearly swooned. "You know that's not actually a good thing, right?"

Nix shrugged, careful not to dislodge his hand as she did so. "It's all tingly, but it doesn't hurt. Not even broken. Just a scratch."

"So tough," he teased, playing with a lock of her hair.

She raised an eyebrow and pressed just a little harder against his shoulder in warning. "Was that sarcasm?"

He laughed and cringed at the same time, saying, "Ah, okay okay! Not sarcasm!"

"How tough am I?"

"*So* tough." Elliot grinned boyishly.

She nodded, satisfied. "That's right. And don't forget it."

From the front seat, Danny praised her, saying, "You did good today, darlin'. Real good."

Rachel's body warmed and Nix felt a pleased blush light her cheeks, a sensation that was more enjoyable than she would have expected. They lapsed into silence, Nix holding in Elliot's blood, Danny driving, and Elliot quietly bleeding.

Watching the road pass by out the window became so entrancing that Nix was startled when Rachel spoke up.

"Thank you," she whispered, so softly that Nix almost didn't hear her. A mixture of uncertainty and gratitude painted her tone as she continued, *"For...for saving him, I mean. Thank you."*

Nix chuckled to herself. Maybe her new doll's manners weren't so bad after all.

Chapter 9

The walls of the motel bathroom were asylum white. Floor to ceiling, nothing but white. A little elbow grease and the tiles might actually sparkle, but this was a motel room that went for forty bucks a day and so the tiles just glowed dull, relentless white. Rachel was dripping on them, her blood fresh and red and pretty.

Nix rooted around in the first-aid kit on the counter, pulling out antiseptic wipes and sterile gauze, remembering the old days when she'd just cauterize wounds with a searing hot chunk of metal if she bothered to do anything with them at all.

Strictly speaking, Rachel's body would heal itself eventually, and until then Nix wasn't exactly hindered by pain or stiffness to any appreciable degree. Even torn to shreds, most humans were still wearable.

But the other hunters had seen Rachel's injuries already, and Nix couldn't very well risk them catching sight of the sigils carved into Rachel's torso—freshly scabby and strengthened after her encounter with Cirrik—lest they start asking awkward questions. If it weren't for that, Nix would have punted the obsessive and extensive first-aid kit out the window and called it a day.

So here she was, trying to decide between ten different sizes of bandages in a neurotically white bathroom that was barely big enough for her to turn around in without tripping over the shower curtain.

Every four minutes or so, Danny would offer to help, and Nix would categorically refuse, relying on respect for Rachel's modesty to keep him out.

Her left arm was pulled tight to her chest and secured by a long triangular strip of cloth, which wasn't making things any easier. Eventually, Nix chose the biggest gauze pad and slapped it to the shallow abrasion over her ribs. Blood was sticky. It would stick. Nix shrugged into one of Elliot's old shirts, covering Rachel's modest assets.

For her next task, the cut on Rachel's forearm was probably going to need something done to it. Not fire, unfortunately. Nix glared at the first-aid kit, bitter at the advances the humans had made in literally everything. Pretending to be one of them had been so much easier even just a century back.

A knock came to the door, two quick taps. It wasn't fully closed in the first place, but her visitor waited for permission nonetheless. Nix toed the door open with her focus locked on a tiny bottle of what may or may not have been antibiotic ointment. The black lettering had all but worn off, and the fabric first-aid kit itself was frayed around the zipper, its plastic inside pockets cracked and melted in places like they'd dragged this sorry little medical bag behind the truck for the last hundred miles of bad road.

A hand reached over her and took the container from her grasp, replacing it with a small tube. "You want the polysporine," Elliot said.

She glanced up at him. "How do you know what I want?"

Elliot smirked and raised his hands in a gesture of surrender. "Hey, just a suggestion, Rach. I'm sure that bug-bite gel will do just as well."

An unanticipated shot of concern curled in Rachel's stomach.

"You're hurt," Nix said, pointing out the obvious. The full extent of the damage was visible now that he was in a t-shirt and no longer wrapped in his thick black jacket. Sure, there'd been blood in the truck and she'd seen the dryad take a few good swipes out of him, but he still looked worse for the wear than she'd expected.

The white glare of the room added contrast to the blood and the dirt and the pale skin beneath. Humans were so fucking fragile, it was ridiculous.

He raised an eyebrow as if she'd just informed him that grass was green. "You too."

She grabbed the first-aid kit—the parts that weren't scattered on the bathroom counter or had fallen into the sink—and pushed past him, delaying bandaging her arm for the moment. Danny had already cleaned and bandaged the major wounds—after eventually finding his misplaced key on the floor of his truck—but Elliot insisted he could take care of the rest on his own. Danny wasn't exactly the gentlest of nurses.

"Sit down, I'll patch you up," she offered, throwing him a look over her shoulder that made it clear she wasn't asking his permission.

Elliot shrugged, but flicked off the bathroom light and took a seat on the edge of the bed. "*You're* going to patch *me* up? You sure about that?" he teased.

Nix pursed her lips, doing her best to look offended. "Don't you trust me?"

He held her gaze for a moment, the mirth slipping from his features, and answered with far too much sincerity, "Of course I trust you." The seriousness disappeared as quickly as it had come and Elliot smiled, nudging her with his elbow as she opened up an antiseptic wipe with her teeth. "Hey, remember when I fell down that ravine when we were kids?"

"Uh...." She didn't, of course, remember this. But Rachel did. The memory swirled and twisted through her thoughts like a ghostly specter. Rachel scrambled to pull it back, but it was already there, torn open and laid out for Nix's inspection. "Yeah, at Aunt Caroline's in Arizona, right? With Billy Gerard and his cousins?"

"Yes. Billy. Man, I haven't thought about him in ages. I swore I'd never let you within ten feet of a med kit for as long as I lived after that incident."

Nix laughed. "I was seven, how was I supposed to know the difference between peroxide and rubbing alcohol?" With her unrestrained hand, she wiped away the grime on his cheek and along the edge of his jaw. Just abrasions. She smoothed a little polysporine over them with her thumb and asked, "Want a Band-Aid? Pretty sure I saw some Hello Kitty ones in there somewhere."

"I think I'll pass," he answered fondly.

"Your loss." Nix shifted closer on the bed next to him, tilting his head to the left so she could dab at a cut that trailed down his neck and slid beneath the collar of his shirt. She tugged at his sleeve. "Take this off."

"Yes, ma'am." The fabric was pulled over his head with impressive efficiency, revealing a broad, muscular chest splattered with scrapes and scars, some new, some old. White gauze was taped over the laceration in his shoulder and another square was held in place near the center of his chest. Elliot folded his filthy t-shirt and set it beside him. "So Pops said you were looking into colleges. What are you thinking of taking?"

Rachel sighed in frustration and told Nix, *"I'm not going to any goddamned college. That was Danny's idea, not mine."* Ah, the trials and tribulations of youth.

Nix nodded her acknowledgement and relayed the message to Elliot, "The college thing is Danny's idea. I'm happy where I am. Just wish he'd give me the chance to prove myself in the field more often."

"You proved yourself tonight," Elliot said. "Pretty damn well, too."

Nix grinned. "You impressed, big brother?" He should be. It'd taken inhuman strength and reflexes, and left her with some really fierce splinters.

When he laughed, she felt the rumble of it beneath her fingertips. "Yeah. Yeah, I have to say, I am. That move with the stick back there..." he trailed off, shaking his head. "Thought I was about to get skewered."

Her hand flittered down Elliot's chest as she wiped at a spot of dried blood on the left side of his stomach. Their positions brought her closer as she reached across. She could have moved to the other side of the bed for easier access, but she didn't.

He watched her. She could feel the weight of his gaze as her hand brushed down his abdomen. His skin was warm beneath her fingers, a testament to the strong human heart pumping blood through his veins. They were messy, high-maintenance pets, but they certainly did have their charms. Warm bodies. Warm blood. Just begging to be torn open and explored. She licked her lips.

He tensed and caught her wrist abruptly. "Your hand is cold," he said, his voice the texture of a gravel road.

She stilled, but didn't move. Rachel watched on with rapt attention. Nix had expected at least token protests, but maybe Rachel here did burn just a bit brighter than the rest. When she looked up to catch his eyes, his mouth was so close to hers that she could feel the hot slide of his breath across her lips.

Nix leaned forward, lowering her eyelashes. Her tongue darted over her bottom lip.

Elliot drew back. She could see his carotid artery throbbing in the side of his neck, a pulse so rapid that it fluttered under his skin like it was calling to her. "I should—ah, I mean..." he stumbled, "I should probably, um, check on Pops—just make sure he's okay, you know."

Elliot nearly threw her off his lap in his escape and it was all Nix could do not to burst into laughter.

She settled for a sly smirk behind his back as she watched him leave. It was only a matter of time.

Chapter 10

When Rachel was eight years old, she set herself on fire.

Still had the flat, shiny pool of a scar on one leg to prove it, though it could have been worse. It should have been worse. Nix watched the memory unravel like a spool of film in front of her as Rachel slept and dreamt and Nix stared up at the water-stained ceiling.

Rachel's parents had been gone for two years, three months, and fourteen days, buried in some shithole called Heavenly Pines where the closest thing in a mile to civilization was a trailer park by the same name.

She wanted to miss them, but she didn't. Oh, there were times when a warm memory would sweep across her consciousness and she'd feel a peculiar stirring in her chest that was reminiscent of what she'd felt when the beloved family cat got rolled over by a semi, but even then she'd just start missing Mr. Fluffers all over again and forget about anything else.

Just because she didn't miss them didn't mean she wasn't *supposed* to miss them. This was in the third grade, before any of her classmates had developed an appreciable capacity for empathy, so every day at school they made sure to remind her of her orphan status, lest she forget and do something foolish like laugh or smile.

And Danny, he tried real hard but he was never around. He'd signed on for the whole godfather gig in the ceremonial sense for a best friend he hadn't seen in years, but he'd never expected to be called on it. Duty, on the other hand, started calling for him long before he and Rachel had met. It never stopped and he *always* answered. Rachel was just one more duty filed away in his house and taken care of, like the collection of cursed coins in the safe beneath the stairs.

He'd be gone for days at a time, weeks even. A tall, austere woman in a long, black coat tried to take her away a few times, claiming she'd be happier in a tiny room crowded with five other girls in a foster home than she would be in a big empty country house with a boy only five years older than herself to watch over her.

Elliot was outside mowing the lawn, and he wasn't talking to her. She'd taken one of his favorite remote-controlled cars and dropped it from the second-story window when he wouldn't play with her earlier in the day.

She could hear the lawnmower roaring beyond her window, the noise oscillating in volume as he worked his way across the front section of the yard, up and down, up and down. The smell of fresh-cut grass filled the whole house.

So there she was, sitting on her bed, waiting for the sound of tires to roll up the gravel driveway, not sure whether it would be Danny coming to save her from the social worker lady, or the social worker lady coming to save her from Danny.

And even at eight, she didn't feel it. Wasn't worried or sad or anxious. Rachel didn't feel anything. She didn't feel the sunlight pouring in through the open window, the gentle summer breeze, the polyester blanket underneath her crossed legs.

The box of matches on the fireplace mantle was her little secret. Rachel felt the fire. She felt it and she liked it, and she knew it was bad and she couldn't tell anyone, but she *wanted* the fire and in some strange way it felt like the fire wanted her back.

Wallowing in her eight-year-old tragedy, working away at her little pyro thing, she lit a match and held it, staring into the flame until it burned down to her fingers and extinguished. The whole thing gave her a special kind of thrill because she wasn't supposed to play with fire, not ever, and it was the only thing she'd felt in days.

It made her fingertips tingle.

Rachel repeated the process over and over, so immersed in her project that she didn't notice when the noise from outside stopped and the sharp cut-grass smell gradually softened.

And as one match ate its way down the wooden stick and met her fingers, it didn't go out like the others had. It burned and burned and burned until the pain was too much, too stark and vivid and real, and she let it fall.

Polyester blankets, as it turned out, are tremendously flammable. This is why the faded tag said in tiny black letters *Caution: Flammable Material, Keep Away From Open Flame*. But at eight, of course, she didn't read warning labels and even if she had she wouldn't have cared in that moment.

When the flames caught, she was too surprised to do anything. She didn't run or scream or jump, she just froze. The fire seared her bare legs and it *hurt* and her hands shook, but she couldn't move. There was shouting coming from somewhere nearby, but it wasn't coming from her.

As suddenly as it started, she was being dragged off the bed, hauled away from the flames so quickly that her feet didn't even touch the ground. Elliot had her around the waist, pulling her away from the fire and into the hallway, stepping over a tray of broken dishes and mangled cheese sandwiches. He dropped her by the railing and stomped out the fire on the bed until there was nothing left but curling wisps of black smoke.

Elliot was breathing hard, panicked, and Rachel couldn't even look at him.

She waited for him to yell, or call Danny and tell on her, or phone the police because setting fires was bad and bad people like her belonged in prison. Instead, he dropped to his knees and wrapped his arms around her and whispered harshly, "Don't *ever* do that again."

Her eyes welled with tears, and even though Danny had told her that she was supposed to be brave and that brave girls didn't cry, she couldn't stop it when they started to slide down her cheeks in slick wet streams, and because she couldn't stop herself, she cried harder. She told him through a series of semi-coherent sobs, "It hurts, Elli, it *hurts*."

"I know. I'll fix it," he promised. And he did.

Nix lifted Rachel's hands in the darkness, examining the tips of her fingers as she held them in front of her face and tried to catch the sliver of dawn peeking in from behind the curtains. Even now, even asleep, Rachel's fingertips still tingled when she dreamt about fire. But because Elliot had asked, she never did play with matches again.

Chapter 11

"Somethin' about this...it just doesn't add up." Danny held a pile of papers in one hand, a couple inches away from his eyes. He'd forgotten his reading glasses again. He regarded the papers suspiciously while steering with his other hand and not bothering to keep his attention focused on the road. The road wasn't going anywhere. Or at least that was his excuse when Elliot pointed it out.

Elliot shifted tensely in the passenger seat, his gaze flicking from Danny to the road and back again. After a few moments and an angrily honked horn from a passing vehicle, Elliot grabbed the papers from him and sat them on the dashboard. "Are...are you sure you don't want me to drive for a while? I *can* drive," he said. The sky was gray and overcast. A light mist of rain landed on the windshield, obscuring the tidy rows of almond trees in the sprawling orchard they drove through.

"I'm fine," Danny responded. "It ain't nice to question your old man. Didn't I teach you anything?"

Elliot sighed. "Pops, we got the, uh...whatever that thing was—"

"Dryad," Nix piped up from the backseat. She watched their faces through the rearview mirror.

"Yeah," Elliot said, "we got it. Case closed. Would you just let it go already?"

Danny, bereft of his files, promptly pulled his phone out of his shirt pocket and started poking at it. "I was sure it was a demon."

Elliot cringed as the truck ran across the rumble strip at the side of the road before Danny straightened their course. "Well, it wasn't.

What does it matter anyway? You never used to care what it was you were hunting, just that you got the job done. Drilades not good enough for you now?"

"Dryads," Nix casually corrected.

"*Mfh*," Danny said dismissively. It was the kind of sound that suggested to Nix that she wasn't going to get off easily. If Danny just dropped this whole thing with Ida and Sonora, just left the place behind with a waved hand and a muttered, *"Good riddance!"* she could call it a day and be on her way. That clearly wasn't going to happen.

Elliot lifted a hand to his head, pressing two fingers against his temple. "Well we can stick around if you really think we missed something. But when Joan called, you said you wanted to check out Modesto and—"

"I know what I said."

The thing was, it was never, ever that easy. Danny wasn't working for anybody, but he checked in with other hunters regularly. There was a whole safety phone-tree thing going on with a group of them, a system to make sure that no disappearance would go unnoticed, no death unavenged.

She'd gotten the hunters off her own trail, but now she was stuck to them. For the time being, at least.

If she ditched the girl unharmed, they'd know to come after her. If she killed the girl under suspicious circumstances with Danny still obsessing over that one little puzzle piece in Sonora that didn't quite fit—Ida, the old bitch, was an endless nuisance—then they'd come after her. Nix briefly considered knocking off Rachel in unsuspicious circumstances, but that didn't sound enjoyable at all. And finally, if she killed the lot of them right now, their friends would come after her.

Even if she could deal with all of that, the risk still remained that somewhere in the middle of this mess, word would get out to the wrong archdemon regarding her location and their little misunderstanding from months ago would end up further biting Nix in the ass.

It was a tight position. These hunters were admittedly amusing, but she couldn't shake the regret over hopping into the girl's skin in the first place.

"Good," Elliot said. "Then you know you can't have it both ways. We can either stick around Sonora and keep looking into that woman's death, *which we've already done*, or we can move on to a real case with people who are still alive and need our help. Joan's waiting on us."

What a charming young man Elliot was. Nix was really starting to like this kid. Unfortunately, he didn't seem to be getting anywhere with Danny in spite of his very rational and helpful protestations.

"Yeah, yeah. We're going, ain't we? Just keep an eye on the papers, will you? If there's something else going on in that town, I want to know about it."

Just one more day, a week at most, and she could call it quits.

Chapter 12

When they finally arrived in Modesto and found that the suspicious activity Danny's pals had them chasing was in fact an anticlimactic and *human* car-theft operation, Danny took a couple hours by himself to decompress from the disappointment at a local dive bar, leaving his kids to pass the time in a 24-hour chain restaurant down the street from their new motel.

Nix'd only had a short period of time to get to know the man, but she suspected 'decompress' was code for 'sulk like a two-year-old denied candy' and didn't actually have any desire to endure that any more than she already had.

"You know," Nix started, as though she and Elliot had already been having a conversation and hadn't been sitting silently across from each other nibbling on fries in a booth for ten minutes, "you can join him if you want. I don't need a babysitter."

"Join Danny?" Elliot asked distractedly, peering out into the night through the large window next to them.

"Yeah." Obviously.

"At a bar?"

Nix eyed him like *he* was the two-year-old. "*Yeah*. At a bar. You do drink, don't you? Hell, I would if I could right now."

He returned his gaze to her, thick eyebrows wrinkling toward each other in confusion.

Nix followed up quickly with a muttered, "If—if I drank, that is. If I wasn't just nineteen and all. Not that I would. Drink, I mean." She shoved a fry into Rachel's mouth and looked away. "My point was that I don't need a babysitter."

He laughed—a deep, startled kind of laugh. He may even have choked a little with all the laughter. Nix didn't see what was so damn funny. Her acting was *spot-on* teenager. Nix knew that for a fact. She frowned at him, but Elliot was undeterred.

His grin was wide and inviting as he got up from the table and nodded to her, saying, "Come on, Rach. Let's go 'decompress' for a while."

She lifted an eyebrow but followed him out of the booth. "You're taking me to sulk in a bar?"

He wasn't, as it turned out, which was both better and worse than she'd expected. Back in their motel room, Elliot set a bottle of vodka on the little table between their beds. Nix plopped down on Rachel's designated bed and stared at the bottle. Rachel was staring, too.

"*This some sort of trick?*" Rachel asked, no small amount of suspicion in her tone. The girl, it seemed, didn't often get the opportunity to imbibe. It wasn't just about age, either—Elliot had been drinking since he was younger than she is now. For Elliot it was like a rite of passage. Danny had practically encouraged him.

No, it was something unique to Rachel, some reason Danny had never felt the need to clarify that had him lecturing her every time she looked too long at the beer fridge or the booze cabinet. Rachel was of the opinion that it was a gender thing, that it was unladylike to drink, and she'd been holding a nasty little grudge about it since she'd turned fifteen and been firmly lectured on the dangers of just one drink by a completely sloshed Danny.

Nix wasn't entirely convinced, because who knew what was going on in Danny's head—not her, that was for damn sure. Fucking pendant.

Elliot dropped down beside her on the bed, kicking off his shoes and angling his body to face her. He motioned to the bottle encouragingly.

Nix hesitated, wondering like Rachel if this was some sort of trick, then after a moment she shrugged, unscrewed the cap—fully sealed, so unlikely to have been tampered with or spiked with holy water—and took a quick gulp of vodka. Cheap vodka. The taste burned in the back of her throat.

Rachel hadn't tried much except beer and her palate reflected her inexperience. Nix'd had a lot of vodka in her time, but none quite this awful. She must have cringed in spite of herself because a chuckle escaped Elliot as he watched her with a wry smile pulling at the corners of his lips.

"Not quite what I was expecting," Nix admitted, handing him the bottle.

"Not a lot of selection at the liquor store," Elliot said, a note of apology in his voice. "Figured vodka would be the best bet. You loved those chocolate martinis at Joan and Jake's place when they used to let you try a sip."

"No, I mean, it wasn't what I was expecting from you," Nix clarified. She leaned into him and added in a mock-serious tone, "I am a minor, you know."

"Don't remind him! I'm nineteen," Rachel said. *"That's legal in some places."* She said it so earnestly that Nix had to fight back the urge to laugh—the kid was cute. Dumb, but cute.

"If we go to Canada, I'll be sure to mention it."

It was Elliot's turn to shrug as he took a swig from the bottle, handing it back to her. "Well, two years was a long time to be away, for me. You were a kid when I left." He paused, eyes flicking over her so quickly that Nix almost thought she'd imagined it and Rachel was convinced she had. "You're...not, anymore."

"See?" Rachel crowed, the metaphysical embodiment of her soul squirming in excitement.

Nix held back a grin, repositioning herself on the bed to face him, legs crossed. She took a deep pull from the bottle, this time careful not to allow Rachel's face to express her distaste for his choice of alcohol. "No. I'm not."

"And I know you don't need a babysitter, but it's been so long since we really got to hang out, just the two of us, I figured now might be a good time to start."

A lazy warmth coiled in Rachel's chest. *"I missed you so much,"* she confessed, but only Nix could hear her. *"Tell him?"*

Nix ignored her. This evening didn't need to degrade into maudlin declarations of longing, and Nix knew Rachel was just itching for the opportunity to pour her sad little heart out to somebody. Nix was doing them all a favor by keeping the girl's mouth shut.

She could feel the alcohol sweep through Rachel's veins, already beginning to take effect on this body, loosening her muscles and distorting her vision. Rachel's ever-churning thoughts gradually slowed until all she was doing was watching quietly as the night unfolded.

Nix didn't tend to feel the effects of alcohol herself, only the physical reactions of her hosts, but somehow she'd stopped being quite so pissed off about being stuck here and started feeling at ease. "Aw," she teased, "you'd rather hang out with little ol' me than go with Pops to a real bar? That still sounds an awful lot like babysitting."

"You've never been in a bar with Danny," Elliot said, taking a heftier swig of the vodka and shaking his head. "I can't count how many bar fights I've had to intervene in just so he didn't kill some poor bastard. Now *that's* babysitting. Hardly even get a chance to drink and unwind when he's there. This is far less stressful, believe me."

"Mmm," Nix offered in commiseration, indulging in another drink herself.

"It was worse with El gone," Rachel told Nix, like they were sharing-friends or something. *"Pops would just come home all bruised and bleeding and there was nothing I could do about it. He'd say it*

was from some hunt, but I knew it wasn't."

Elliot leaned back, propping himself up on one arm and causing his shirt to ride up a bit. Rachel didn't fail to notice, which meant that Nix noticed too. Smiling, Elliot said, "You remember that time in LA when you broke your wrist?"

Chuckling, Rachel said, *"Not well after those shots of tequila Jake gave me. Sure cut the pain, though."*

"It's a little blurry," Nix told him with a grin. "Hurt a lot less with the alcohol."

"Danny was so mad at Jake for that!"

"Nothing like tequila after a rougarou hunt, Jake always says."

"Like Jake always says: nothing like tequila after a rougarou hunt."

Elliot's laughter trailed off and he tilted his head to the side, eyes squinting at her in the dim light. "That one wasn't a rougarou. That was a demon."

Nix stilled. Caught off guard, she tamped down her annoyance with Rachel long enough to smile disarmingly and reply, "Well, like I said, it was a little blurry."

Rachel hung on Elliot's reaction as Nix quickly calculated nine possible weapons within reach to kill the boy.

Something passed through his gaze but vanished just as smoothly as it entered, replaced by a quirked eyebrow as Elliot reached over and tugged the bottle from her grasp. "I think I'd better cut you off if you can't even remember *that*," he said, teasing.

Nix smirked, taking a moment to offer a curt warning, *"Try that again and I'll slit your boy's throat."*

Rachel went silent, a chill trickling down her spine, cold sweat beading in response to her sudden fear. Nix couldn't control involuntary things like that—didn't usually need to. Once, she'd accidentally scared a host into a heart attack, but generally speaking, involuntary responses were pitifully pointless against Nix's grand schemes.

"Hey, don't blame the vodka!" Nix said, leaning forward to recapture the bottle and encountering only token resistance from Elliot. "It's just been a while, is all. You missed a lot when you were gone."

"How many hunts did Danny bring you on when I was away?"

Nix thumbed through Rachel's memories and decided, "Not many. Mostly just the long ones for research and stuff. He doesn't like to leave me by myself at home, but he doesn't like me being in the field, either. Hard to find a balance like that. Especially with all the activity lately. He's hunting almost all the time now."

Elliot glanced down at his hands, suddenly serious as he asked, "Has he...has he been acting weird to you? More distant, I mean. Secretive?"

Nix considered this, but she didn't have much basis for comparison. With Rachel's thoughts less guarded under the haze of booze, Nix didn't even have to pry to know that while he'd been a bit more intense about work lately, if he was hiding anything from her, he was doing a fairly good job of it. For lack of a better option, Nix pointed out, "Danny's not exactly the sharing-and-caring type."

"No, I know. It's just, don't you see a difference in him? He's changed since I've been away."

"Maybe he's going senile," Nix suggested reasonably. The man was old, after all, and humans rapidly degraded in quality with age—that was just common knowledge.

Elliot stared at her askance, as though Danny wasn't already way the hell over the hill and flirting with all kinds of crazy.

"I'm...kidding?" she amended.

"Well I'm not." Elliot waved his hands around animatedly, the effects of the alcohol becoming apparent in his exaggerated mannerisms. "He's been talking about 'the end of times' and reading the book of revelations and—and *texting*. I mean, Christ, Rach, maybe it is the end of times! I didn't even know he knew what texting *was*."

"You're right, that is a bit worrying," she agreed, another sip of vodka burning her tongue. "At least he's not sexting?"

Elliot grimaced. "Argh, why would you even—no." He raised his hands. "I do not need that image in my head, thank you."

Change could be difficult to recognize from too close a perspective. It was insidious that way. Just because Rachel hadn't noticed much change in Danny's behavior didn't mean Elliot was wrong. Maybe Danny was hiding something.

If that was the case, Nix wanted to know about it. Nix shrugged and suggested, "Maybe we should check his phone?"

Elliot gawked at her. "Are you serious? He'd kill us. He'd kill us and bring us back to life just to kill us again."

"But if you're really worried about him..." she pushed.

"I don't...I mean, well...*hmph*," Elliot trailed off, bringing the bottle to his lips and holding it there for a long moment before tipping it up and drinking. He stared at the wall for a while, so Nix considered the conversation ended and snatched back the vodka. It had been a long shot, anyway.

Minutes of silence passed before Elliot spoke up again, his tone unreadable but soft. "If we do this," he said, "we're in it together. And we'd have to do it right."

Now Nix was gawking, mouth partly ajar, eyes wide, head tilted in attempt to get a better angle on him and discern his intent. The kid was not fucking around. He was really willing to do this. "I can't believe you're taking me up on it," she admitted. "You'd really rifle through an old man's text messages without his permission?"

Rachel, deep inside her own head, shouted, "*Damn it, Elliot! Clue in—that's not me!*"

Nix, thoroughly entertained by both her and her adorably earnest brother, told Rachel, "*He likes me better, kid,*" just to make her cry.

Elliot looked stricken. "What?"

"My my, there just might be hope for you yet." Nix grinned. "I'm teasing. I'm in. Let's do it. But not tonight."

"Yeah. Not tonight. Tonight's for vodka," Elliot declared, passing her the bottle.

Nix gladly accepted his terms, smiling as Rachel whimpered and her tear ducts started to water. A gulp of bottom-shelf vodka excused that nicely.

Chapter 13

Elliot breathed slowly and evenly in the bed next to hers, a sheet pulled up to his chest and an ugly, stained comforter pushed down to the end of the mattress despite the chill in the night air. The room was dark but for the glow of the streetlights slipping through the crack between the curtains. Nix was lying on her side, pretending to be asleep as she watched him in the darkness.

Every time she shifted on the bed, it groaned and Elliot stirred. He was such a fucking light sleeper she couldn't even sneak out of the room without him knowing, in spite of the quantity of alcohol he'd consumed before bed.

She was considering drugging him—maybe slipping him one or two of her knockout pills just so she didn't have to lay here and stare at the damn ceiling every night while these precious humans got their beauty rest and Rachel's inane dreams twisted though her head—when a shadow swept past the window.

Nix canted her head to take a peek, but saw nothing but a brief flash of red lights, probably taillights. There weren't a lot of people around here. In fact, Nix was willing to bet that these hunters were the only ones with low enough standards to subject themselves to such a rattrap.

Still, someone had passed by. Someone rather small. Could there be a pintsized ax murderer outside? Oh, she hoped so. But more likely, that was wishful thinking. Stare into the darkness long enough and all the shadows start to look like something frightful and entertaining. But they were just shadows. Boring goddamn shadows.

The alcohol had knocked Rachel right out. She was dreaming about being chased down winding roads by a monster she couldn't see. Nix was no Freud, but the symbolism seemed pretty obvious there.

Boredom made Nix quietly scratch at the shadowy places inside Rachel's mind, seeing if she could coax a bit of that darkness to the surface. Nix had never been a fan of locked doors, and lucky for Rachel, Nix's curiosity was cheaper than a shrink.

Rachel twitched toward consciousness but Nix soothed her back down, telling her, *"Shh, just sleep, pretty doll, just sleep,"* telling her, *"you're safe, everything is all right."*

Rachel's mind was so much easier to see clearly when she was like this, when her guard was down and she wasn't putting up a fight.

The clutter of boxes inside her head cleared away, shifting into a wide road bracketed by a desert that stretched into eternity on either side, just like the ones they drove down in rural California every day. Nix didn't see the appeal, but to Rachel it felt like home. It was safe and familiar, and all those rolling hills of dirt and sand and emptiness were where she belonged.

For a while, Nix was there with her. Elliot breathed, slow, steady, in and out. Rachel ran, bare feet slapping against the asphalt in the borderlands of her mind, her own breathing fast and stilted. Nix followed at an easy pace, the shadow at Rachel's back, admiring the barren landscape and the way the wind swept across the road and rustled through the bushes.

Rachel panted, terror pouring off her like sweat. She tripped over nothing—not a surprise, the girl was as graceful as a three-legged chupacabra—and fell hard to her knees. Nix wandered up behind her, watchful, intrigued. Rachel glanced up and scrambled to stand, tracks of dirt and tears staining her face.

She gasped, but she wasn't looking at Nix.

Nix turned, following her gaze, and from the shadows emerged a tiny figure.

A little girl with long, dark hair walked up to them. She was smudged with soot; her hands, her cheeks, her white nightgown. Nix could smell the sharp, acrid scent of ash on her, like an entire forest had burned to the ground with her in the middle of it. Wisps of smoke rose from her skin. In the creases of her lacy dress, embers still burned, slow but bright.

The girl's gaze was far away, her eyes a glazed white as pale as her skin. Nix couldn't even tell if she knew they were there. Rachel stared wide-eyed at the girl, her lips parted in horror, though Nix didn't really get what the big deal was—the kid was a little creepy, sure, but not exactly intimidating. She was what, three and a half feet tall? *Pfft.* Nix could take her.

Suddenly, Rachel turned and caught Nix's gaze. She stretched her hand out, palm up as if in supplication, and Nix startled at the unexpected attention.

"Please," Rachel sobbed. *"Stop me."*

The little girl's head tilted to the side, dropping until it rested awkwardly on her shoulder, thick black veins bulging out of her neck. Her mouth opened wide, cavernous and—

Something tapped against the window.

Nix snapped back into the room, drawing Rachel from her nightmares. Rachel's mind was still reeling with images from her dreams, but they dissipated quickly as consciousness rose up to meet her.

Elliot was already sitting up in bed, the white sheet pooled at his waist.

"You hear that?" he asked.

Nix nodded, then realized he probably couldn't see her nod in the darkness, and whispered, "Yeah."

Elliot cringed. "What's that smell?"

The foul scent of putrefaction breathed into the room like a whisper, barely there but unmistakable.

Nix listened. A huff of air sounded from beyond the door, almost a grunt.

Elliot tensed, slipping silently from the bed and pulling a .45 out from underneath his pillow.

He raised a finger to his lips and caught her eyes. Nix nodded her understanding, adrenaline already working its way through Rachel's veins like a bright light through the lingering haze of booze. This was so much more interesting than watching Elliot sleep and enduring Rachel's stupid trauma-dreams. If there was anything less than an ax murderer out there, Nix was going to be pissed.

Elliot moved soundlessly toward the window with such practiced grace it was as though his feet weren't even touching the ground—an impressive achievement for someone who'd downed half a bottle of vodka only hours before. Nix rose to join him and the bed springs shrieked with such malice it was like she'd personally offended them. Elliot glared in her direction but all she could offer was an apologetic shrug.

A scratch at the door.

Nix and Elliot both looked to the deadbolt and chain securing it, even though she'd watched Elliot check it three times before turning the light off and again before getting into bed. With swift, precise steps, Elliot leaned against the wall and peeked past the yellowed curtain.

Nix and Rachel waited, thoughts churning with anticipation and dread, respectively. Elliot's brow furrowed as he glanced at her then back out the window.

He snuck over and leaned down to whisper into her ear, "I can't see anything, there's nothing out there," just as that nothing slammed itself into the door with a resounding *bang*. Elliot stumbled into her, but recovered just as fast. "Get into the bathroom and lock the door, I'll line the threshold with salt." When she didn't move Elliot said, "*Now*, Rachel! Go!"

Nix was unimpressed with the whole being-trapped-in-a-bathroom-behind-a-salt-line idea until she heard the barking. It started off as a low growl then rose to a sharp, feverish pitch that made Rachel's ears ring and Nix's borrowed blood run cold. She knew that sound.

The adjoining motel room door slammed open and Danny emerged in his rumpled clothes from the day before with a shotgun in his hands, looking exactly like the kind of person that should not be holding a shotgun.

Elliot looked to him. "Pops—"

"Shh," Danny admonished, creeping up to the window himself to take a look. The *shh* abruptly turned to "*Shit*. Stay back from the door," he commanded, voice raised above the increasingly haunting cries from outside.

The whole bathroom-salt-line thing wasn't looking nearly as bad as it had been a moment ago, but Nix was still caught unprepared when firm hands gripped Rachel's shoulders and walked her backwards into the bathroom. Elliot was already pouring the salt across the threshold and passing her a loaded revolver before Nix really caught up. "Wait—" she managed, a weak and unconvincing protest, but it was already too late.

"Stay there," Elliot told her, as if she had any other option at this point. The banging against the door grew louder as Elliot and Danny shouted to each other, Danny barking commands and Elliot following them almost faster than they hit the air.

"Pops, what is this thing?" Elliot asked over the noise.

"Just stay back! Give me that salt—I said stay away from that door, boy!"

They were just lucky it was too stupid to have gone right through the window, but that was only a matter of time. The salt line wouldn't hold it for long.

It was here for her. It had to be. They didn't just appear out of nowhere; there were always masters controlling their actions, puppeteers to pull their strings. This was not a creature of independent thought. Nix had managed to avoid detection this far, and she didn't think they could possibly have caught her scent—if they had, they'd have found her quicker than this.

But somehow, there was a hellhound on the other side of that door, and she was completely, irrevocably *fucked*.

Oh, she was fucked on all possible levels. Not only was she fucked on the one hand, with the hellhound tearing down the door, ready to drag her back to its master for Lucifer knew what atrocious and *unfair* punishments, but even if the hellhound didn't get to her now, she was trapped behind a damn salt line!

Rachel started to fuss in her head, the alcohol still buzzing a bit in her veins and making her bold, but Nix pushed her down, unwilling to expend valuable time dealing with her endless 'Oh no, my family is in danger!' nonsense.

She dropped to her knees on the bathroom floor, trying to think, she just needed a moment to *think*.

At least she had Danny and Elliot. They could buy her time, delay the creature's entrance, and if she was very lucky it might even stop to chew on their corpses long enough that she could get away. There was no window in this tiny bathroom, which *had* to be a fire hazard, but it still left her with no means of escape, unless perhaps the wind might sweep through with the hound's arrival and stir the salt just enough to—

"The hell is that racket?"

The room stilled. Danny and Elliot turned to stone, guns raised, bag of salt spilling out on the floor. Even the hellhound went silent.

The voice had come from the other side of the door. Light footsteps followed, the even *clomp clomp clomp* of heavy boots across cracked pavement.

Danny inched back toward the window. Nix pulled Rachel's body up from the floor, leaning into the doorframe as much as she could to get a better view.

The low growling started up again, like the smooth rev of a finely tuned engine.

"What the—" the man's voice returned in a startled shout.

The night dissolved into screams.

Danny flew out the front door, Elliot close behind, guns firing with loud, jolting blasts. A light gust of wind swept through the room as the door opened, the reek of death and rot following swiftly behind, so pungent that Nix had to temper Rachel's gag reflex. The salt didn't even stir.

Nix paced in a tight circle on the pitifully small bathroom floor, trying to get a good view of the action so at least she could see it coming. Rachel's eyes had long since adjusted to the darkness, but Nix could see nothing but obscured shadows dart past the window behind the curtains, and the occasional flash of burning red eyes.

The reek of the hound was so powerful Nix could taste it at the back of Rachel's throat, like it was trying to crawl down inside.

As quickly as the noise had started, it vanished.

Water swished through the bathroom pipes. Cicadas hummed in the distance. The shrill buzz of too many fluorescent lights carried from the restaurant down the street. A passing motorist honked his horn from half a mile down the road and the first notes of a police siren rang far, far away.

Then she heard the breathing and for a terrible moment she couldn't discern its source. They were dead, all of them, and the hound was coming for her. She had to get away, had to—

Danny's voice carried, ragged and halting, through the open doorway, saying, "Get up. You hurt? Let me take a look at you."

"I'm fine, Pops. Can't say the same for that guy, though. Wasn't he from the front desk?"

"Yup, looks like."

Nix sighed in relief—relief that the hellhound appeared to be either chased away or out of commission, that is. Though she supposed she didn't mind terribly that the two hunters survived. That thought gave her pause but she didn't have time to dwell on it.

"Shouldn't we call a—an ambulance...or something?"

"There'll be some on their way, I'm sure, what with all the ruckus. Can already hear the sirens. We'd best leave before they get here," Danny declared, as though the salt that was spilled all over the floors and the bullet casings and the general state of disrepair the rooms were in wouldn't be at all suspicious to the authorities. How they were still alive and hunting was in so many ways a mystery to Nix.

"But, Pops—"

"Man's dead already, son. We did what we could." Oh good, a body. They could add that to the list of not-suspicious-at-all.

"Yeah. Okay."

But Nix wasn't out of the woods yet. Now was not the time to fret over human idiocy—now was the time to bank on it.

As she heard their footsteps round the corner toward the open door, she clutched the gun tightly in her hands and dropped back to her position on the floor with Rachel's knees tucked under her, as far back from the threshold as she could get. She stared at the floor in front of her.

Nix took a deep breath, focused.

If she played this right, there was a chance she could still make this work. If she didn't, if they realized she couldn't cross the salt line, she was doomed. Not eaten-by-a-hellhound doomed, but pretty fucking doomed nonetheless.

"Rachel?" Danny's voice called to her. "Darlin'?"

She ignored him, schooling Rachel's features into a convincing portrait of shock. Throw in an orange shock blanket and she could get an award for this performance.

"Rach?" Elliot said, moving closer to her. She didn't look up when his shadow towered over her. "Hey, come on, we've got to go." He stopped in the doorway, staring down at her. "Rachel?"

"What's wrong?" Danny asked, coming up behind him. He took one look at her and turned to Elliot, whispering, "Do you think she saw him? Oh Christ, all that blood, I didn't think she'd see from here. Must've snuck up to the window?"

Elliot nodded. "Rach?"

"Darlin', we did all we could for the man, he just didn't make it."

She swallowed hard and stared at Rachel's hands, letting her eyes well up with tears.

Danny made a pitiful sound in the back of his throat, like he was distressed but didn't know what to do about it. Hushed, he told Elliot, "Get her up and packed. Fast. We have to leave."

"Rach, hey..." Elliot prodded, moving toward her. She watched his shoes inch toward the salt line, and she held her breath.

Like it was nothing, Elliot crossed over, scattering the line and wrapping his arms around her, pulling her to her feet.

Nix sighed deeply and threw her arms around him, and if that wasn't part of the act she'd never admit to it. "I saw all the...the blood, El," she lied to cover for her enthusiasm. The only blood she could see was on him and it didn't appear to be his own, but she could smell the sharp metallic scent of it, an identifiable undertone beneath everything else.

Elliot murmured into her hair, "Hey, it's okay, it's going to be okay, but we have to move."

"What did you do to it?" she asked him, genuinely interested and expecting him to tell her they'd scared it off somehow.

"Killed it. Pops took it down. I think it was a hellhound, you know, like in the books."

"I—I didn't know you could kill those," she said. There were ways, of course, but she hadn't expected these hunters to be aware of them. Most humans never had to deal with a hellhound, and if they did, they sure as fuck didn't live to tell about it. Hellhounds were virtually impervious to harm. They were savage and brutal and deadly. Maybe she'd underestimated these hunters.

"You know Pops, he can kill anything."

"Yeah," she said, staring up at him. "I guess."

Elliot released her and walked back into the room, throwing things in his bag. Nix glanced down at the now-scattered salt line. She crossed it. Not being jolted back into place with the sensation of having been lit on fire was extremely gratifying.

Danny and Elliot rushed around both rooms, gathering their things as the sirens intensified. Nix walked straight up to the door and looked outside, not quite believing their claim that the hellhound was dead—and also admittedly intrigued now by the prospect of 'all that blood' waiting just outside their motel room.

Staring up at the blanket of stars lay the unmoving body of an older man. He was Danny's age. Rachel's gut clenched. Nix walked past the threshold, over another broken line of salt, and nearly stepped on a stray finger. Several feet to her left, an arm was lying neatly in the middle of the parking lot.

Nix glanced down at the man, noticing for the first time the dark shape of the hound resting near him. Its red eyes were dull but open. The rest of it was indistinct, only really detectable in her peripheral vision. It smelled just as bad as it had earlier, so it was hard to say whether it was actually dead or not. But it was *still*. Impossibly still for something living.

The man's corpse steamed, still-warm blood hitting the cool night air and rising up in billows of faint white clouds. Condensation had already begun to form at the edge of the window above him.

Gingerly, Nix nudged the hound with Rachel's foot. Its head lolled.

She glanced up at Danny as he scurried past her toward the truck, the man who'd taken down a hellhound in but a few short minutes and walked away with little more than some scratches. Maybe the things Rachel said about him really were true.

Danny caught her gaze, seeming to just notice her, and Nix promptly found herself being dragged toward the truck. "Just don't look, darlin'," he was mumbling to her, soft and concerned with a touch of apology in his voice. "You don't need to see all that. Stay in the truck."

Behind him, Elliot emerged with two bags slung over his shoulder, his and Rachel's. "What do you want to do about that?" he asked, motioning with a grimace down at the hound.

"Throw it in the back. We'll burn it when we get someplace safe."

Elliot nodded but there was something like suspicion in his eyes.

Danny seemed stressed but unphased. A hellhound should have been just as jarring for him as it had been for Nix, if not more so, but the man was stone. She couldn't read him.

She climbed into the backseat and looked out at the stars. She was taking this too far, following them like she was. She was an imposter who couldn't be overlooked forever, but Nix couldn't stop now.

She could feel it stirring in the air, itching in her veins, twitching under her borrowed skin.

She was getting close to something.

Chapter 14

Danny sat next to Nix and across from Elliot in a little restaurant off the interstate. She'd ordered the pancake breakfast and drowned it in a sinful quantity of butter-flavored syrup. Danny barely batted an eye at her but she could sense his disapproval.

It wasn't that Nix cared or anything, but she couldn't help noticing the tension in the air this morning. Neither man had spoken more than a few words to the other since last night's little fiasco and the burning of the hound that followed.

Nix idly fingered her dull breadknife as she sliced into the pancakes, wondering if the tension could, indeed, be cut out of them with a knife—or however that saying went. Plus, Rachel's stomach was positively reeling with anxiety and it was beginning to hinder Nix's enjoyment of the pancakes, which was unacceptable. She was about to call them out on it, or maybe test the knife theory, when Elliot beat her to it.

Elliot, in rare form, burst out with, "Pops, what is going *on*?" so loudly that half the other patrons turned to stare at them. He fidgeted in his seat, glanced around, and hastily lowered his voice, saying, "All these jobs and all in the same area? We've never seen this much activity before, let alone had things seek us out. I mean, a *hellhound*? Why would there be a hellhound sniffing around our motel?"

Danny didn't even look up at his son. The absentminded way he pushed his bacon around on his plate was even more disconcerting. Nothing had been speared, skewered, or decimated since they'd sat down. Even Nix was a little concerned by this.

Mumbling around a mouthful of halfheartedly chewed eggs, Danny replied, "What are you talkin' about? We had that werewolf just a couple years ago. And how about those vamps before that?"

She reached over Danny to grab a napkin and covertly slip a hand into his pocket, heedless of his personal space before returning to her own and dabbing the syrup from Rachel's chin.

Elliot shook his head. "Those were years apart. This is down to weeks. And it was a hellhound. It isn't *normal*."

Danny let his fork fall with a clatter to his plate. "Well we aren't in the business of *normal*," he spat.

Nix nibbled on her pancakes, mildly entertained by the display of their obvious distress. She was feeling great, riding the high of invincibility. She'd just survived a hellhound attack. She was unstoppable.

Danny and Elliot weren't sharing her enthusiasm. Humans really did need their beauty sleep to be at their friskiest.

The best part of all this was that no one had even thought to turn their suspicions on her. Danny didn't seem bothered by the hellhound incident at all, and Elliot was blaming dear old Pops. It was...interesting.

"Pops, if—if you *did* something, if—if that hellhound was there for a reason, you...you could *tell* us. I mean, not that—it's just..." he trailed off, this voice betraying his confusion and lack of sleep. He sighed. "You can't tell me you don't think something is going on here."

The old man raised his head, giving Elliot an intimidating glower. "I don't think something is going on here. End of discussion."

A pause. Elliot's jaw tightened. He nodded. "Yes, sir."

Danny rose from the table, tilted his head toward the restroom and said, "Be ready to leave by the time I get back. There's work to be done and I won't have us running outta daylight."

Once Danny was out of earshot, Nix asked Elliot, "Really? You're just going to let that go?"

Elliot shrugged and didn't meet her eyes. It wasn't until he noticed what her hands were doing that he finally glanced up at her.

"You stole his phone?" he demanded, seemingly flabbergasted in spite of the fact that they'd already agreed to this.

Rachel's fingers flitted over the device as Nix sought out Daniel Whipsaw's deepest, darkest secrets. "Yup." There had to be something here. Anything.

"I can't believe you stole his phone."

Phone contacts were a dead end. So was the call history. No numbers popped out at her. The only repeated names were Joan and Kevin, and a bunch of the same private listing over and over again. "We did agree to do this, or did the vodka blur your memory?"

Elliot looked toward the restroom then back to her and back to the restroom again, gnawing on his bottom lip the whole time with wide doe eyes. It was possible he was having a stroke or something, but Nix was too preoccupied to play doctor at the moment, however fun that may have been.

"Well?" he prodded.

"Oh, so now you're interested?"

Damn. Text inbox was empty. So was the outbox. Too empty, actually. Suspiciously empty. She'd seen him sending and responding to texts like a neurotic teenage girl. Danny was deleting texts as he received them *and* as he sent them. If that wasn't suspicious, Nix didn't know what was.

"Plus side," Nix offered, "he isn't sexting—unless he's really, really good at hiding the evidence. *But* there's nothing useful on this phone, either." She'd been half-expecting some compromising nude photos to be on here, but there weren't even *uncompromising* nude photos. What a disappointment.

"Nothing at all?"

"Nada," Nix confirmed. "For sure he's hiding something, but I still don't know what it is. Whoever he's talking to and whatever he's talking about, he doesn't want anybody to know."

"Damn, you think you can slip that back into his pocket without him noticing?"

Nix huffed, slightly offended by his lack of faith. "Obviously."

Elliot leaned forward, resting his chin on his hands and staring at her. "When did you become such a capable little thief?"

Sliding the phone out of sight as Danny returned from the restroom, Nix winked.

Chapter 15

Nix had been with the hunters now for almost three weeks, and all to no avail.

Danny wasn't talking and Elliot had stopped pushing him. Nix was starting to think she'd overinvested in this whole thing. Maybe there really wasn't anything suspicious going on with them. Maybe they were just regular, run-of-the-mill, overdramatic hunters. Either way, Nix was bored, tired, and pissed.

All she really had for entertainment was the feeble and emotionally volatile mind of a nineteen-year-old girl to play with.

For her part, right at this moment, Rachel was swimming in the emotionally volatile depths of shame. Nix could feel the clenching in her chest, a fist gripping her heart. Every time Nix brought up the subject of Elliot with her, a pit grew in Rachel's stomach, heavy and uncomfortable, but her pulse still drummed with exhilaration, sang with it.

Rachel denied it, of course—they always did. But it was hard enough to deny physical reactions without the added icing of all those sinful thoughts and fantasies that flitted through her head. The more Rachel tried not to think dirty thoughts about her surrogate brother, the more she was unable to think of anything else. Then she'd go on a self-flagellating rampage for a few hours and cry about what a terrible, oh-so-wicked and naughty person she was.

It was all very maudlin. Nix was kind of enjoying it.

On the longer rides, when the conversation had died off and the radio wasn't working and the only sound was the dull, sputtering roar of the engine, Nix would dangle Rachel's self-loathing in front of her like a carrot. She would poke and prod and demand entertainment. Rachel, being an increasingly satisfactory hostess, jumped onto her cross all too willingly.

Nix especially liked getting her worked up by threatening to kill the two men. Depending on her mood, Rachel would panic or beg or threaten or just go totally silent and retreat into what little realty remained in the dark time-out corner of her mind. Unfortunately, she was getting less and less fun to play with, rarely rising to that particular bait, which meant that Nix was getting even more bored. And a bored Nix was a dangerous Nix.

Elliot was in the shower, behind the thin door of yet another motel bathroom in an endless string of motel bathrooms. This one was in Fremont on their way to La Grange, their safe house of sorts.

Because Danny still treated his children like children, they were once again sharing a room with two double beds. Normal siblings would probably have been separated around puberty and allowed some modicum of privacy, but not with this family, no sir. Danny was convinced Rachel needed 24/7 protection, but he had his own secrets to keep and a wall to abuse with tacks and bits of yarn, so this responsibility fell to Elliot.

And Elliot, well, he took Danny's orders very seriously. When they were younger, Rachel and Elliot would share a bed if they had to accompany Danny on a job. They'd slept back to back on tiny, shitty mattresses, Elliot telling her scary stories before lying to her and telling her that they weren't true. Rachel's disbelief in the boogies could be sourced straight back to her irresponsible big brother. Sometimes, he'd walk to the nearest 7-Eleven to buy her milk, and then warm it up in the burrito-scented microwave, and the memories were so appallingly cute that Nix threw up a little in Rachel's mouth.

With these sleeping arrangements, the temptation was unbearable, for both Rachel and Nix. But Nix was determined to draw this out, waiting for the perfect moment to execute her plans—and lock Rachel into forever keeping her peace about her little vacation from responsibility, lest she completely destroy her relationship with Elliot. One day's hesitation would become *decades*, and Nix would get off scot-fucking-free.

Nix was curled up in one of the beds with a book, wearing nothing but white panties and a tight t-shirt artfully rucked up to well above Rachel's waist. The book was only for show—something about an orphan falling in love with her fanged Prince Charming that just screamed to Rachel's *id*. Being a sad little orphan girl herself, Rachel seemed to identify with the protagonist. Nix would have teased her about this relentlessly, but she was too focused on pretending to read while listening to the splatter of water on tile.

Elliot usually came out right about now in a puff of fog with a tiny scrap of a towel wrapped around his waist as he searched through his bag for something clean to wear, as if the bag wasn't already obsessively organized.

He wouldn't mention the fact that he knew she was watching him out of the corner of her eye, and she wouldn't mention the fact that he could have brought the change of clothes into the bathroom with him in the first place and avoided strutting around nearly naked. It *was* a fantastic sight. Certainly worth fake-reading for.

Tonight was different. The wait drew longer and Nix's focus waned until she found herself accidentally reading a page of the book she wasn't reading, and secretly enjoying it. Then she heard a sound from the bathroom. Her interest piqued immediately. Rachel didn't quite catch on, which made it even sweeter.

Nix held perfectly still on the starchy white sheets, holding Rachel's breath and listening.

A moan. Low and male and heady. A shiver flickered up her spine and heat pooled in her belly, landing her thoughts firmly on the other side of that thin door.

A gasp. Nix bit her lip—or rather, Rachel's lip, but Rachel wasn't exactly complaining. The moment it had occurred to the girl what big brother was up to in the shower, she stopped caring about Nix completely.

But as Nix had already made known, she didn't *like* being ignored.

She stood up slowly, careful not to make the bedsprings squeak, flicked off the bedside light and padded in the dark over to the door. She pressed an ear against it, listening to the pitter-patter of the water, the shifting of feet on the shower floor. The water fell in uneven waves, lighter and heavier in turns as it splashed to the ground in sheets.

Nix didn't even have to prod Rachel's imagination for this one. Images of Elliot poured through her head; naked and wet in the shower, washing and scrubbing and wrapping his hand around his dick, jerking off in fast, slick strokes.

Rachel's body ached for him. Nix could feel her face flush with heat and embarrassment. Embarrassment for listening, fantasizing, noticing it in the first place. Rachel's bodily reactions would have been annoying if Nix weren't also enjoying the burn of arousal between the girl's thighs.

This night was going better than she expected, and when she leaned against the wall beside the door, it only improved.

In a choked voice, Elliot said Rachel's name.

The sound was barely discernible over the pounding water, but it rang as loud and clear as a bell in Rachel's ears. Rachel was salivating over the thought of *him* thinking about *her*. When she realized where her thoughts had strayed to, Rachel promptly went about detailing a list of reasons why Elliot could not possibly be masturbating in the shower while thinking about her. It was an easy denial. Easy to construct and even easier to believe.

But while Rachel contemplated the sound levels and the acoustical properties of the bathroom, then declared her own hearing to be lacking, Nix was spreading her legs open and slipping a hand into her panties.

Rachel jolted at this—internally, of course. Externally, Nix had all the control and couldn't be swayed by backseat drivers, however zealous they may be.

It was an odd state, sharing one physical form between two beings. There was an undeniable intimacy about it. Every rush of arousal pulsing through Rachel's veins, Nix felt as though it was her own. And it was, now. Hers to own, to steer, to drive, to *crash*. She'd have Rachel's broken and shattered body wrapped around a light pole by the time she was done, and Nix would feel every glorious second of it.

They both felt Nix slide Rachel's fingers beneath the waistband of her underwear. She tilted her head back against the wall and pumped her fingers in and out, trying to match the sounds coming from just beyond the door.

For a moment, Rachel was completely enthralled by the sensations, but Nix made sure to point out the fact that Elliot could open that door at any moment and *"—find his kid sister next to the bathroom door with her legs spread wide, finger-fucking herself while listening to him jerk off in the shower."*

Rachel started to worry, but Nix's ministrations only sped up as she continued, *"Are you sure you heard what you think you heard? Even if he is getting off right now, you really believe he'd be thinking about you? He's probably picturing that busty waitress by the docks, or that young mother you interviewed in Fresno the other day. Even that homely little truck-stop whore is more likely to be on his mind than his sister is. Do you think it will disgust him to see you like this? What would he think if he could see the sick, twisted thoughts in your head?"* The words landed like blows, just as Nix had intended them to. The satisfaction swelled as she felt Rachel withering and trying to pull away, but Nix held tight and dragged her along.

Elliot's breathing was audible—rough and shallow. As was the slap of flesh on flesh—hard and fast. Another moan followed, this one muffled, like he was pressing his hand against his mouth. Nix stretched herself with another finger while the meat of her palm crushed and rubbed her clit until sparks of light and bliss were filling the darkness of the room for the both of them.

The shower stopped. Rachel went cold with fear and panic, but the fire in her belly didn't fade.

"Or maybe you did hear him right," Nix offered sympathetically, just to keep her off balance. *"Maybe if he sees what a little slut you are he'll take pity on you and fuck you into this wall like you wish he would. Should we wait and see?"*

The shower curtain screeched on the metal rod and the thump of feet followed. Rachel begged her to stop, begged her *not* to stop. A litany of confused, aroused pleas spilled out of her and tumbled around in her mind. A final flick of her thumb and they were both falling, climax slamming into her with an unanticipated force.

A gasp escaped her lips, and Nix wasn't sure if it was hers or Rachel's.

The door handle turned.

Nix was across the room and under the covers before a sliver of light could penetrate the darkness.

Chapter 16

This was it. Danny hadn't brought up Sonora in two days. He was meeting up with friends, either for a hunt or to share makeup tips, she wasn't sure, but the point was, after tonight Sonora would be far enough from anyone's mind for Nix to make a clean break for it.

Nix was more relaxed than she'd been in days, but now it was Rachel who was on edge. It was a pity. They'd had a nice thing going, in Nix's opinion, but Rachel had now regressed to bargaining.

"*If you just leave,*" Rachel said, "*I promise you, we won't come after you. Danny doesn't need to know. I mean that. You—you could just, you know, fly away or whatever it is you do, without anybody knowing you were here in the first place.*"

"*Sure,*" Nix said. "*Because you hunters are so trustworthy.*"

"*How can you even—fine, okay, fine. You can read my mind, right? So read it. I'm not lying. You know I'm not lying!*"

"*No, I know you believe you aren't lying. Not really the same thing, kid. Certainly not a guarantee. Besides, where's the fun in just leaving?*"

Rachel huffed. "*Then...then take me instead,*" she pleaded. "*They haven't even noticed that you're here. Just crash the truck or drive off a bridge or something. Make it look like an accident and they won't even think to come looking for you and there'd be no way I could tell them otherwise.*"

It was cute how much she cared. The whole martyr thing she had going was just adorable. Unnecessary, because Nix was mostly just teasing—three dead hunters was begging to be caught—but still adorable.

"*Hmm,*" Nix pretended to consider, "*well, I suppose you have a logical argument there.*" Rachel hung on her every word, tensed up like a turtle in its shell. "*But...I think I'll stick with the murder thing. Can't be too careful, you know.*"

Rachel deflated, and her body tried to cry. Nix made it stop. "*Why are you doing this?*"

Nix snickered. "*Pfft. Come on, you're not seriously asking me that? All our quality time together and now you're asking me my motivations?*"

"*Well, don't you have any?*" Rachel said. "*If you just wanted us to leave you alone there are easier ways of doing it. Maybe...*" Rachel trailed off contemplatively and Nix wondered where she was going with this as-yet-unformed thought. Not that she cared, or anything. Curiosity had always been a character flaw of Nix's, that was all.

Nix gave in. "*Maybe, what?*"

"*Maybe you were lonely,*" Rachel proposed in a soft, entirely too nonjudgmental voice.

"*Fuck you, kid, I'm not lonely. Jeez. What kind of dumb explanation is that?*"

Stupid, insolent brat. Honestly.

"*It's not like you have a family, do you?*" Rachel said. "*It's okay—I mean, not wanting to be lonely. Everybody wants to belong somewhere. Maybe what you've really been searching for is that place. I understand what that feels like. Danny and Elliot, they...they're all I have, but they're enough, you know? They're everything.*"

Nix scowled. "*Yeah, well, you won't have them for long, will you? Now shut up. I liked you better when you were silent and broody.*"

Rachel made a sad little sighing-whine noise that wasn't as gratifying as it should have been.

Nix didn't *not* belong. She belonged perfectly fucking fine. She had friends. Sort of. Okay, frenemies mostly, but that was practically the same thing. Family...it's not like she needed that. She'd had one once, so long ago she could barely remember, and it wasn't as great as Rachel made it out to be. Caring was a weakness. She shook her head, irritated that Rachel insisted on projecting her emotional issues onto Nix like they had anything whatsoever in common.

What Nix really wanted was just something that was *hers*. She'd tried on hundreds of bodies, thousands. She'd slipped beneath the skin of strangers time and again, felt their muscles clench around her, their bones grant her shape, but the fit was never quite right; they were never hers.

She'd always wondered if the right fit was a one-time thing, something she'd had once and could never find again. It seemed appropriate, in a way, like this was the cost of her eternity, the perpetual itch of not-quite-right, of something fundamentally lacking. There were worse fates.

Nix had accepted it, mostly. Maybe not as easily as the others, and maybe there were still those days that passed slower because she couldn't help but lament the way her borrowed bodies hung wrong off her frame and were tight in places, loose in others. Nix wanted to *fit*, but not in the way Rachel thought.

In her younger years, she'd tried to tailor them herself, but she'd never been much of a seamstress—or a surgeon. Their bodies never could stand up to the cutting and stitching and rearranging; infection turned to rot quicker than one might expect, then pieces would start to fall away and flesh would slide off bone until there was nothing left of it but decay.

Nix didn't like them cold, anyway. Once the warmth leeched out of them there wasn't much point in staying. Some lasted better than others—Nix wore a cardinal for nearly a decade, once upon a time. The nun she'd stolen next had been stone-dead in a fortnight.

Even Rachel wasn't as warm as she used to be.

But now wasn't the time. Nix pulled up to a little farmhouse on the outskirts of Yosemite. A small white van was parked just up the road. Nix rooted around the passenger seat to find the scrap of paper she'd left there.

Confirming that the address scrawled on the paper matched the one in white block numbers on the side of an overflowing, coal-black mailbox, she drove up the driveway then killed the engine.

The blinds were all drawn shut across the front of the house. The white siding was caked in grime and the brown paint along the railing and on the front door was gradually chipping away. It figured that Danny would find the least habitable place in rural California to hole up for a few hours.

These hunters weren't exactly the classiest bunch, bless their little redneck hearts. If anyone ever found out that she was playing chauffeur to these moronic humans, she would never hear the end of it. Nix tapped the horn to alert them to her presence, then waited.

After thirty seconds of admiring the impressive expanse of weeds and dead grass that constituted a front yard, Nix got restless. She tapped the horn again.

A gentle sigh stirred up the dust in the corners of Rachel's mind. *"Why haven't they noticed? They didn't even—"*

"Didn't I tell you to shut up?" Nix scolded, then she sighed, too. "The place looks empty. Maybe we came to the wrong one."

"No, I mean, why haven't they noticed I'm not me?"

Nix shrugged, tilting Rachel's head to get a better view of the covered windows. No suspicious shadows fell across them. Hmm. "They probably don't care about you at all," Nix suggested.

Rachel threw her a dirty look, which was an indescribably odd sensation every time it happened—*feeling* a look without *seeing* a look. Just because Rachel was lacking in a countenance of her own as of late, didn't mean she lacked the capacity for expression.

Maybe they *had* come to the wrong place. This was supposed to be the home of a hunter named Valerie McPherson, known by her friends as Val and by her enemies as The Evil Hell-Bitch. Nix had never heard of her but Rachel had met her a month or so back, and wasn't particularly fond of the woman. The house's general state of disrepair made Nix doubt that it was home to anyone, but who was she to judge?

Val had come out of nowhere last night, spirited Danny away, and left Nix on chauffeur duty while Elliot tied up some loose ends on their last case. Nix got out of the rusted piece-of-shit Ford that she'd so admired upon first laying eyes on the thing, and slammed the door—not out of frustration, but by necessity. The metal frame was warped at the bottom and required a little extra heft to get the damn thing to close.

Nix dropped the keys into Rachel's purse and walked up the front steps. Danny had said to just stay in the truck until he came out, but Elliot would be waiting for them back at the Wildfire Motor Inn and Danny should have been finished whatever he was doing by now.

Rachel added that she desperately hoped he wasn't doing *Val*. Apparently, she lived up to the title of Evil Hell-Bitch, but was attractive in a hardened, Amazon-warrior kind of way. A pretty face with a Glasgow smile. Nix took Rachel's word on it.

When her knocking received no answer, she went to ring the doorbell, only to find it hanging from the wall with one wire detached and the other frayed. This was getting ridiculous.

She was about to go back to the truck when she heard what sounded like a muffled scream coming from beyond the door. Nix tested the handle, found it unlocked, and eased inside.

There was a messenger bag sitting by the front door with a blue-and-white USPS logo stamped across the front of it. Nix dropped Rachel's purse on the table next to it and wandered through the foyer. The old hardwood slats creaked and groaned under her weight, but she could hear other voices, loud and irate, that drowned out any small noises she made.

Nix wondered if Cirrik had come around to cause problems for her, as per usual. If he had, Danny and Valerie were probably dead or dying already, which was no great loss but a bit of a disappointment. Danny was hers. Val, well, Nix supposed Cirrik could have her.

She followed the noise until she reached the open basement door.

Chapter 17

Nix peeked down the stairs and was decidedly unprepared for what she found.

Cirrik sat in a steel chair in the center of the room. No ropes or chains held him, yet his every movement was that of a caged animal, locked in place and wild from restraint.

He screamed behind a cloth gag, writhing in the chair and jerking his limbs against invisible bonds with a raw desperation Nix had never seen from him before. Blood and spit dripped down his chin, oozing out from under the gag. He was still dressed in the postal worker, but postal workers didn't have eyes like that.

Danny and a tall redhead stood with their backs to Nix. The redhead hurled a few choice insults while splashing around a bottle of water—holy water, judging by the smoke rising from Cirrik's lap where it fell—while Danny chanted something in a foreign tongue, reading from sheets of paper. The redhead was holding something in her other hand, a small something that glowed pale blue and fluctuated in brightness with Danny's words.

Nix immediately recognized the chant as an exorcism, but though she heard it too, she felt nothing stir or unfurl inside of her. It was directed only at Cirrik, the power tight and focused like the beam of a laser. She didn't know this version, but something about it felt familiar. The words looped and swayed in the air, heavy, but as smooth as silk.

There was no salt line encircling him, no restraints to hold him down. Cirrik should have been gone by now, miles away, hiding in somebody else's skin, not riding inside a dying civil servant.

Cirrik choked, throat visibly seizing up and compressing as though hands were wrapped tightly around his neck.

Danny kept chanting.

The putrid smell of cooked flesh hit the air, overwhelming a peculiar perfume scent that Nix hadn't noticed at first. It took less than a second for Nix to pinpoint the source of the foul stench.

Cirrik's postal worker was melting.

Blisters raised across the backs of his hands, red and livid. The skin cracked and peeled, curling up and blackening at the edges like burnt newspaper, and still Cirrik didn't jump ship.

Nix didn't know what he was waiting for. She didn't know if she should try to stop this, if she even could. The hellhound had been a jolt to the system, but this was something she had never in an eternity expected to witness. The room reeked of burning carrion topped with the heavy tinge of sulfur, the combination so strong Rachel nearly gagged.

She had to do *something*.

And then Cirrik was looking at her. His eyes softened when they met hers. She felt him calling out to her, desperate and afraid and just so terrifyingly unlike the Cirrik she knew.

She could see Cirrik's true face, the one behind the mask, and that was burning, too.

The ball in the redhead's hand flashed, filling the dark, dank basement with a blinding, sky-blue light.

Nix gasped.

Cirrik shuddered violently, and it was over. Just like that.

The postal worker was limp and mutilated and empty. Neither host nor passenger had survived. It was impossible. Cirrik couldn't have died, not really, not *irrevocably*. Nix glanced at the hunters in the room. They paid her no mind. She could still get away. This didn't have to be her end, too.

Danny said, "Don't even need the script anymore. Think I've got the thing memorized."

"About time," the woman replied.

Danny added, "That went better than I thought it would."

Nix edged backward, toward the front door.

The pale-blue glow softened, then ceased, leaving a glossy sphere the size of a cue ball in the redhead's hand. She took the papers from Danny and set them on a long workbench with a note of finality, tucking the glass orb into the pocket of her long leather jacket. "Told you it would get even easier. Once they start coming to us, it cuts our work by half. You should've seen the ones we got earlier this week. There'll be more where they came from, just you wait."

Nix took a step, skulking backward into the dismal living room.

The floorboards squeaked.

Danny looked up at her.

She made a break for the truck.

He called after his daughter, bounding up the steps while shouting, "Rachel! Hey, just wait a minute, would you?"

She was halfway to the truck when it occurred to her that she didn't have the damn *keys*. They were sitting on the table next to the door with everything else. Nix froze. Danny's heavy footfalls were approaching. But they didn't know, did they? He'd still called her Rachel. She'd been careful—she should have been *more* careful. *Shit*.

Danny grabbed Rachel's shoulder as Nix debated leaving her host behind. But with that kind of power, who knew what else they had at their disposal. If they trapped her, she was fucked.

Deep inside her own body, Rachel kicked up a bigger fuss than she'd managed in days, screaming for her Pops like shrillness could save her.

"He does that to us, and we both die," Nix snarled, slapping the little brat down. *"Melted, toasty, stir-fried Rachel pieces, and it'll*

destroy him to do it."

Rachel went silent, but the unnerving buzz of her complete attention made Nix feel like her skin was going to crawl off. She hadn't noticed how much the girl had been disassociating until Rachel snapped back, and Nix didn't like it, wanted her little dolly to be fucking *docile*.

"Rachel, stop. I'm sorry you had to see that, darlin', but there's no need to run off."

When the redhead walked out, Rachel recognized her as the infamous Val. The woman leaned against the doorframe and lit up a cigarette, cupping her hand around the flame of an old banged-up lighter. She opened her mouth and smoke slid out from between her lips. "Don't baby her, Daniel," Val said, her words punctuated by small gray clouds. "She's part of this now."

"Part of what?" Nix demanded. And she wasn't panicking. This was not panicking. Nix *did not* panic.

She shrugged Danny off of her, took a step back.

Danny's hand dropped away from her shoulder and he looked to the ground, scuffed his foot against the dirt. Rachel winced at the flash of hurt in his eyes, but she was just as shocked as Nix by what they'd witnessed.

He cleared his throat and said, "Well, it's, uh, hard to explain."

"You just—you just *killed* him," Nix spat. But no, he couldn't be dead, that was wrong. So what if she wanted him dead in the first place, Cirrik was not *theirs* to kill. Cirrik was *hers*.

"Guy was dead anyway," Val said. "It's not like that filthy demon was just going to let him go. Thought you said she was the smart one, Daniel."

"Rachel," Danny interrupted, moving to block her sight of Val, "this is the big project I've been working on, the one I had you do research for last month without asking any questions. I'd have told you and Elliot about it sooner, but you have to understand how dangerous this is."

Nix turned her attention inward to Rachel, accusing, *"You knew about this?"*

Rachel was mute, still stinging from Nix slapping her down. It seemed impossible that Nix could have overlooked any of Rachel's secrets, but everything about this seemed impossible. Maybe the girl had found a way to hide things from her.

Danny said, "We...we've found a way to exorcise demons; a way that doesn't just pull 'em outta folks. It destroys them. Forever."

"That's *impossible*," Nix contested, glancing around for an escape route while not panicking.

"I thought so, too," Danny agreed, then shrugged. "But it works. You saw it." He grabbed both her shoulders this time, forcing her to look at him. "This changes the whole game, darlin'. And it's not just individual demons it can kill. It's everything."

Nix narrowed her eyes and asked evenly, "What do you mean *everything*?"

"All the wickedness in the world, all the evil we've fought for so long, we can end it. We're still collecting enough power to pull it off, and every dead demon gets us closer to our goal, but if we can make this thing work we can cleanse the earth of darkness."

"Cleanse the earth..." Nix repeated, the words scratching at a long-faded memory buried just beyond her grasp.

The grass rustled at her feet as she paced in a quick circle, its brittle stalks crushed beneath her shoes. For a moment, Danny just watched her.

Nix's gaze flickered up to Val's where she leaned against the threshold. Flecks of brown paint chipped off and fluttered to the ground as Val made herself comfortable. A puff of her cigarette, then her face was blurred by the smoke. In the moment Nix couldn't see her clearly, Val almost looked familiar, Rachel's memories blurring into Nix's.

Nix couldn't recall ever having crossed paths with the woman, but she'd crossed paths with a lot of people over the centuries, it wasn't impossible that they could have met before. Even if they hadn't, Nix now had the distinct feeling that she'd come to regret ever having made Valerie McPherson's acquaintance.

Val opened her mouth, saying, "You see it now, don't you?"

Nix stilled, wondering suddenly whether Val might feel the same dormant recognition. The wind brushed through the tall grass, tilting the green and gold stalks and causing the weathervane on the old house's roof to spin counterclockwise. The air smelled like graveyard dirt, ashes and dust in coarse ground bone.

Nix considered her options, found them lacking. Carefully, she asked, "See what?"

Val's lips parted and the thick pink scars that pulled at their edges made her look like a grinning Cheshire cat even though her voice was serious when she clarified, "Why we have to do this. Like your Pops said, this is big. Bigger than anything you've seen before, anything any of us have seen. This is the great war of our generation. You should feel proud to be a part of it."

"Proud?" Nix repeated softly. These humans were well and truly deranged. Rachel swelled within, stirred by their words, and Nix shoved her down hard.

"We have the chance to make a real difference," Danny added. "We've been chosen."

At this Nix turned her attention back to the man standing a mere three feet from her. "Chosen...chosen by whom? Where are you getting your information? How do you even know that what you're doing is safe?"

Danny glanced at Val.

When no answer seemed forthcoming, Nix demanded from Rachel, *"Tell me what you know about this."*

"You know everything that I know," Rachel said, sulky but responsive. *"I've been helping to translate some things now and then from real old-school Italian. Danny asked me to, but didn't say why."*

This was absurd. *"And you just obey without question, naturally?"*

"*If Danny says this is the right thing to do, then it is.*" Rachel offered no indication of deceit, and Nix *knew* deceit. Any other time she would have been confident in her ability to effortlessly detect the lies of a human, but now she wasn't so sure.

A buzzard beat its wings overhead. Val frowned at it as much as she could with a permanent grin carved into her face, looking up into the sky where the huge creature circled.

"You're just going to have to trust me on this one, darlin'," Danny said. "I can't tell you more without putting you in greater danger."

She was Rachel. They saw her as Rachel. Rachel was not a suspect. Rachel was fine. Therefore, Nix was fine.

Nix sighed, and being sweet, innocent, caring Rachel, she asked the obvious question, "Why did you have a mailman in the basement?"

"The man was possessed," Val said plainly. "The demons, some of them have been trying to track us as word has gotten out about the revolution. He showed up on my property. I had to deal with him as necessary, you see." She nodded to Danny, adding, "You sticking around for cleanup this time? I'm going to need a hand moving the body and getting rid of that van he drove up in."

Danny nodded. "The body, of course, yeah, I'll uh, find a shovel."

"Out back, by the garden shed," she instructed. "We can put him next to the others for now, but someone might come looking for him if he was actually on a paper route. We'll have to burn everything."

Danny stepped toward her again and Nix was careful not to show her hesitancy to be too near to him. "Rachel, help Valerie start up a fire, I'll do the digging." He paused, his big hand settling once more on Rachel's shoulder. "I need you with me on this, darlin'. No more questions, understand?"

Nix nodded dumbly. Danny raised his eyebrow with an uncharacteristic sternness toward his daughter, as though he was trying to act tough in front of Val to make up for his previous show of unmanly tenderness and concern. Nix relented, "I understand."

"Good girl."

Danny walked off toward the back of the house, and Val moved from her position in the doorway, nodding at her to follow. Nix complied, taking the steps cautiously.

Val looked her up and down, obviously unimpressed by what she saw. "Don't look so traumatized. It was only a demon."

Nix glared, biting her tongue. Survival was what mattered now.

Instead of telling Val to fuck off and slicing the psychotic bitch open, Nix asked, "What about the man?"

Val tossed her cigarette onto the wooden planks of the front porch, grinding it in with the toe of her boot. "Every war has its casualties. You'll understand that someday. Until then, I don't have time to hold your hand and neither does your Pops, so you better get your shit together. You're a soldier now, kiddo."

Chapter 18

Danny carried the body outside. Val, as far as Nix could tell, was acting the part of supervisor over the whole thing. Nix licked Rachel's lips distractedly, glancing out the open front door and staring at the truck for a long moment. Just in case, she slipped the keys into her pocket for a quick getaway.

Nix rummaged through Cirrik's big messenger bag like she'd been asked, fingers glancing over envelopes and postcards, newsletters and flyers. They'd have to burn it all, just to make sure.

Her fingers brushed against something hard and round buried at the bottom of the bag and Nix pulled it out.

When the light caught the polished surface, she quickly lowered it back into the bag to shield it from prying eyes. It looked like a small marble of some sort, blue and not unlike the larger orb she had seen in passing in Val's basement. It glowed brightly. Not the sort of innocuous trinket she might expect to find in a mail carrier's bag.

Nix rolled the ball between the palms of her hands for a moment, feeling Rachel's skin tingle at the contact, then decided to discreetly tuck it into Rachel's purse. John Smith's business cards were arranged neatly in a front pouch. She pulled one out and examined it with, perhaps, a touch of fondness. But just a touch.

Nix stuffed the contents of the bag back inside it and walked through the house to the door in the kitchen.

Danny was already a few feet into a fresh grave of his own making. Nix couldn't help but admire the poetry of it.

He was clearly experienced at this particular task and worked swiftly, sweat pouring down his face and discoloring his shirt, the shovel tossing dirt over his shoulder like clockwork. Val smoked her cigarette next to a burning pyre nearby, her red hair drawn back into a ponytail at the nape of her neck. The air was thick with smoke.

Val glanced up and caught her eye, like she'd sensed Nix watching.

Nix opened the door, trying to move briskly, not making eye contact.

She looked around the small garden at the back of the house. The earth there was almost entirely tilled. The dirt was churned and spread over two hundred square feet. Much of it was covered by young bushes and flowers, all a sickly shade of yellow like they'd just been planted and hadn't yet adjusted to their new environment. It was the only part of the property that looked at all tended to. The rest was weeds and old oaks, stretching on for miles. No neighbors nearby, no one to hear the screams. It was a good setup.

Nix figured that Val could probably fit about ten bodies in this section of the property, if she stuck to one body per grave. Who knew how many plots she'd already used up, Evil Hell-Bitch that she was. Under other circumstances she and Nix might just get along splendidly, but Nix wanted nothing to do with her level of fucked-up.

Danny tossed the shovel out of the hole then pulled himself out of the fresh grave and wiped the sweat off his brow with the dirty rolled-up sleeve of his shirt.

Val patted down the dead man's legs, pulling out his wallet and a cell phone then tossing the objects to Nix. "Get rid of these, will you? And disable that phone."

She nodded, cracking open the phone casing and popping its insides out. She threw the objects into the fire, including the bag full of letters that would never reach their destinations. Some things melted, others popped and shifted in the pile as the smoke stretched toward the sky, black and heavy with the foul scent of burning plastics and synthetics and paper. But it all burned just the same.

She stared into the fire for a long moment. Rachel's fingertips tingled.

"Did you do it?" Val asked, suddenly close enough that Nix could feel her breath brush over Rachel's ear.

Nix turned around, stepping back and putting a little distance between them. "It's done," Nix confirmed, motioning to the bonfire. She glanced at the body. Val had stripped him of his clothes, placing them in a separate pile to be burned. Nix looked away.

Val watched her for several seconds before replying, "Good."

Val stood there, arms crossed. She had an unreadable expression on her face for what felt like forever.

Then Val turned away, humming a light tune beneath her breath and moving to toss the discarded clothes into the fire. Val's song pierced through her and for a moment Nix was frozen and breathless on the precipice of a memory. The melody...she knew it.

She remembered apples, the clean scent of them, and flowers, so many and so fragrant. The air had been warm and light. There were flowers everywhere and laughter and celebration because...because it was the spring festival. Yes, and she was in a quaint little village just north of Florence where they celebrated life any chance they got because they knew it would be short but hoped to make it sweet. Everyone was dancing and singing and placing flowers in her hair.

Nix remembered feeling welcome and happy, even though the festivities weren't really her style and none of the humans had any idea of the danger that lurked among them—but that just made it sweeter, really.

Cirrik had been with her, in a boy not much older than her own young hostess. He held her hand and twisted a flower into her braided hair and smiled innocently up at her, like they hadn't just drowned a fair maiden in a well after bashing her skull in with a heavy stone, though Nix could see the sparkle of humor lingering in his eyes.

It was...romantic. Nix had forgotten just how romantic it had been because...of everything that happened afterward.

The fire popped loudly and embers scattered into the air. Recollection sparked behind borrowed eyes and suddenly the nameless dread that had been itching at her insides since she'd run into Cirrik finally had a name: Florence. The foreign tongue that had seemed so familiar when Danny was chanting it in the basement suddenly found its home in her memories.

Nix had been lucky; she'd chosen a politician's youngest daughter as a host and that was the only reason they hadn't exorcised her. They were afraid of killing the little girl, too. Nix hadn't understood it at the time, hadn't realized that her brush with exorcism had been an actual brush with death—*"Real death, my love"*—but now it made more sense that Cirrik had run out of town so quickly and left her there.

Nix hadn't been exaggerating—the priest really was an honest-to-Lucifer whackjob. He'd been neck-deep into some plot to end the world, the whole world, not *just* demons. His own village had burned him to stop his attempt at ending the plague of humanity and wickedness on the earth, to cleanse it....

A murder of crows squawked on their perch at the edge of the roof, watching them work, the same buzzard still circling expectantly overhead. Nix finally released the air in Rachel's lungs.

Val and Danny...they had to be recreating the priest's efforts. The pronunciation was nearly impeccable considering the exorcism had been ancient even back then, and the chant, Nix was sure it was the same one. She wracked her brain, dimly aware that Rachel was still there, watching Nix's memories spin open and burst like fireworks, so wanton and uncontrolled that she would otherwise have been embarrassed to have a host witness, but Nix didn't have time to care about that now. Now, she was panicking.

Were they trying to end the world? Was that what this revolution was? But no, they couldn't be, at least not knowingly, right? And what about that exorcism, where could they have gotten it after all this time?

And the glowing sphere thingy. What about that? The priest, too, must have had the sphere, or something like it, something to trap the souls inside, to harness their power. Nix couldn't remember seeing it, but things had been so chaotic, and there was that blindfold for part of it...no, wait. There had been something glowing, in the beginning. She just never got to find out what it was because by the time the priest was dragged away by angry villagers and his followers ran off, it had been gone.

Surely they knew that they were harnessing not just the demons but the human souls of their hosts as well? If they were working from fragmented notes in an archaic Italian dialect, translated by an American teenager with a stellar lack of language skills, then maybe it hadn't come up.

Or maybe Val did know but, being crazy, didn't give a fuck. But how could Val have known that song? Nix barely remembered it and had never heard it since. She must have researched the time period and location thoroughly, or maybe one of those followers escaped and passed on all that knowledge through generations, or...or....

Danny and Val were staring at her. Nix felt the blood rush to Rachel's cheeks. Danny glanced down at the naked, mutilated corpse laying on the lawn, then back at her, his brow furrowed and his eyes tentative, and Nix realized she must have been staring at it this whole time. And oh fuck, was she hyperventilating?

"Darlin', why don't you, uh, go inside for a little bit and sit down while we finish this up? You don't look so good."

Nix swallowed and looked up at him, nodding. She turned away and toward the house, moving at a calculated pace and carefully listening behind her to make sure they didn't suspect that it wasn't *Rachel*, per se, having the only-panicking-a-little meltdown in the yard.

"She has a thing about blood and dead bodies," she heard Danny whispering to Val. "Gets all pale and shaky sometimes. Sensitive disposition, my girl has, just 'cause she's got such a good heart, you know."

"Hm," Val responded. "Let's just finish this."

Nix gingerly closed the door behind her and stumbled around a bit until she found a bathroom tucked in between the kitchen at the back and the living room that wrapped around the front. She shut that door, locked it, and turned on the faucet, splashing water against Rachel's face.

Rachel started, *"Are you—"*

"I fucking swear," Nix warned, "if you ask me if I'm okay, I will *end* you."

Rachel was silent for a moment, long enough to make it obvious she was changing tactics, then said, *"Are you...sure...about this ending-the-world thing? Seems kind of rash, and Danny's not the type."*

Nix had to agree with her. They mustn't be aware of the far-reaching consequences of their actions. At the very least, Danny would never risk his kids' lives and ending the world would certainly do that and more. Not Danny's style.

"They think they can end evil and monsters and things that go bump in the night. They probably don't realize how much 'cleansing the earth of darkness' really encompasses," Nix said, mostly to herself. She sighed and stared at her reflection in the mirror. Well, Rachel's, but possession being nine-tenths of the law and all....

"But how do you know that's what will happen?"

Nix didn't. Not for sure. It was so long ago and she'd only been tangentially involved in the whole thing. But there had been no doubt at the time that the priest's workings had been a bad idea. And whether humanity was at stake or not, Nix was very much a part of the 'evil, monsters, and things that go bump in the night' constituency and the destruction of that was not okay.

Sweet, innocent Rachel, of course, wouldn't understand that. Rachel was scandalized by her own naughty-bad fantasies, and thought trespassing in Pops' motel room was terrible because he told her not to. She was just...naïve.

"The world isn't as black and white as you hunters think it is," Nix tried to explain, though she knew it would be futile—she knew it but couldn't help but continue. "The line between us, between what you are and what I am, it isn't...we're just not as different from each other as we seem at a glance, okay, kid?"

Nix rubbed Rachel's hands over her face roughly, splashing water on the mirror, then turned the tap off.

"You...you were human once," Rachel said, a hint of a question at the end of her words, but she stood by her assertion.

Nix had forgotten how perceptive Rachel had seemed when they first met. So, okay, naïve but perceptive. Not a bad combination. "There's...a balance. Between light and darkness. Mine tipped a little hard to the left, and here I am," Nix told her. "Got the good end of the deal, if you ask me."

"Did you sell your soul?" Rachel asked, pushing a little harder than Nix was really comfortable with under the circumstances.

"Something like that."

"Why'd you do it?"

"Why would you?"

A pause. *"Oh. You did have a family. Someone you loved."*

Nix dried Rachel's hands off on a crusty old towel with tiny red roses sewn along the edge. She hated this house, this place, everything about today. "A...sister," she admitted. She was off her game today, was all. Plus, it wasn't like Rachel would live to tell about it anyway. Nix wasn't going to be able to let the girl go back to free-range now, not if it meant her own destruction.

"Kid sister," Nix added, useless clarification. She remembered that much. The rest of the family could rot in the darkest depths of hell for all Nix cared, and when she was finished with them, they did.

Rachel radiated sympathy, all warm and weak in a way that stirred the oldest of Nix's memories.

"She was..." Nix trailed off, lost in fragmented recollections, then shook her head. Fuck, she had to get ahold of herself. This was getting embarrassing. "Doesn't matter now. Long dead. Better off that way. Water under the bridge and all that. You and I have bigger things to worry about right now than dead relatives. Well, maybe you don't, but I sure as hell do. Don't worry too much about your Pops and Elliot, I'll get around to killing them soon enough. For now, I need you on point."

The sympathy burnt out abruptly and Rachel sighed, part frustration, part anger, just where Nix wanted her.

There was no good way out of this. No clean exit strategy. This was only going to get messier.

It was a delicate situation. They wouldn't believe her if she told them straight out. Coming from Rachel, she'd lack credibility if only because the girl had no reason to know that their special little cleansing ritual would bring about a bloody and permanent end to all existence.

If Nix revealed herself, of course, they wouldn't trust her motivations. They wouldn't understand, because they were laboring under the mistaken impression that any creature of her disposition would be inherently dishonest, would *want* the world to end. And sure, maybe this was true of some, but not of Nix.

To say she wanted humans erased from the face of the earth was preposterous. It was like saying that a butcher hates animals because he kills them, when in reality the butcher loves animals, or why else would he take such pleasure from slaughtering them? Nix loved humans. But like the butcher, what she loved most about them was the warm, wet feel of their insides, the weight and taste of flesh between her teeth, the way their veins hummed with life before she tore them open.

"*I wouldn't open with that,*" Rachel recommended.

"Too honest?" Nix asked.

"*Sure, too honest, let's go with that,*" Rachel agreed. "*But you know, honesty might work if you don't make it sound quite so...evil.*"

Nix doubted this. Honesty was rarely the best policy. Honesty didn't sit well with most humans. People far preferred to be lied to. "You think I should tell them their stupid plan is going to destroy the world and I know this because I was there the first time some idiot tried it? In 1863. In Florence. In somebody else's body."

"*Yeah.*"

The poor girl was truly a lost cause. Had Nix ever wondered why she was never taken very seriously by those around her, she now knew without hesitation that it was because Rachel was a fucking moron, well-meaning and perceptive though she may be. "You realize if they try to exorcise me, you'll die too?" Nix pointed out.

"*I do.*"

Definitely a moron, no survival instinct to speak of. But then, maybe it wasn't her own survival that drove the girl, but Nix's destruction. "You'd die just to see me die?"

"*In a heartbeat,*" Rachel returned.

Wow. That was cold. Not unexpected, but damn cold. So much for bonding. Nix smirked, feeling the weight of the day and the awkwardness of the last ten minutes lift just a bit. "Gotta say, I'm a little offended," Nix told her. "Proud, but offended."

"*I wish you'd just kill me.*"

Nix rolled her eyes. "Come on, silly girl, don't be rash. We've still got plans to see through. Fun, happy plans. Plans involving your Pops and your brother. I know you wouldn't want to miss that."

"I hate you," Rachel told her, but Nix knew better than to take her seriously—no one ever did, after all.

Chapter 19

Nix gradually made her way out of the bathroom and took a moment to glance down the stairs into the basement, just to see if the sphere or the papers Danny had been reading from were down there.

She didn't dare go down herself—she still had no idea what they'd used to bind Cirrik in place like that—but she had to look. From the top of the stairs it was hard to tell, but the shadows across the workbench were impeccably smooth and nothing seemed to be on it. Val probably wouldn't have been so careless as to leave those things lying around, anyway.

All that remained in the basement was an empty chair. Nix tried not to stare at it for too long. Eventually she had to close the door to walk away.

She needed a new game plan.

Nix found a dusty old couch to sit on in the living room. This just wouldn't do. Not the couch—the couch was fine, as far as couches went, but everything *else*.

She'd let herself be drawn off course and sucked into human concerns. And okay, so the world-ending ploy was pretty much inevitably her problem too, but that didn't mean it was only *her* concern. Cirrik was working with someone—multiple someones—by his own admission. Surely they had this handled...though if Val's word was to be trusted, maybe they didn't. However many bodies she had buried in her garden, it was a good bet that they'd all had demons inhabiting them when Val got to them.

Nix peeked out the window, saw that Danny and Val were still suitably distracted by poking at the fire, then she reached into Rachel's purse. She pulled the little glass ball out and held it in her palm. It was still glowing. The power it gave off was gentle but focused. Inside the purse, Nix couldn't sense it at all, but in her hand...the power was directed at some kind of goal.

Maybe Cirrik had been using this to track the larger sphere. Moonlighting as a mailman was a stupid way to go about it, but if this thing only worked based on proximity, perhaps he'd used the mailman gig as an excuse to wander around the area seeking it out.

If it was so well hidden that they had to try and track it on foot, Val and Danny must be using some powerful countermeasures to keep their whereabouts concealed. Nix tucked the ball back into the purse, making sure this time that the glow didn't show through the fabric. She couldn't afford to be reckless anymore.

So demons were just inadvertently killing themselves off, then, thinking they were cleverly seeking Val and Danny out to stop them, while actually bringing what the two conspirators needed right to their doorstep. It was...cunning. Nix had to give them that.

And here she was, sitting in the Evil Hell-Bitch's living room, breathing in the smoke of Cirrik's failure, lured in just like him. They didn't seem to suspect her so far, and she was confident that her sigils were strong enough to keep her true nature securely hidden, but just being here was still a significant risk. One might even go so far as to say a *stupid* risk.

It occurred to her that she might very well be the only one left to stop this. It was a humbling notion. Activities like this, *destroying* demons and humans like they were, couldn't go unnoticed for long, of course. They'd probably have all manner of creatures up in arms, not just Nix's kind.

And maybe they already did. Danny had been hunting non-stop lately, and it was rare to find nonviolent creatures like dryads killing people, even when they did have valid reason to be pissed off. Trouble seemed to flare up wherever these hunters went. It wasn't impossible that it was them trouble followed and not the other way around.

For the first time, Nix wondered if that hellhound hadn't been sent for *her* after all. And she had to admit, in spite of the distance she kept from her own world by losing herself in human ones, she'd felt that something was off about these hunters the minute she laid eyes on them.

It was like a subtle pull, a curiosity she just couldn't shake. Under any other circumstances she'd have been long gone by now, not sticking around and playing chauffeur to a bunch of hunters just for the hell of it. Something about them called to her. Maybe it was this.

Danny and Val were making a mess of things and they hadn't even executed their big plan yet.

Nix didn't want to be involved in any of this. But now, she wasn't sure she had a choice. She couldn't just let them destroy everything, not the whole *world*. She lived in that world. She liked that world. And what if no one else stepped in to stop them in time?

Nix pondered, thinking of the creatures she knew, trying to figure out if any could play savior. None of them worked—Nix had to be *hidden*, that hadn't changed, and the world being on the edge of destruction wasn't anonymous-note material.

Well, she'd just have to be the hero then.

Nix stopped abruptly at the idea and accidentally laughed aloud. The sound was almost as jarring as the sentiment. If they heard her they'd think she'd lost her mind. She almost certainly had.

Hero? No no, that was absurd. She didn't need to go *that* far. She was going to give herself some weird hero-complex or something if she continued down that road. No sir, she would go no further.

Heroics. *Pfft*. Those were for suckers and do-gooders.

Well at least she could still see the humor in things even when the world was ending. See? Silver lining.

Now, the real problem here was that a bunch of incompetent humans were making a damn mess and acting out some moronic god fantasies like they had any right to inconvenience her with their bullshit. They'd had the audacity to kill *her* frenemy, when Nix had been first in line for that pleasure for over a hundred fucking years. Who did they think they were?

No, Nix was not going to stand for this. Fuck them. She was going to butcher every last one of them. No more excuses. The fate of the world was at stake.

The back door creaked open. Nix sat up a little straighter.

Of course, she wouldn't start with the killing *now* or anything. No, best to wait for the opportunity to present itself. Couldn't just rush into these things. She had to play it smart.

Plus, Nix needed to know how many others were involved in this plot. There was no telling how far this thing reached. If she was going to confront them, she'd have to do it right, make sure all her bases were covered.

But she'd have to do it pretty fast, too. This wasn't the sort of thing one wanted to put off for too long. Wouldn't she feel foolish if she was late to the world-ending party?

"Rachel, darlin'? It's time for us to move out."

Danny and Val, though, they appeared to be at the heart of this, so she wasn't about to piss them off. Not until she had all the information she needed to act, and act wisely.

Val didn't say a word to her.

If Nix followed Danny a little more eagerly on their way out of the house and away from the Evil Hell-Bitch, well, it was for the sake of The Plan.

She handed Danny the keys as they got in the truck. He acknowledged her with a grunt, which Nix found oddly reassuring.

They started back on the road, leaving the corpse garden and the circling buzzard behind. When they pulled out, the white van was gone. She didn't ask about it.

Danny was covered in mud and soot, and looked—and smelled—very much like a man who'd just dug a grave and lit a lot of things on fire. Nix debated the likelihood that they'd actually get pulled over by a cop and decided, why mention it? It would only stress him out. Could really use a shower though, *wow*.

As the miles clicked higher, Nix started to relax.

The sun was still fairly high in the sky. There were no clouds. Danny opened the windows and let the roar of the rushing wind into the cab of the truck. Rachel's hair followed the breeze as Nix stared out the window at the trees, then the bare hills.

The roads looped up and over the terrain like a black ribbon, endless and winding. And it was on this endless road, where the asphalt turned rough as they crossed between counties, that Danny finally spoke.

"I don't know how much you remember, from when you were young," he said. "With your folks, I mean. Your mom and I, we were real close when we were your age now. She was...she was like a sister to me. She was a special woman. But we grew apart, you know. And I didn't...I didn't realize when she changed." Danny stopped.

Nix turned to look at him, but for once he was staring at the road, fingers tight on the wheel. His lips moved like he was trying to form some thought into words, but nothing came out. Rachel hung on his words, confused and intrigued. It wasn't often he spoke to her with this strange note of vulnerability in his tone, so she knew what he was saying had to be important.

Finally, he said, "I wasn't there for you when I should have been. Wasn't there for her, either. And I regret that more than you know. I know they weren't...I mean, what they did, I don't—they had no right...I...I just wish...." He stopped again and adjusted his grip on the wheel.

They went over a dip in the road and the truck groaned in protest.

He took a deep breath. "But I know they loved you in their own way. And I know you loved them. What happened to them was a tragedy. It was a terrible accident. But in a way—God rest their souls—it all worked out for the best. I got a second chance with you. One that I didn't get with your mom."

Nix asked what both she and Rachel wanted to know, her own tone a careful, fragile match to his, "Pops, why are you telling me all this?"

He cleared his throat once, twice, glanced over at her, glanced away. "I just want you to understand, darlin', why it's always been so...so *important* to me to keep you safe. I thought that if I kept you close, kept you away from all the things that could hurt you, that I'd be able to protect you from...from everything." He chuckled and the sound was out of place in his voice, too high-pitched, too empty.

"But that was hard to do, you understand, in this line of work. I tried to stop for a while, but I never could. And I thought for a long time that maybe you'd be safer far away from this life, but I guess deep down I knew that you wouldn't be able to escape it any more than I could. And at least this way I always knew you were safe with Elliot or me lookin' out for ya. I know it's selfish of me, but I just wanted to make sure you always had somebody to take care of you."

This was the most Nix had ever heard him say in one go. The way his pulse was pounding in his neck and his hands were slick on the wheel, she was approaching Rachel-levels of worry for the man's health. What was happening here? "Pops—"

"No, just...just let me finish. Now, I know I haven't always been the father to you that I should have been, but I've always done my best to do right by you and your brother. I'm not always gonna be around. And in this job, that time's probably gonna be sooner rather than later. Part of the reason I'm working with Valerie is to try and make sure that this world will be a safe place for the two of you when I'm not there. And—and I know you don't like to talk about this sorta thing. I don't either. I just want you to know, darlin', that I can see now that I've been holding you back. I've tried so hard to protect you from everything, that I never considered that you were a strong enough...young woman...to—to handle things for yourself. And you are. You've got a good head on your shoulders and a kind heart. I was wrong not to trust in those qualities earlier. And...I'm sorry. I just want you to always know how proud I am to call you my daughter, Rachel."

Danny turned to look out his window and oh shit, Nix thought she heard a sniffle beneath the wind whipping through the truck. That had gotten unexpectedly maudlin really fast. Nix had to fight back Rachel's tears and her sinuses were just a mess—if she had to sniffle herself, somebody was getting thrown from this vehicle.

To placate the both of them, Nix awkwardly offered, "Th—thanks...*Pops*."

Danny nodded resolutely, still not looking directly at her. "Yeah, well...." He coughed, hocking something up in his throat and spitting out the window. Half a mile passed without either of them talking, but Nix couldn't stop staring at him. Finally, Danny glanced in her direction and asked, "Elliot get everything worked out in town?"

"I, uh, don't know. I can call him?"

Danny grunted his agreement and they were back on solid ground again. The pavement smoothed out underneath the truck as they crossed into Stanislaus County.

Fuck. What a weird day.

Chapter 20

It was eight o'clock on Saturday night, and Nix was getting drunk with a bunch of hunters. This was becoming a running theme, the drinking thing. Danny gave her the side-eye of mild disapproval when some guy named Jake handed her the first beer, but true to his word, he seemed to have loosened up on policing Rachel's every move.

Nix liked to think she'd earned the girl a little credibility with her Pops during their time together and maybe that was what really drove Danny's overly earnest declaration of pride or whatever the hell that was back in the truck. If nothing else, Nix was quite content in the knowledge that Danny still thought she was Rachel, because wouldn't *that* have been an awkward conversation otherwise.

Nix leaned into the corduroy couch and took a pull from the bottle, taking in the scene around her. La Grange was a quaint little one-horse town in the middle of nowhere, with a saloon and a general store and not much else.

Joan and Jake, owners of what Danny considered one of their safe houses, lived far enough away from La Grange that it was a good trek to get into the place—and Lucifer help you if you blinked on the way through—but close enough that they still fell within the community.

Their home was situated atop one of many hills, isolated like the people who lived there. Old house, old furniture, old people. Nothing fancy, but the place certainly had its charm. Among an array of fake fruit on the dinner table lay a disassembled Glock on a strip of oil-stained cloth. Little china figurines of cows lined the mantle of the fireplace just below a mounted sword set polished to a shine.

It was strange seeing this side of the hunters; the side that collected tiny cow ornaments and sat around the living room reminiscing with old friends. She wasn't about to let this catch her off guard, of course. They were still a bunch of murderous psychos. But here, laughing and chatting like they were now, they put on a good show.

Danny, freshly bathed and better-smelling, was standing in the kitchen speaking in hushed tones with 'Uncle Kevin' and a woman named Joan. Danny's hand rested on the other man's shoulder, the touch lingering, and the way they stood so close to each other suggested a level of comfort between the two that Nix didn't realize Danny was capable of.

Kevin Rousoe, the man of legend, was fierce and resourceful. The *real* Kevin Rousoe, the old man standing around his friends' kitchen only a few feet away from where Nix was now sitting, he was nothing like the formidable opponent she was expecting.

He was thin, with a face that wanted to smile but rarely did. He never looked angry or mean, just sad and ancient like the life had been draining out of him for years and somewhere along the lines he'd stopped caring.

He was about Danny's age, and Rachel had known him as long as she could remember. One of her earliest memories was of her Uncle Kevin with her small hand engulfed in his own, his skin a warm contrast to the cold wind that lashed at her black dress as strangers prayed and lowered her parents into the ground.

He glanced over and caught Nix's gaze, nodded in a sort of fond acknowledgement—or something else entirely, hard to say with this guy—and turned back to Danny. Kevin was an odd man. For some reason, Nix instinctively liked the guy.

Joan was much more animated. She was the collector of porcelain cows in this household and something of an informational hub for other hunters. Rachel didn't know her as well as she knew Uncle Kevin, but Danny and Joan went way back and constantly kept in touch.

And occasionally, like tonight, they dropped by her little house in the hills and stayed the night between hunts. From what Nix could tell, she seemed to be the center of the little safety phone-tree that had caused Nix so much trouble in the beginning.

Joan's husband, Jake, provider of beers, sat across from Nix in an armchair, already pretty smashed from a couple of drinks and looking a bit worse for the wear. He had a bad knee and tended to lurch and limp wherever he went, but he was younger than Joan by five years or so, putting him around forty. Whether or not Joan and Jake were involved in the whole ridiculous war thing Danny and Val had going, Nix couldn't say. But, better safe than sorry. She'd deal with each of them in turn.

Elliot had disappeared into the garage, leaving her on the couch with Rodney, the last of tonight's crew. Twenty-five with the intellectual and emotional IQ of a thirteen-year-old, Rodney was wiry and lanky and lacking in any appreciable social skills, but here he was. Against all odds, this guy was, in fact, a hunter—and apparently a good enough one to warrant a seat here with the rest of them. He was Jake's grandfather's brother's step-grandson once removed, or something.

Rachel had met him twice. The first time, he'd nearly hit her with his truck, and the second he'd drunkenly propositioned her in the presence of Danny, which ended well for no one. She didn't much care for the boy. He wasn't drinking tonight, though, which was a plus. Something about hoppy beer making him gassy.

Nix shook her head and sipped her beer. These idiots were going to end the world? Fuck, what had her existence become? This was a goddamn joke. It was all so...ordinary.

She took a deep breath, inflating Rachel's lungs with air then releasing it slowly.

Rodney was sitting next to her; too close. Whether or not it was intentional was up for debate. Nix was undecided as to whether he was just a smarmy little bastard, or if he had some kind of social impairment that prevented him from understanding the concept of personal space. Rachel was undecided on the matter as well. Nix took a moment to enjoy the sense of camaraderie before Rachel got grumpy again.

Rodney was sitting on the edge of her sweater. He smelled like the inside of a garbage truck on a hot day. She stared pointedly at him, then at the length of unoccupied sofa next to him. He grinned—or was that his equivalent of a leer? Hard to say.

Oh well. She'd just have to kill him. He *could* be involved in The Plot of Idiocy—he *was* an idiot, after all. No sense in underestimating the depths of that crater in his head where his brain should be. Rachel didn't even protest at the thought.

She took another swig of beer. Jake made a clever joke about crossbreeding a werewolf and a chupacabra and for some reason this struck her as funny. Nix laughed, and it was genuine. Then she thought about slitting their throats wide open, and she laughed some more; laughed until she couldn't get ahold of herself, because the mental images of their gaping windpipes and their flailing arms were even more hysterical with the haze of booze and the slight, trembling recklessness that the day had instilled in her.

Jake beamed, clearly under the impression that he was just *that* funny. "You're in a good mood tonight," he said.

Nix considered this, and yeah, sure, why shouldn't she be in a good mood? "Well, we're alive, aren't we?" she pointed out, sitting in the middle of the lions' den, blending with the lions, because she was just that goddamn good. "It's only fair to celebrate. After all, we could die tomorrow."

Rodney half-smiled, a little awkwardness in the curve of his lips. "Well, uh...cheers to that!"

"Cheers!" Jake chimed in, leaning across the coffee table and clinking his beer bottle against hers, then tapping it against Rodney's can of coke.

Elliot strode up to them and passed her an open bottle of beer before she'd even realized she'd finished hers. Such a good boy. She'd have to reward him for his obedience later.

The condensation was cold and wet against Rachel's palm. With one hard look at her couch-buddy, Elliot had Rodney scooting over to the other end of the sofa. Some sort of alpha-male thing, she imagined. Whatever Elliot had done, it worked effectively enough that Nix wanted to bottle that look up and sell it. Imagine the demand.

Elliot dropped down next to her; too close. A grin pulled at the corners of her lips, but she held it down. He, too, was sitting on the edge of her sweater, keeping her pinned in place. Rachel's heart fluttered at his proximity. She could feel the heat of his body next to hers and goosebumps prickled over Rachel's skin.

"Thanks," Nix said, raising the beer in her hand. She held his eyes and took a long pull from the bottle, tipping it up, her lips forming a tight seal.

His gaze flittered between her eyes, lips, and throat as he answered in a low voice, "No problem."

Nix thought about crawling into his lap and fucking him right there in a room full of witnesses while her hands tightened around his neck—but she was going for subtlety. Still, she doubted the poor boy would stop her.

"So the last time I seen the guy, I told him, you know, you don't just borrow somebody's rifle and up and leave, right? I mean, can you believe the nerve..." Jake was saying, and this was about the point that Nix tuned out.

Elliot shifted next to her, his leg brushing against Rachel's in a manner that could have been accidental if not for the way his gaze flicked up to hers for a split-second as he nodded and said, "Hmm," in response to Jake's ranting.

Elliot leaned back and propped his arm up behind her along the back of the couch. Considering how jumpy he could be, Nix was rather impressed at how smooth his actions were tonight. The alcohol probably helped.

Not to be outdone, Nix nonchalantly rested a hand on his thigh as she reached for a coaster, and this turned into a game of subtle touches and lingering glances when no one else was looking. Nix was winning 8 to 5 by her count, though in Elliot's defense, he may not have realized it was a competition.

At some point, Joan wandered up and sat on the arm of her husband's chair, talking about the Mustang she was working on in the garage. It was all very tedious. A couple hours in, and Nix was already getting bored and antsy, looking for an opening to get one of them alone. As the alcohol dwindled, she found one.

As it turned out, 'beer runs' were common occurrences for these humans. Nix prided herself on staying up to date with human social norms and popular culture, but in all her years she'd never actually had the opportunity to engage in this particular ceremony.

There was a whole social ritual attached to it with unique roles for each participant. It was necessary to have a driver, to start with, and the driver was expected to be stone-sober when called upon as supplies waned. Providing alcohol to minors was fine, but drinking and driving, *that* was where they drew the line.

This all made little sense to Nix—what benefits were achieved in this role if the purpose was to purchase alcoholic beverages for others yet never consume them oneself? There had to be some sort of intangible reward involved, but Nix had yet to identify it.

Whether this soberness policy was a universal rule was up for debate. Rachel insisted it was the norm, but also pointed out that the last time Rodney had been here drinking, she'd heard he'd been responsible for the demise of a particularly valued porcelain cow, so it could have had more to do with Rodney than the role the group had volunteered him for.

Regardless, the driver, it seemed, also required the company of at least one additional participant whose state of inebriation appeared largely inconsequential. She understood the basics just fine; humans were notoriously illogical, but Nix could certainly get behind the common cause of celebratory beer. It made Rachel all pliable and hazy, which was an improvement from the nearly constant state of anxiety and stress this body had been in since Nix had commandeered it. It was in this spirit that Nix volunteered for the role of companion when the opportunity came.

"I'll come with you," Nix offered happily, standing as Rodney fiddled with his keys. He grinned at her—this might have been another leer, the kid hadn't really mastered that particular art yet.

"Yeah...me too," Elliot said, voice flat and vaguely suspicious. He stood up behind her, hand on her shoulder.

Still staring at Rachel, Rodney told Elliot, "Sorry, man, only got room for one. And the lady did call it first."

Elliot's eyes narrowed.

Nix turned to him, patted him patronizingly on the chest and said, "See you soon, El."

Reluctantly, Elliot sat back down. "Don't forget your phone," Elliot reminded her. "In case we need to...get ahold of you," he added unconvincingly, leveling a final glare at Rodney that Rodney didn't seem to notice.

Nix followed the young hunter out the door and into the cool night air. It was chillier now than it had been during the day. The windshield of Rodney's truck was spotted with raindrops. A thin splatter of stars brightened the night sky. They were alone.

The ride to the liquor store in Snelling was quick and involved a lot of tiresome small talk directed at Rachel's breasts, and though they lacked the means to respond, Rodney seemed undeterred by the one-sidedness of the conversation. It was excruciatingly dull, but it was an opportunity Nix couldn't pass up.

They'd taken the longer route from Joan's house in the hills, lingering over the twisting roads between nowhere and somewhere. The truck rattled as it went over the bridge across the slow-moving river that cut through the town, and then they were close enough to civilization to locate an open liquor store. Nix waited in the truck as Rodney went to retrieve the alcohol.

Despite being slightly drunk, Rachel still took the opportunity to complain to Nix, saying, *"Rodney has nothing to do with any of this. Just let him go."*

"He could," Nix contested.

"You know he doesn't. He couldn't fight his way out of a wet paper bag. Of course he isn't involved. He's harmless."

Nix sighed a sigh of long suffering. *"No offense, doll, but we're talking about the end of the world here. Not exactly the best time for me to start taking your advice, quaint and well-meaning as it is."*

"You...you can't just go around killing people for no reason!"

Nix considered this. *"Um, actually, I'm pretty sure I can. Besides, he's an ass. I'm doing you a favor. Now shush."*

Characteristically, Rachel declined. *"You don't—"*

Luckily, Nix wasn't asking politely. She slapped a muzzle on the girl and took a moment to enjoy the blissfully non-self-righteous silence.

The seats of Rodney's truck were made of cracking vinyl. The cold of the plastic seeped through her jeans as she plucked at the frayed edge of the backrest. She watched the boy walk across the nearly empty parking lot. The rain-wet asphalt gleamed beneath the gaudy florescent lights of the liquor store, a blur of blue and red.

The second he walked into the store and out of her line of vision, her hands darted out to the glove box. She rummaged around inside, fingers searching for familiar shapes in the darkness.

Deck of cards, packets of condoms, leather gloves—not what she was looking for.

Nix unsnapped her belt, turning around to dig into the crowded compartment behind the seat. Dirty clothes...more dirty clothes...fuck, did he even own clean clothes? In the front window of the liquor store, between the posters and metal bars and the naked florescent dancing cowgirl, Nix could just make out Rodney's plaid jacket at the checkout.

She slid down, reaching under the seats and feeling around the gravel-encrusted carpet. Her fingers touched on something cold and long—a shotgun, which was great but not exactly meant for use in close quarters. A little farther back—there! Nix pulled out a chunk of chilled metal, flipping it open to release the blade. Every hunter carried a switchblade somewhere and Rachel's pitiful Swiss Army knife just wasn't going to cut it for this one.

Rodney was walking toward the truck. Nix straightened, snapped her seatbelt in place and tucked the opened switchblade between the seats.

Rodney climbed back into the truck, gracelessly dropping two 24 packs of beer onto the seat between them and leaving Nix to catch them before they tipped over. She moved the beer to the floor.

The entirety of the ride back was composed of an unending monologue on Rodney's part. Nix paid this no mind, focusing on the winding road. The occasional "Hmm," and "Ah," seemed to satisfy the boy as they drove back toward Joan's house.

"—as if I'd leave that lying around, can you believe that?"

"Nope," Nix responded absently. The truck turned left at a crossroads.

"So that's exactly what I told him. I mean, the thing had to be twelve feet long and totally ripped with muscle, but I cut him down because that's the job, right?"

"Mmhmm." They were nearly at the bridge. A half a mile, at most.

"And the lady was like, super grateful, obviously, because I saved her life and all. And I just told her, 'ma'am, no need to thank me, I'm just doing my job,' you know?"

"Mm." They passed a deer-crossing sign. Ah, yes. Nearly there.

Nix watched the electric poles as they drove, dark blurs at Rodney's speed, and she counted twenty-three, counted twenty-four....

Twenty-five was still ahead of them, but Nix called it anyway.

"Pull over," she said, still looking out the window, watching the headlights gleam off the water in the darkness. They rolled over the wooden bridge. Nix unsnapped her seatbelt.

"What? Why?"

Nix sighed, letting her fingers drop to the hem of Rachel's black sweater. In one smooth motion, she pulled the garment over her head without bothering with the buttons, shook her hair out and tossed the sweater onto the pile of clothes behind the seats. "Just *pull over.*"

Eyes locked on Rachel's lace-clad breasts, Rodney muttered, "Absolutely." He tore off the road at the end of the bridge and stopped so suddenly she nearly slammed into the dashboard. The beer bottles clattered against each other on the floor of the truck.

Rodney threw the truck into park and killed the engine even though it was chilly out tonight, his hands just the slightest bit unsteady on the wheel. Nix glanced at herself in the rearview mirror and smirked as Rachel struggled pointlessly, unable now to complain verbally but still plenty distressed. Nix crawled over the space between herself and Rodney, tossing one leg over Rodney's thighs, straddling him as he sat ramrod straight in the driver's seat.

The air was cold against Rachel's skin and she could see their every breath like tiny clouds in the confinement of the vehicle. She licked her lips, then Rodney tilted his chin up and licked them for her. He tasted like grease and Cheetos, not terrible, but not pleasant, either. For all that he seemed like a nervous teenager, he knew exactly where to put his hands and didn't waste time positioning them on her breasts. His fingertips ghosted over the sigils carved into Rachel's skin, but if he noticed, he didn't mention it.

His fingers were soft and surprisingly uncalloused for a hunter. But then again, the kid exaggerated his conquests every time he and Rachel spoke, as if in attempt to woo her with tales of his rippling, unchained masculinity. Rachel couldn't have been less impressed by the boy and Nix had to agree that he left much to be desired.

"I had no idea you were so wild, Rachel. Christ, you're hot," he mumbled into her mouth. "Knew you wanted me."

"Shhh," Nix warned him. He was ruining the moment. She lifted one hand and brushed it across the side of his face. "Close your eyes."

Rodney eagerly complied, a stupid grin breaking out on his face like he'd won the lottery and Nix supposed that in a way, he had. He was convenient and accessible—so, lucky him, he got to go first. Nix considered taking him for a quick ride, poking around in that brain of his, but the idea of it was a bit repulsive and she knew Rachel was right; he didn't know anything. She didn't need to bother. No, this one was just for fun. And if she happened to take a semi-relevant pawn off the board, well, that was icing on the cake.

She took his bottom lip gently between her teeth, teasing, as her left hand reached down between the seats, gripping the hilt of the switchblade and savoring the weight of it in her hand. Rodney's eyes threatened to flutter open. She ground Rachel's body against him, drawing out a long, throaty groan as his head tipped back over the seat.

Nix lowered her lips to his neck, pressing Rachel's mouth against his carotid artery and pushing her tongue against it until she could feel the rapid hammering of his pulse. He opened his mouth and she could feel the vibration of words coming up his throat.

She covered his mouth with her free hand, palm pressing against his lips. He swallowed and Nix tracked the movement of his Adam's apple. Rodney's hands reached around her, gripping Rachel's ass in his palms and urging her closer.

He wasn't a pretty boy, not the way Elliot was, but he wasn't horrible to look at, either. Nix had an idea of how to make him a bit more handsome, though. She lifted the knife, holding it just a centimeter from his skin, right over that lovely pumping artery calling her name.

A hint of arousal stirred in her, encouraging Rachel's heart to beat a little faster in anticipation. Rachel thrashed inside her head, but Nix was pretty sure it was more perfunctory than anything else. She had no real connection to the boy. There was no reason for Rachel to care so much about a mere acquaintance, particularly one she didn't even like. She put on a good show, but Nix knew that Rachel wanted this just as much as she did.

Rodney bucked up against her impatiently and she could feel his arousal straining against the denim of his jeans.

The windows fogged with their breath, the sheen of condensation making the rest of the world blurry and surreal.

For a moment, everything was simple. She was the predator and he was her prey, and there was a certain delicious balance to it, a rightness. Nix wondered if he could feel it too, the way the world narrowed down to just them and the roles nature gave them.

She'd stilled and his lashes fluttered open to seek her out. The blade glimmered in his eyes prettily as Nix drew it back, and then it was sliding into his throat hard and fast, cutting through flesh and veins and cartilage, sticking out the side of his neck.

He tried to push her away, but his strength waned rapidly and Nix could not be moved. Her weight kept him pinned like a butterfly beneath her. His every movement sent hot shocks up and down her spine.

He choked on the blade, on the blood, his airway partially blocked as he bled out on the cold vinyl seat.

Gaping windpipe. Flailing arms. Nix smirked. She was right, it *was* hysterical.

Blood attempted to spurt out around the buried blade. Nix quickly pulled a dirty shirt from behind the seats to shield herself, but blood splattered against her bare skin regardless. She'd have to wash off before returning to the lions' den.

Rodney clutched at his neck weakly, one arm flapping as he squirmed and jerked, spasming and wide-eyed as he came in his pants. Too soon, it was over. His head fell forward against his chest, lifeless. The way his body stilled as the last drops of blood trickled out of him was practically pornographic.

Rachel went quiet.

Nix sighed and wiped her bloody hands down the front of Rodney's checkered red-and-white flannel shirt. His blood pooled in the creases of the vinyl, tendrils of steam rising up.

She dismounted Rodney's still-warm body and crawled across the seat, pushing open the passenger-side door with a loud creak and letting in a burst of fresh air. Rachel's head cleared as Nix took a deep breath.

She licked her lips, tasted blood, and the gratification of that warred with the regret that she hadn't drawn things out a little longer. But Nix didn't have time to worry about that now.

There was work to be done.

Chapter 21

Nix sauntered into the lions' den after ditching the truck in the river and walking back. She dropped the cases of beer next to the coffee table, content in the knowledge that she had fulfilled her social obligations as the bringer of beer.

"So he had me in his sights—oh," Joan paused, reaching for a beer and patting Rachel's shoulder approvingly, "thanks, honey. Where'd Rodney go?"

Nix shrugged, handing a beer to Elliot and grabbing one for herself before plopping down into her vacated seat on the couch, discretely checking her shoes for bloodstains. "Got a call and took off real fast," Nix said, carefully making eye contact. "Said not to worry about him or anything. I think it was a girl on the phone."

"Of course it was," Jake said with a knowing smile. "Kid's just like I was at that age."

"Real lady-killer," Danny joked, nudging Kevin with his elbow.

Joan turned back to the group and picked up where she'd left off, saying, "So he had me in his sights, gun aimed square at the center of my chest, with this cocky grin on his face. And lo and behold, there was the lever not two feet away from me. And this was a big car hanging over him, too. I'm talking 1982 Ford pickup—thing was a friggin' tank, just a big ol' hunk of metal and he was standing right underneath it. It was almost too easy. One good pull and the bastard was flattened like roadkill."

She laughed, beer sloshing down the side of her bottle as her hands moved to illustrate the flattening. "Didn't even get a shot off!

I can just imagine the security guard's face the next morning, pulling up to find that mess oozing out from under five thousand pounds of scrap metal." Another chuckle, the others joining her, and Nix knew she was under the radar.

Nix leaned back into the couch, her shoulder pressed flush against Elliot's, and it was almost like Rachel belonged there.

Nix was still buzzing from the satisfaction of a fresh kill. She'd ungagged Rachel during the walk back, but the girl still wasn't talking. The whole brooding-teen thing was not a very becoming trait, in Nix's opinion.

Kevin raised his glass of bourbon and clinked it against Joan's bottle, giving her a little salute. "Remind me never to piss you off, Joanie."

Joan beamed and asked, "What about you, Kev? Best ever?"

He joined the others in their reminiscences, contributing to the conversation when it was required of him, but there was something false and empty in his mannerisms. His pale blue eyes were flat. It was as though he was never entirely present. According to Rachel, he'd checked out, so to speak, when his wife had died a couple years back. Hadn't been the same since. Even now, he looked like a withered skeleton in his chair next to Danny, disappearing into the paisley fabric, a ghost trapped in human form. Nix would be lying if she said she didn't know that feeling.

Kevin glanced at Danny for a second, then turned away. "Ah, I'd have to go with Tallahassee. No cars or fireworks," he disclaimed, shrugging, "but we exorcised it nonetheless. This was with Marybeth, mind you, and you know how clever that woman was. Always gave me a run for my money.

"We'd cornered this demon in a church—it was possessing the nun, see—and we had it in an iron-enforced salt trap, but the thing was gonna off the nun before we could get through an exorcism ritual, so we had to find another way to pull it out.

"Marybeth had doctored the sprinkler system beforehand, so as soon as I lit up a cigarette, it started raining down holy water. Hand to God, up to that day, I'd never heard a demon scream so loud as I did then. It ditched the nun, but was still trapped, see, and burnin' up from the water like it was an acid bath.

"Managed to get the nun out safe and banish the demon back to hell in time for supper." He smiled and sighed wistfully. "Those were the days."

"I hear ya," Danny answered with a nod.

Nix rested Rachel's head on Elliot's shoulder, wondering at the possible mechanics of an iron-enforced salt trap, but not overly surprised that Rousoe would be the one to come up with something like that. Elliot reached for one of her hands and squeezed lightly, a gesture Nix had come to recognize as a sign of support or affection. Experimentally, Nix squeezed back.

"Okay, okay," Jake said. He raised his hands theatrically and announced, "Oklahoma City!"

"Oh, not Oklahoma City," Danny pleaded. "We've heard this one a dozen times."

Jake just waved him off, undeterred. "Nah, the kids haven't. Have ya, kids?"

Elliot shook his head and Nix followed his lead when she realized that she counted as part of the 'kids' constituency in this group.

"See? Gotta teach the next generation how to do it right. So there I was on top of the WR Bank in the dead of night, just on the outskirts of the city, searching for a wendigo. Middle of winter. Wind was blowin' somethin' fierce. And I know the thing came up here, but there's no sign of it anywhere.

"Then I see it! There's a rope hanging down the ledge where the bank connects to the old town hall about twenty feet down—the wendigo could've jumped it and survived, but not without damage, so I go to check if it's tryin' to escape down this rope, and sure enough, there it is 'bout five feet down. Thing sees me starin' at it and suddenly it leaps right at me, all claws and teeth—damn near lopped my head off!

"Now, I see that the rope's still hangin' from the roof and—no, wait, I'm getting ahead of myself here...so, I'm strugglin' like mad, half pinned to the roof, half hangin' off of it, and at first I'm thinkin' I'll stab the fucker in the heart, right? A good spike of silver through the ticker would've been plenty, but here I am reachin' around to find my knife and gettin' nothin' but air—never did find that knife, by the way. Damn shame, that."

Danny frowned. "You've gotta get over that knife, Jake. It's gone. Let it go."

"Yeah, yeah. So I'm reachin' around until I feel somethin' scratch against my fingers. The rope's still hangin' from the roof! The wendigo's got her claws gouged deep into my right arm—thing's useless to me as tits on a man at that moment, so all's I got is my left to work with. I let the bitch think she's got the upper hand for a minute, you know, let her chew on me a little to keep her occupied—"

Joan tutted in disapproval. "The kids don't need to hear about you getting gnawed on, Jake."

"Ah, Joan, the kids are fine!" Jake defended. "Where was I—right, the wendigo's chewin' on my arm somethin' awful but when it wasn't lookin' I was pullin' the rope back up and wrappin' it around the wendigo's neck.

"Soon as it felt the rope go round, it started jerkin' away from me, trying to escape, but I wouldn't have any of that. I grabbed that rope and pulled hard, 'til I got her off balance, then I pushed her right off the roof! I hear this *whoosh* as she's fallin', then a sudden horrible *snap*!

"When I looked down, I could see the wendigo's spine poking out where the rope looped around its neck, body barely hangin' on by a thread of flesh. And that, kids, is how you kill a wendigo without fire or a silver knife. Many a man will say it can't be done, but no sir, no sir, they ain't never tried to hang one before and I can promise you that."

He gulped down the rest of his beer, rolling the bottle between his hands thoughtfully.

Suddenly his eyes lit up and he sat forward in his chair, saying, "Oh, and let's not forget about Wichita! Now there's a story."

"Okay, okay," Joan said, hands raised. She looked to Danny with a quirked eyebrow. "I think it's high time the kids were off to bed."

"But it's only—" Danny said, then abruptly stopped at Joan's glare. He turned to Elliot and Nix. "G'night, kids."

Elliot nudged her with his elbow and stood up. Recognizing this as a social cue, Nix followed suit, edging out from behind the coffee table.

She watched him walk in front of her toward the stairs as the other hunters continued their conversation in hushed tones until they were out of earshot. The muscles in Elliot's shoulders shifted as he reached for the railing, taut against his tight cotton shirt, and Nix remembered the feel of Rodney pinned beneath her, straining and reaching and convulsing.

Nix wondered what it would feel like with Elliot, to have him pinned, at her mercy, and decided she needed to find out.

Chapter 22

The walls here were thin. Paper thin. Even now, she could hear the chattering from downstairs continue, the sound flowing up to the second story like smoke and slipping under the door.

This could either end very well, or very, very badly. Nix grinned. It had been a long day—a long few weeks, actually—and she was excited to see which way things would go. No more waiting, no more sitting on the sidelines, it was time to act.

Elliot had followed her borrowed body into her borrowed room, close behind her the whole way, so as soon as she got the door closed it was all too easy to shove him up against it. Elliot gasped, staring at her with wide, uncertain eyes.

"Rach?" he breathed.

He stood there, all compliant and painfully handsome. She wanted to fuck him as much as she wanted to kill him, the body she was wearing burning with young lust.

She pressed against him, and he melted back into the wood of the door. His jaw tensed.

Rachel's eyes followed the line of his jaw down to the tight tendons of his neck, to his collarbone, then back up again. For Elliot's part, his eyes hadn't strayed from her lips. Pupils blown wide, when he finally did catch her eyes, Nix leaned in and captured his mouth.

He didn't withdraw, but he didn't participate, either. Elliot just stood there like a stone statue and it became quite apparent why nothing had ever happened between them before.

Addressing Rachel, Nix said, *"Well, now we're here. Shall we continue?"*

Rachel didn't respond, but her body did. Nix could feel Rachel's arousal twisting together with Nix's own, terror mixing into helpless need and making it utterly irresistible. She considered, for a moment, passing the reins over to her host, but it was too much of a risk, what with Rachel still being all pissy about the Rodney thing.

A spark touched her lips as Elliot's tongue darted out and his mouth parted for her. If the hard line straining through his jeans hadn't been indication enough, this was damning proof of his desire. Naughty boy. Nix nipped at his bottom lip and Elliot pulled back, breathing hard.

Nix palmed him through his jeans. Elliot moaned at the touch, wrapped strong hands around Rachel's biceps and pulled her closer. His tongue slid into her mouth again, probing and exploring and it occurred to Nix that she could grab the .45 he kept tucked in the back of his jeans and press the barrel underneath his chin and pull the trigger before he could even realize what was happening. She'd never blown someone's brains out mid-kiss before, but the idea struck her as oddly romantic. But the sound would be too loud, drawing the others before Nix could finish with him, and that wouldn't do. Rachel's shiver of terror at the image she shared was nice, though.

She slid her arms around his waist, pushing up the hem of his shirt and sliding her hands underneath. His arms were corded with thick muscle, all valleys and hills beneath her fingertips. His skin was hot against hers. Rachel's body had cooled gradually the longer Nix was inside of her and the contrast was grand.

His fingers stumbled over the buttons of her sweater, attempting to simultaneously pull it open and push it off her shoulders, but Nix didn't bother to help. Instead, her focus drifted to the rest of him and her mouth followed, licking and biting her way down his neck. His pulse jumped every time her teeth grazed his skin.

She moved down his chest, sinking to her knees before Elliot could get the sweater past her shoulders. He watched her, his lips slick and parted.

Nix smoothed her hands up his legs, over his thighs, reaching around to grasp his firm ass, then higher. Her fingertips brushed against the hilt of the gun, metal warm from Elliot's body.

She held his eyes. Elliot didn't move to stop her. He didn't move at all. She pulled the Ruger from his waistband and cradled it in her hand.

Elliot licked his lips. Gently, Nix placed it on the ground next to her and with her left hand she flicked open the button of his jeans. The fog seemed to clear suddenly from Elliot's eyes and he reached out to still her wrist.

For a moment they waited like that, Nix looking up at him, Elliot looking down. He was clearly trying to formulate words, but, well, the boy wasn't much for talking in the first place. Eventually, he managed, "I—we, we shouldn't...be doing this." The last part was said with something approximating conviction and Nix could see the war in his eyes.

She pulled her wrist away carefully and ran her fingers across the palm of his hand, then reached out with her tongue and sucked his index finger into her mouth.

His eyes darkened. Army-boy's hand was shaking. She'd have giggled if her mouth wasn't otherwise occupied.

Somewhere in the back of her mind, Rachel made a small desperate sound. Nix asked her, *"Do you want me to stop?"* not because she would comply, but because she already knew the answer. Rachel maintained her silence, but Nix persisted, *"All you have to do is say so."*

Naturally, Rachel didn't say so. She watched. A voyeur in her own body. Like with Rodney, Rachel didn't have to say anything for Nix to know that they wanted the same things. It was only natural, to *want*.

"*That's what I thought,*" Nix told her.

She released Elliot's finger with a pop, leaving it slick and wet.

"Rachel," Elliot whispered, "please."

"*Please don't,*" his little sister echoed uncertainly. Nix ignored her. Rachel'd had her chance.

Nix didn't know what Elliot was pleading for. He didn't seem to, either. She slid two fingers from each hand through the belt loops and tugged his jeans down slightly.

Laughter swirled up from downstairs. Glasses clinked loudly. Nix wondered what it would take to make Elliot scream. She grinned at the thought.

"*Just don't hurt him,*" Rachel pled, her heart fluttering with anxious energy. It made Nix feel all tingly and warm inside. "*They're right downstairs. You'll get caught, and Danny'll kill us if you get caught. So you can't hurt him. Right?*"

Elliot's hand landed gently on her head as though he wasn't sure what to do with it. His fingers tangled into her hair and pushed it away from her face. Nix leaned into him, batted her lashes and asked in as innocent and uncertain a voice as she could muster, "Do you want me to stop, Elli?" Nix used Rachel's childhood nickname for him as an extra-special touch—it really added something to the moment.

His brow furrowed and his fingers tightened. Elliot swallowed, Adam's apple bobbing with the movement. He shook his head. His face was flushed and his lips were red and swollen from her kisses. The very picture of debauchery.

It made her want to slice him open and see how *warm* his insides were, see if he would twitch and shudder at the intimacy of her hands tightening around the soft wet weight of his heart. Nix wasn't about to let this one go to waste; she'd do it right this time, draw it out the way she couldn't with Rodney, make it *last*.

Nix shuffled closer on her knees. She made a show of dragging his jeans all the way down, and wrapped one hand firmly around him. Soft skin, hard flesh, and the sight of it had Rachel squirming like a worm on a hook, utterly mortified and so turned on that it was making *Nix* hot.

Elliot made breathy little noises as she worked him in her fist, but not the wall-shaking moans she wanted. Rachel's body was edging on breathless, the chill of Nix's presence in her abating as nerves fired up and left her almost feverish, dripping with eagerness that Nix was going to taunt Rachel for. Later.

Intent on her goal, Nix leaned close enough for her breath to breeze over his flesh, hot and moist. Her tongue darted out, slicking spit over his shaft and Elliot jerked back, slamming into the door with a bang.

They both paused, listening for signs that they had been overheard, but the chatter from downstairs continued. Holding his eyes, Nix brushed her tongue over him again. He flushed and looked away with a pained expression. It was a good look on him, so she did it again, licking from bottom to top with her tongue flattened, lingering and probing until his gaze flickered back to her.

"Oh god. He's going to think—he's going to...." Embarrassment made Rachel hot. Nix laughed at her in the privacy of their shared skull, her host shivering, body aching as her shame flared higher. When she finally took him into Rachel's mouth, Nix watched him swallow hard. She took him deep and swallowed too, clenching around him in a vice. It hurt, Rachel whimpering inside her, but she didn't ask Nix to stop.

"What if he doesn't like it?" Rachel whispered. *"What if he goes downstairs and tells Pops?"*

Nix felt his veins pulsing against her tongue and lips, could taste his heartbeat as it skyrocketed. She dragged her nails down his thighs, deep enough to be risking blood, not quite hard enough to be certain of it.

"*Trust me,*" Nix said.

He had one hand resting on the door handle as though he was planning a quick getaway. There were no locks on these doors. The weight of Elliot's body leaning up against it was the only barricade they had, and with a house full of hunters, if they *wanted* in, they would get in.

Nix desperately wanted to get them caught, especially by Danny, but if they caught her now, she'd be thoroughly fucked—and not in the sexy-fun way. Still, the danger made the ache between Rachel's legs nearly unbearable. In between sucking and licking, Nix slid her hand into Rachel's jeans to try and ease the tension.

Elliot moaned and flinched when he saw, looking away from her while biting his fist and muttering, "Oh Jesus fucking Christ, Rach, *fuck.*" He twitched in her mouth and Nix moaned theatrically, fighting the urge to bite, reminding herself of the plan as she dragged Rachel and herself toward the edge finger length by finger length.

"*This is sick,*" Rachel snarled, feeling every second of it with Nix, the dirty, twisted things in her heart fueling every bit of her body's reactions. "*He doesn't want this! You're making us want this!*"

"*Oh yeah, this is some black, black magic,*" Nix whispered to her sweet little dolly, affection blooming in her. She loved virgins. "*He needed so much convincing to let you suck his cock like some random bar-whore. You didn't need any, but like I said: bar-whore.*"

The fingers in her hair lost their previous gentleness, and Elliot forced himself in to the hilt. Rachel choked, throat seizing around him, saliva spilling down her chin and dripping onto her sweater, and she mewled in shocked pleasure, a rush of liquid coating the hand down her jeans.

Nix grabbed his hand out of Rachel's hair and pressed it against the door, taking back control. The boy was no blushing virgin, and after two years in the army she had higher expectations of his stamina, but it didn't look like he was going to last long.

Her own fingers slicked over Rachel's aching nub, wet and sticky as her climax built, but it wasn't enough. The blue jeans were too fucking tight to get the movement she needed, and Nix was sorely tempted to just rip the damn things off.

Nix's cheeks hollowed as she sucked hard, swallowing around Elliot one last time and then he was cursing, hips bucking, coming undone.

After a moment, he pulled away from her, which was no small feat since she literally had him pinned to the door. Elliot was panting, thighs glistening with sweat as he kicked his pants off and dragged her to her feet.

Nix had no idea what he was going to do to her, but she hoped it would hurt. Rachel was so excited, she was on the edge of passing out, and her body was *on fire*. A lick of punishment would only make it better.

"He's going to tell," Rachel predicted grimly, missing her mark by a solid light-year.

Heedless of Rachel's terrified musings, Elliot gripped her arms with bruising strength, eyes dark and feral, and fucking *growled*. Like a fucked-up dog or something, all bared teeth and curled lips. Who knew the boy had it in him? Nix liked this sudden take-charge attitude of his.

He stared into her eyes, the foot of height he had on her suddenly more impressive than it had been only minutes earlier. One strong hand wrapped around her wrist. He lifted her hand and sucked a sticky-wet finger into his mouth, twisting his tongue around it and stroking the sensitive webbing between her fingers. When her brain finally caught up with the fact that he was tasting her, a whole new swell of heat spread through Rachel's body.

Elliot shoved her backward until the bed hit the back of Rachel's knees. She'd have fallen to the mattress, but he held her up, crowding her as one hand slipped to her waist and jerked her pants down her hips, panties along for the ride. When he released her and his grip wasn't holding her up anymore, she fell back on the bed, her legs still trapped between him and the mattress, jeans tangled around her knees.

Elliot grabbed the tangled knot of blue jeans and underwear, and tore it off her, tossing it to the side, completely unconcerned by the clatter of the brass buttons on the wooden floor. Conversations below continued uninterrupted, but Elliot didn't pause to listen.

As he dropped to his knees and nudged her thighs apart, something in Rachel's brain short-circuited, and Nix was left dumbfound. She hadn't been expecting quite this level of success. He hadn't even touched her yet and already Rachel was sky-high and writhing with fear and anticipation. Rachel *was*, of course, a blushing virgin—though based on Nix's performance, Elliot probably didn't even realize. *"Oh God, is he going to...?"* Nix couldn't tell if Rachel was excited or terrified.

"Shh," he hushed her, rubbing a stumbled cheek against the soft skin of her inner thigh, "they'll hear."

She had no idea where this Elliot had come from, but Nix liked him a lot more than the boring soldier-boy version. She might just have to keep this one around for a while.

Less than a mile away, in a truck submerged in water, Rodney's body would have already begun the process of decomposition. Nix had left his eyes open, in case he wanted to watch. She was thoughtful like that.

A voice from downstairs rang above the rest for a moment and a chorus of drunken laughter followed. Someone banged something against a table, probably a beer mug. She listened for footsteps on the creaky old stairs but heard none. Elliot's hands pinned her knees against the edge of the mattress, positioning his face right where she wanted him and ensuring she held still. His breath blew across her skin and a chill ran up her spine.

Nix had every intention of enjoying this—a fringe benefit, and a pleasurable one at that, but nothing more. Rachel, on the other hand, was coming unglued. A few fumbling teenage encounters in the back of a pickup truck being her total experience, Rachel had never even touched a guy's dick, much less had anyone go down on her. The novelty of Elliot's lips pressed against her in a sloppy but reverent kiss had her writhing.

It was all Nix could do to keep her still. Elliot's tongue slid inside her and flicked over her clit with the precision of experience. The sensation sent Rachel skyrocketing. A high-pitched moan escaped her lips in spite of Nix's attempts to keep her quiet. Nix promptly bit her tongue in warning. She couldn't have the girl getting any ideas about regaining control over her own body.

If Elliot would just stop sucking like that, she could invest a lot more mental effort into that goal. She squirmed as pleasure built up in her, the overflow from earlier rising to unmanageable proportions.

Elliot pressed a finger inside her, pushing in slowly and twisting. Rachel was so tight that even one finger stretched her, nearly painful but mostly *not enough*. It wasn't until Elliot pulled away and nipped her thigh in admonishment that Nix even realized she'd been making an increasingly loud litany of breathy little sounds that weren't entirely Rachel's fault.

She put a hand over her mouth to keep quiet. Normally she'd delight in the possibility of some curious passerby walking in on them, but if anyone interrupted them right now, Nix was going to have to fucking kill somebody. Again.

Elliot's finger returned, slick, and another pressed in alongside it without warning. The stretch burned deliciously and her back arched off the bed. The tip of his tongue flicked over her clit and she dug her fingers into the old pink bedspread, sensation starting to cascade down her body like the light of a sparkler.

She propped herself up on her elbows to get a better look at Elliot.

Nix hadn't noticed before, too intent on the sensations splitting her skull, but he was making noises too, murmuring against her skin. She caught Christ's name and Rachel's, blended together in some sort of prayer and the prospect made her laugh. He drove his fingers into her while simultaneously torturing her clit with quick flicks of his tongue, and Nix's laughter turned into a choked whine halfway out of her throat.

The tension was unbearable, twisting through her insides until she was writhing on the bed, hips bucking against his mouth as he tried unsuccessfully to keep her pinned with one hand pressed into her hip.

She couldn't feel the bedspread or the mattress, just a pervasive tingling all over her body that was driving her nuts. His fingers pumped into her harder, faster, until every thrust blurred together, and still Rachel teetered on the edge.

The breeze blowing through the open window was just a tease. Her skin sizzled and ached, everything ached, and she needed—she needed...if he would just...Elliot licked her as his fingers plunged in to the knuckle, stretching Rachel's body wide, and suddenly Nix was floating somewhere off in the distance and Rachel had the reins.

Climax ripped through her and before she could shout out, Elliot's mouth covered hers. His fingers didn't stop, drawing out the pleasure, thumb continuing the work his mouth had left. Rachel could taste herself on his tongue, along with the beer he'd had earlier in the night.

It was only for a moment, a moment that seemed to stretch and expand over each second, drawing it out to three times its actual length. But it was enough. It was too much.

Nix snapped into the driver's seat, sending Rachel plummeting back into that little corner of her brain that she still claimed as her own, and it was over. Rachel's body was still riding the high, drifting down slowly as Elliot guided her with his mouth and hands, Nix breathing hard through the aftershocks.

Chapter 23

Croissants littered the breakfast table. A pitcher of orange juice and an assortment of fruit were arranged neatly in the center. Joan was quite the hostess. Maybe Nix should have jumped into her body instead.

Nix got the impression that Joan didn't get to do this sort of thing very often. Something about the stacks of pancakes and French toast delivered at sporadic intervals to the table gave it away. Joan brushed by Nix's elbow, laying out some sort of sugary confectionary on the tablecloth next to her.

"You should stay a while," Joan was saying, attention directed to Kevin. "Jake and I, we like the company. Gets so quiet out here, you know?"

"I'll think about it, Joanie, thanks. I've got a couple of errands to run in town, but nothing time-sensitive, maybe I'll drop by afterwards before I head up north again. I appreciate the invitation."

"I know you do," she agreed cheerfully. "That goes for you too, missy," Joan added, patting her hand lightly on Nix's shoulder and gracing her with a motherly smile that made Rachel's chest constrict with latent longing. "You and Elliot are welcome to stay as long as you want." She cast a glance to Danny, who was busy carving into a pile of French toast covered in syrup and bacon. Rachel grumbled silently about cholesterol, but Nix didn't care enough to relay the message. The man wouldn't live long enough to die of a heart attack, anyway. "You can leave the kids with us, Daniel, if you need to."

"Ah, Joan, don't worry about it. I need my boy in the field. My girl, too," he added quickly. "Don't know what I'd do without them."

Joan made a little *'hmph'* noise that Nix couldn't decipher.

"Shouldn't we be on the road already, Pops?" Elliot said, buttering a piece of wholegrain toast with broad strokes. He hadn't made eye contact with her all morning, though she'd caught him staring at her twice when he thought she wasn't looking. Amusing as the boy was to play with, Nix couldn't help but wonder if she'd been too rash, tipped her hand. It was an easy fix if she had, though Nix kind of wanted to sample him a bit more fully before she was finished with him.

"I won't let you hurt him," Rachel said, as though she had any say in the matter. Nix grinned, amused by the kid's daydreaming.

Danny looked down at his plate, waved a hand dismissively, and decided, "Those folks ain't getting any deader. Finish your breakfast."

The man was a touch mercurial. Only an hour ago he'd gone on about how a succubus and a half-dead goat were giving the good people of Manteca all manner of grief, but apparently that didn't mean he should be rushed through breakfast.

Joan picked up the plate of bacon and set it at the far end of the table, then served some egg whites on her husband's dish despite his protests. "You'll keep in touch about the case, won't you?" she asked Danny.

Nix had yet to see her eat anything. All Joan seemed focused on was the continuous production of food for her guests, and being smotheringly creepy in her affection. Joan had hugged her *three* times this morning—that was three times too many, by Nix's estimation.

Rachel may have been dying for a mother figure in her life, but Nix sure as fuck wasn't, and hugs...well, hugs were just *weird*. The whole prolonged physical contact was understandable under the right circumstances, but this hugging thing involved standing perfectly still while Joan caught her in a vice and squeezed the air out of her lungs for between ten and thirty seconds.

Every time they passed the ten second mark, Nix was suddenly convinced that Joan was on to her and she was about to get stabbed with some sacred anti-demon knife dripping with holy water or something equally sinister. With Rousoe around, these hunters probably had all manner of nasty weapons in their demon-killing arsenal. The hugs had to be a trap of some sort, but Joan had yet to make her move. It was very stressful.

Danny didn't look up from his meal when he responded, "Of course. Should get there by mid-afternoon. Ain't far. If we find anything noteworthy, you'll be the first to know."

Nix sipped her orange juice gingerly, her gaze brushing over each of them in turn. Joan continued to fuss. Jake still looked a little drunk from the night before. Elliot was expending a tremendous amount of focus on salting his eggs. Danny attacked his meal with an embarrassing intensity.

Kevin...Kevin was a bit of an enigma. He sat quietly, politely contributing when it was required of him but never initiating conversation. Nix had a feeling about this guy. Whether Joan or Jake were in on The Plot was debatable, but Kevin...she could see this guy involving himself in some diabolical end-of-the-world ploy.

Nix glanced up at Joan. She needed to know for sure whether she and her husband were involved in this.

"Joan?" Nix asked.

"Yes, dear?"

"How's the car coming along?"

Joan smiled, broad and sincere. "Oh, fine! I just replaced the spark plugs and the distributer cap last weekend. Going to change the oil then work a little under the hood after breakfast." Joan brushed her hands off on her apron and a wispy memory of Rachel's mother doing the same flittered through her head.

Nix smiled back at Joan. "That sounds like fun," she said.

"It will be!"

Nix poked at the egg on her plate and tilted her head, tone both hesitant and tinged with hopefulness as she asked, "Do you think you could show me sometime?"

Joan beamed, eyes brimming with trust—and maybe a little pride. "I'd love to, honey. I could use the help," she added, pointedly glaring at Jake, but there was no real animosity in it.

Jake shrugged, sipping his coffee.

Nix turned to Danny. "Hey, Pops, do you think I could stay with Joan and help her with the car? I can catch the bus to town after."

"Nonsense, I can give you a ride!" Joan offered, looking thrilled by the prospect. "How about it, Danny?"

Danny glanced between them. "Well, I suppose we can't do too much today anyway. Coroner isn't in until tomorrow morning. Elliot can pick up the slack, can't you, boy?"

"Sure thing, Pops," Elliot replied absently, carefully examining his fork.

"So I can stay?" Nix asked, excitement thick and out of place in her voice.

Danny looked at her with squinty eyes, but he seemed pleased if not a touch suspicious that his daughter was exhibiting excitement over something so mundane. "Don't see why not," he said.

"That's great!" Joan enthused. "We can get started as soon as the boys leave. It'll be nice to have some girl time, just the two of us."

Nix smiled and nodded her agreement. They were all so easy. It was like taking candy from a baby—and that was pretty goddamn easy, in Nix's experience.

Kevin glanced down at his watch then wiped his mouth with a paper napkin. "I'd better get going. Thanks for the breakfast, Joanie."

The table erupted in social pleasantries. Everybody had to say goodbye and chat and wave. It wasn't just for Kevin, either. They did this little show every time somebody left the table and it was getting rather tedious.

Nix sighed inwardly. Of all the things she did not have time for when the world was potentially ending and her entire species and that of her hosts was about to be wiped off the face of the earth by a bunch of well-meaning morons, social pleasantries were at the top of the list. But she played the part, just like always.

And when Kevin left and insisted on *hugging* each and every one of them individually for the apparent minimum of ten seconds, Nix endured. And when Danny slowly dragged himself and Elliot away from the table and out the door, Nix waved and said, "See you soon," and "Be safe," and all the other pedestrian bullshit she was socially obligated to say.

Because she was a professional.

She could handle this.

And by tonight, this would all be over.

Chapter 24

She caught Joan alone in the garage after everyone had left. Jake was napping away his hangover upstairs and after a brief examination of the house, Nix decided that the only way to know for sure whether these two were involved in anything was to ask.

And by ask, of course, she meant crawl up inside them and poke around their brains for a while. For some reason, Rachel found this tactic offensive and started protesting before Nix even got to the garage. She was convinced Nix was going to butcher her two little buddies, and while this was true, Nix didn't appreciate the assumption. For Rachel to think she *knew* anything about Nix was just insulting.

Engine oil and other car smells painted the air in thick, broad strokes. When Nix took a breath she could feel the grease, sticky and slick in Rachel's lungs.

Rustling fabric and clinking metal were a soft background music that broke the silence. She reached into Rachel's pocket, pulled out two knockout pills, and swallowed them dry. She waited until she felt the change start, the little shift in Rachel's head that blurred her vision and made her limbs heavy. She didn't want her ride wandering off.

Nix walked around to the front of the car facing the garage door. It was a 1971 Mustang fastback, stock 302 V8, candy apple red with white racing stripes right down the center. The hood was up. The paint was chipping off bit by bit and the rust bled through, because she could paint it all she wanted, but she could never completely erase what lay beneath the surface. And yet, Joan seemed determined to try. Typical human. From the looks of it, she'd been at it for a while. Tools were scattered in a semicircle on the concrete. A pile of dirty rags lay near the front of the car.

The woman was tucked beneath the front of the precariously jacked-up vehicle, reaching up to screw with its insides, so far under that only her legs were visible. At the light shuffle of Nix's footsteps, a voice floated out from beneath the car, asking, "Rachel, that you? Can you hand me my wrench? Just be careful of the jack—my ramp's busted, so this isn't very stable."

It was almost too easy.

"Don't hurt her."

Nix glanced around and grabbed the requested item, pressing it into Joan's open hand. She met Joan's eyes when she tilted Rachel's head to glance past all the rusting metal.

"Thanks, honey. Almost finished down here, then we can get to the fun stuff under the hood. Hey, I forgot to ask, how's that arm of yours?"

"Feels fine," Nix said. That was ages ago. Humans were strange with their injury obsessions. So far as Nix was concerned, if it didn't fall off, it was still good.

Joan shimmied out from under the car. She sat up and wiped her hands off on her jeans. Nix could hear oil spilling out into a pan. "That's good to hear. Your Pops was worried. He's real proud of you, though." Joan smiled, like she was sharing a secret. "I think you impressed him with that dryad. He was all puffed up and bragging about his girl last night. Don't tell him I told you—you know how he is." Joan chuckled.

"My lips are sealed," Nix promised. "Hey, how does this thing work?" she asked, pointing at the jack. "I've never used one before."

"Please don't hurt her."

Joan raised an eyebrow. "Really? I thought you worked with Danny on that old truck?"

Nix nodded. "Oh, yeah, I did. Never let me touch the jack though. Think he was worried I'd get crushed under the truck or something."

"Don't do this." The pills were kicking in. Rachel's presence was dimming and her vision was spotty in places.

"I see. Well," she motioned toward the jack, "it's pretty straightforward. Usually I wouldn't be using it to hold the car up while I change the oil, but you work with what you've got, right? If you ever need to use one, chances are it'll be to change a tire not oil. Just *don't* tell your Pops you saw me doing this. I'll never heard the end of it. Anyway, you have to be extra careful not to jostle it when it's like this. Just make sure the car isn't going anywhere—that's what the bricks behind the back tires are there for—and position the stock jack under one of the jacking points next to the tires. Then you crank the handle, making sure it's nice and tight where you want it to be and it'll scissor open 'til the car's lifted up. It's not too dangerous so long as you know what you're doing. Once I'm done under here, I'll let you test it out, if you want."

"I'd like that."

Joan hummed in what Nix imagined was approval, then eased back under the car. "Oh, there's a filter over on the workbench, do you mind passing it to me?"

Nix walked up to the jack, tilting her head to determine the most effective angle.

"Stop!" Rachel pleaded, voice slurred and distant.

Nix smiled. "I wouldn't mind at all."

One solid kick with Nix's strength powering it, and nearly two tons of metal crashed to the floor.

Pain spiked through Rachel's foot but it was *so* worth it. The sound reverberated through the garage as the tires bounced on the concrete and the jack clattered against the wall, knocking over a tin garbage can. The open hood slammed shut.

It was all so sudden and so loud that Nix couldn't even hear Joan gasp or cry out. She wondered if she'd overdone it. It wouldn't be the first time she'd meant to injure an animal and accidentally killed it in the process. Rachel was paralyzed by the shock and utterly quiet, though, so Nix considered this a win.

Red blood and black oil twisted together, seeping leisurely into the dirty rags and down into the thin cracks that ran like veins through the concrete floor. One of the Mustang's windows was fractured in a lightning bolt pattern from the abrupt impact, and the back bumper had almost fallen off. The car was a lost cause, anyway.

A soft choking noise slid out from under the vehicle, the sound of fluid-filled lungs fighting for air.

Both Nix and Rachel sighed in tentative relief, though for different reasons. Nix knelt down on the cold concrete and looked under the car. A chunk of metal protruded from what Nix could see of Joan's chest, crushing her and keeping her pinned.

Joan's left hand reached out, grasping at nothing.

Nix took the leap. Joan's neck was at an odd angle, making it a bit more of a process than usual to slip down her throat and oh my, yes, that was an awful lot of pain.

There were more broken places than Nix could count, but it wasn't the body she was interested in right now. Nix poked around Joan's brain while Joan was still too distressed and injured to notice the intrusion.

Like her home, Joan's mind was surprising cozy and dotted with cow ornaments, though much deeper than the surface implied. There was a dead daughter in here, a number of other hunters, a long history with paranormal intervention, and was that an early career in porn? Fascinating. Joan was much more interesting—and flexible—than she let on.

Unfortunately, however, she didn't seem to know anything more than Nix did about any coming war. Joan knew *of* it, but only what she'd heard in passing. Danny had warned her not to get involved, it wasn't safe, he didn't want her getting hurt, blah blah blah. The man was so predictable.

Joan also knew that Danny and Val and...oh, of course. So Kevin *was* involved. No great surprise there.

A sharp stabbing pain in Joan's chest drew Nix back to the surface. Joan's throat filled up with the metallic tang of blood. She stopped breathing.

For one lonely, quiet moment, just as Joan slid away into nothing, Nix was the only voice inside this head. Her body was shot and Joan had nothing left to offer her, so Nix gathered herself up and pushed her way out in a messy gurgle of blood and death until she was slipping back into Rachel's comparatively more comfortable young body.

Two down.

Nix picked Rachel up off the ground and brushed her off. The girl was spinning and grasping at air, hopeless to be sure, but still she tried to regain control. The drugs pumped through her system, leaving her body groggy and uncoordinated, but Nix maneuvered her without much trouble.

"Joan?" Jake's voice came from somewhere deep inside the house. The noise must have pulled him from his drunken stupor long enough to cause him some concern.

Nix tucked herself next to the stairs, out of sight to anyone coming down them, and looked around for an appropriate weapon. Footsteps sounded nearby, coming down a flight of stairs. Nix glanced at a corkboard wall laden with various tools, but found nothing of interest. Her gaze fell on a hammer—too small. The car bumper—too large.

The door handle to the house twisted open.

A tire iron was tucked against the stairs—*just right*.

"What the—" Jake's voice trailed off, then he erupted into a nonsensical stream of panicked curses as he lumbered down the steps calling to his dead wife.

Nix stepped forward as Jake's heavy foot hit the bottom step. She swung the tire iron.

Jake shouted and tumbled backwards, falling onto the last few steps, then down them. Nix dropped the tool, letting it clang to the ground as it settled.

She stepped toward Jake, stood over him, and felt that exquisite sense of peace come over her as she stood looking down at her prey.

Nix let go, let Rachel crumple to the ground like a fallen coat, and she felt renewed, like a snake shedding its skin. The air was heavier with Nix in it, electric and tinged with sulfur. Jake moaned on the concrete, a hand pressed to his head, and his lips were parted just enough for her to slip between them.

Jake choked on her.

He flailed and gasped for air and tried to fight, but already it was too late.

She shrugged him on and lifted her new body from the ground, brushing his hands off on his jeans for him. The world had a slightly different look to it through these eyes. Everything was a little fuzzier around the edges and Nix wondered if he was still drunk from the night before. Jake's ears rang from the blow, the lingering sound sharp and piercing.

Rachel lay where Nix left her, still and silent.

Jake's mind was like a sloppy, inebriated mirror of his wife's. Joan took up hobbies after their kid died, Jake took up drinking. He knew even less than Joan did, which wasn't really a surprise. Nix stood a moment longer, snooping through his thoughts, trying to spark the relevant synapses to see if anything popped up, but nothing did. Ah well, can't win 'em all.

Satisfied, Nix stepped over the discarded girl and rummaged through the hefty drawers of Joan's workbench.

The pool of blood and oil spread languidly from beneath the car. It didn't take long to find the rope.

Nix smoothed her fingers over the rough weave, loosening the knot while keeping it tidily wrapped and easily forming another. Three twists and the noose in her hand was just waiting for its hangman.

Rachel stirred, the fabric of her clothes rustling against the concrete as she made some of the confused little gasping noises that Nix had grown accustomed to. Her body hadn't been hers for a while now, so it would take some getting used to, some reconnecting of familiar ties. Nix smirked at her as she lay there. Rachel's fists clenched and unclenched at her sides in attempt to drag herself back up to consciousness.

Even if she ran, she wouldn't get far, so Nix wasn't overly concerned about leaving her be for a moment, but she still didn't want to draw this out any longer than necessary. She had places to be, people to kill. Plus, Jake's bum knee seemed to be troubling him today and it was getting annoying already. *Click-click-click* with every step.

Nix wrapped her hand around the end of the rope and flung it into the air, over an exposed rafter. The rope fell into place with a soft but solid *whoosh*.

Nix climbed onto the car, feeling it sink beneath Jake's weight. She heard something crack and shift, wondered if it was the car or Joan's skull, then pulled the rope nice and tight, securing it in place and tugging on it to test its strength. Finding the noose met her specifications, Nix grinned, Jake's lips lifting into a macabre mimicry of a smile.

She glanced down at Rachel as she wrapped the noose around Jake's neck. Rachel met her eyes, looking lost and confused, and rather like a skittish kitten. "No worries, doll," Nix reassured her in Jake's deep voice. "Won't take a moment."

Rachel clawed weakly at the ground, pulling herself to her knees and wobbling, her bearings still out of reach. "No," she said.

Nix frowned, standing on the sleek metal hood of the Mustang, socked feet planted firmly on either side of one of the white racing strips. "No, what?"

Rachel panted, and this was the first time Nix noticed the tears glistening in her eyes. Poor dear'd had a long day. But it would be over soon.

Rachel pursed her lips, squeezing her eyes shut and looking away for only a moment, probably still fighting off the vertigo and skull-splitting headache that generally accompanied these transitions. Rachel ground her teeth together, looking awfully fierce all of the sudden considering the pitiful position she was in.

"I—I won't let you do this, I won't!" Then she was scrambling to stand and—oops! Rachel fell back to her knees, hitting the hard concrete with a surprised yelp. Quietly, with a hitch in her voice, she added, "I won't."

Nix adjusted the noose, tugged the rope again to check that it would support Jake's weight and she was about to step off the hood of the Mustang when a rumbling sound reached Jake's ears through the dull ringing that remained there.

A car was coming up the driveway.

Nix caught Rachel's eyes in a second-long standoff. Rachel bolted, stumbling into the work bench and diving toward the stairs leading back into the house. Nix jumped—physically and metaphorically, as it were.

Without her to hold Jake's body up, he crumpled and the noose tightened. Jake made a strangled sound in the back of his throat as she left him and just before Nix could climb back into her naughty little hostess, Rachel screamed.

Halfway through the bloodcurdling sound, Nix was cramming herself back down Rachel's throat. The scream short-circuited, transforming into a watery cough as Rachel's body tried to reject her, and then she was back.

Nix pulled her on quickly, not worrying about getting the fit right, just getting her hands back on the wheel.

Rachel keened in frustration.

Nix took a deep breath, tasting the engine oil and blood on the air, blinking away the tears Rachel was insisting on shedding. Jake twitched, swinging back and forth, back and forth.

Even if he did manage to wake up now, the oxygen would be cut off from his brain and his muscles, deprived of that oxygen, would be useless to pull himself up or try to get free. Though he was unconscious at the moment, Nix admired the man. Even alive, he had seemed determined to dig himself an early grave. He'd recognized his own hopelessness, embraced it.

That's what Rachel wasn't getting; the cold hard fact that there was nothing she could do to change her fate or that of anyone else. If she'd just accept that one immutable truth, things would run a whole lot more smoothly for the both of them. But then, hopeless as Rachel was, Nix didn't really expect any great self-insights from her any time soon.

A car door slammed outside.

Footsteps rushed across gravel, pounding on the wooden porch by the front door.

Someone had heard Rachel scream. Nix took a look at the mess around her. She smiled.

Chapter 25

When Nix slipped back inside through the garage door, she'd hoped to make a quick break for it before getting caught by whoever had pulled up in the driveway—or at least buy herself some time for a little recon—but as with so many best-laid plans, it didn't quite work out how she'd hoped.

She flicked off the light and eased the door closed, backing up into the dark foyer, nearly tripping over a discarded boot. For a moment, she stilled, listening for any sign of her visitor, and for that moment, she thought she was alone.

The click of a revolver cut through the silence, quick but loud and resounding in her ears.

Nix turned to see a gun staring back at her, and beyond it the pale eyes of Kevin Rousoe. She stumbled back with her hands raised, adopting a terrified and confused expression.

"Uncle Kevin, what are you doing?"

His eyes narrowed, gaze wavering almost imperceptibly, something haunted still lurking deep down in there. If he was pointing a gun at her, he already knew something was wrong, but he looked unsure. "Step aside," he demanded.

For lack of alternatives, Nix did. He moved past, gun still trained on her, and with an impending sense of dread, she recognized the twisting lines of sigils and crosses and Latin etched into the silver. Rousoe was known for his weapons, but Nix hadn't imagined this was one of them.

An exorcism in a bullet. Is that what this was? It couldn't work, could it? Maybe he was bluffing. But this was Rousoe, not a man to pull punches. And if he was in on the whole cleansing-the-earth plot, who knew what tools he had at his disposal, or how far he would go.

Kevin grasped the door handle and pulled it open, shooting her a suspicious glance before looking inside. She peeked past his shoulder, trying not to smile at the thought of the lovely mess she'd made.

A bit of illumination filtered through the two windows on either side of the garage, but each was covered by thin yellow curtains that only served to make the light look pale and sickly, and the old cans of oil stacked up on the windowpanes blocked the light out even more. It wasn't enough to see inside very clearly, but Kevin didn't make any moves to reach for the light switch.

She could still hear the soft bumping sound of socked feet brushing against the Mustang as Jake's body continued to swing.

The expression on Kevin's face didn't change as he looked into the garage. He sniffed, pursed his lips, and she thought she saw his eye twitch just slightly at the corner, but she couldn't be sure.

If he'd stop pointing that stupid gun at her, she'd have a lot more options. But he probably couldn't even see Joan from this angle, what with the majority of the woman currently crushed and dead under that car. So it was just Jake who was the obvious issue on first glance. And Jake, of course, was a sad drunk most of the time and it wouldn't be such a stretch to think that maybe he strung himself up on the rafters, perhaps even after accidentally killing his wife.

Yeah, that was good. It could work. A nice little twist ending and everything—people loved that shit.

Kevin looked away from the macabre scene in the garage, letting the door slam shut as his attention locked back on her. The way his shoulders loosened and he sighed, he almost looked...relieved...like it wasn't as bad as he'd expected. But Nix must have read him wrong. The eyes were harder, though, than they had been before, and his jaw cracked as he ground his teeth together.

Nix opened her mouth, ready to make her case.

"I don't know what you are, but you aren't Danny's girl," he said, voice tight with conviction.

"Yes!" Rachel cheered, deep inside her mind. A bit prematurely.

This was it, time to shine. She widened Rachel's eyes, letting them well up with tears courtesy of Rachel's current emotional distress, which made the annoying internal whimpering and trembling almost worth it. "What are you talking about? I—I just found them like this, I swear! Jake, he was drunk and he went into the garage with Joan and I heard this...this loud bang and..." Nix lied, quite convincingly, in her opinion. The tears started to trickle free and she let a note of hysteria leak into Rachel's voice, "I don't understand what's happening! Uncle Kevin, please, I—"

"Don't," he warned. His eyes narrowed and his lips formed a flat, even line, a line impervious to bullshit. "Just drop the act."

Nix almost wanted to applaud the man. She'd met eight self-proclaimed professional hunters in the last few weeks, boarded with two of them and wore one for all that time, and no one had questioned her. Not once. Mr. Rousoe, here, had just earned himself a bit of her respect. She considered pushing the act a little further, but she'd met his type before—he wouldn't be so easily persuaded.

She smirked and lowered her hands, hooking her thumbs into the pockets of Rachel's jeans. "Got to say, I'm impressed. Here I thought all hunters were bumbling morons with gun fetishes. I see you've avoided the bumbling moron part. Lucky man."

"The kitchen," he instructed gruffly, shaking his gun at her in what seemed to be an attempt to communicate directions.

Nix sighed, then shrugged, wiping at Rachel's blurry eyes. "All right, fine. Kitchen it is." It wasn't like she was worried about the gun, or anything, nor was she obeying his commands, it was just that the kitchen was probably the better venue for this so she figured it couldn't hurt to go along with it.

He pulled a chair out from the dinner table by hooking his foot around one leg, never taking his eyes off Nix, and whipped it around to face her. Kevin looked at her then nodded to the chair, and this was getting a little ridiculous at this point. Surely he didn't actually expect her cooperation.

Nix pursed Rachel's lips and stared him down. "Oh come now, you and I both know you aren't about to shoot an innocent girl in the head just to waste little ol' me. What good would that do?"

"Don't underestimate me," Kevin said.

"You could at least tell me what gave me away."

He sniffed and replied, "Sulfur," not bothering to mask the disgust in his voice.

Damn, she hadn't thought of that. Doing so much body-jumping in a confined space like she had, it was unavoidable. Point was: her acting skills were not in question here. Not that they'd ever been, but confirmation was nice.

He motioned with his gun for her to sit. And okay, maybe the gun was getting a little intimidating.

Nix complied. She waited for him to pull some ropes out of his ass and start tying her up, like that would do any good, but he didn't. Kevin held the gun on her and just stood there.

"What, no bondage?" she asked.

"Don't need any."

"Well that's dull. Thought we could at least have a little fun before I killed you," Nix said.

She glanced around the room, eyes landing on a row of cow ornaments close to her right—a series of three with matching porcelain bows that sported the names *Betsy*, *Hefty*, and *Moe*—and if she'd had any doubts about killing Joan before, they were now thoroughly wiped from her mind. She'd just done good taste a huge favor.

Her gaze swept over the mounted sword set across the room as well, but it was too far away to be of any use. The gun that had been on the table the night before had since been moved and she couldn't see anything else to use as a weapon. The thing about weapons, though, was that if she could just disarm him, she wouldn't need one. Kevin pulled out another chair and moved it to sit in front of her, just out of reach, a lunge-and-a-half away.

"The quiet type, hey?" Nix commented. "You know, the quiet ones always have the weirdest kinks. What does it for you? Bowls of jello? Life-size Barbie dolls? Latex cat suits?"

He dug around inside his vest, pulling out a small vial that had exorcism written all over it—not literally, of course, though she wouldn't put it past these hunters to do something so asinine. Kevin unscrewed the cap with one hand and a sweet scent emerged, like cheap perfume, heady and sharp.

Before Nix realized what he was doing, a stream of liquid splashed onto her face. She jerked back in the chair, an offended hiss partway out of her throat when she realized it didn't actually hurt. Not holy water, then. This was a welcome change, as far as Nix was concerned.

She sniffed the air and grimaced. "Smells like knock-off Chanel. That's the best you've got?" She rubbed her hands together and moved to stand up, saying, "Well, it's been fun, Kev, but—"

An invisible force pulled her back into the seat. Nix paused at this. Kevin's face gave nothing away, as usual. She tried again to stand, only to achieve the same result.

"What did you do?" she asked.

The perfume smell intensified, seeming to wrap around her, fastening her to the chair. This was some kind of bizarre-ass black magic Mr. Rousoe was playing with here. Nix struggled but got nowhere. Bondage was far less frustrating than this.

Kevin's lips parted, like he was finally going to answer her, but all that came out of him was a string of old Italian. Her eyes snapped to his.

"Wait, wait, wait," Nix warned. "I know this exorcism—I've see it done. It kills the host. You're *not* going to kill Rachel."

He paused in his chanting only to say, "I'll do what I have to. Rachel would understand."

"Uh, *no*. I have it on good authority that she would *not*. She's still in here, you know," Nix pointed out.

"No, it's better this way," Rachel said, bravely facing her imminent death with the self-sacrificing calmness of a saint. Nix, not being an idiot, didn't repeat that.

Kevin had the decency to look apologetic, but he continued, undeterred, and Nix could feel the beginnings of the exorcism taking root. The words slid under her skin, insidious and sharp, tugging at threads and pulling, pulling, *pulling*.

Nix tried, "What do you think you're accomplishing, exactly? You don't even have your little glowy blue ball thing, huh? You need that, I'll bet. No worries, I can wait here and you can go grab it, hey?"

"Shut up, demon whore," he spat.

"Now that's just rude," Nix said. "We barely even know each other."

He said something else in Italian—either 'damned' or something about taxes, Nix wasn't as up on her languages as she used to be, but it hurt like a son of a bitch. Nix hissed in spite of herself.

"I'll bite her tongue off," Nix said, but they both knew it was an empty threat—she kind of needed the tongue part of Rachel at the moment. She tried again, "I can make this a hundred times more painful for her than you can for me."

Kevin didn't even acknowledge her.

"So what, you're just some soulless killer?"

No response. She felt Rachel's throat tighten as a suffocating heat started to build up inside. That taste in her mouth was some sort of internally generated smoke, which was a bit disconcerting.

"I mean," Nix continued, "under other circumstances, I'd find that kind of hot, but you've known Rachel all her life. You've known her longer than Danny has," she choked out. Still nothing. "How are you going to explain this to Danny? I can promise you he'll be less than thrilled that you fucking *killed* his *daughter*."

He kept chanting, and the burning grew, but it was all going to be fine. Nix had talked her way out of tougher scrapes than this. She just needed to focus, needed to strike him deep.

A thought occurred to her. "What would your Marybeth say?" Nix asked.

Bull's-eye. "Marybeth understood," Kevin said, and every moment that the words between them stilled, the tugging lessened and the scorching heat cooled. Nix took advantage of the brief respite.

Nix repeated his words, seizing on the opportunity to draw this out. "She...understood?"

"I had no other choice with her, just like I've got no other choice now. She knew I had to do it. She begged me to, even though she knew the cost. Sacrifices must be made for the greater good."

It hit her then, the realization, the truth: "You killed her."

Kevin looked away. "I saved her."

Oh, this was wonderful. This was fantastic. This was even more than Nix could have hoped for. "You sick bastard," she said, a congratulatory note in her voice. "I knew there was a reason I liked you."

Still avoiding her gaze, Kevin said, "Rachel will understand, too."

"Really?" Nix challenged. "Well, you can just explain it to her yourself, then."

Nix drew back, shrinking in on herself and leaving Rachel the space to take the reins.

Blinking and still disoriented, Rachel lifted her head and looked around, eyes falling on her captor. "Uncle Kevin?" It all seemed to hit her at once, and the confusion melted into that hysteria that had been building since the moment Nix took her. She tried to move as Nix had done before, but she could barely shift in the chair. "Where—where's Pops? Where's my brother?"

Kevin's mouth hung open a bit, and though he didn't look like he was going to let her go, his expression had changed from deadpan to deadpan-with-a-side-of-shock, which Nix considered progress.

Kevin told her, "They can't be here right now, kid. It's just us."

Her eyes filled with tears. Her bottom lip trembled. Oh yeah, she was doing a way better job than Nix did. This was like method acting or something—or not acting at all, Nix supposed. Rachel was genuinely this distressed. It was perplexing that the human species had managed to survive this long with so much achingly maudlin emotion oozing out of them all the damn time.

Rachel stared at him imploringly, begging in a small kittenish voice with the edge of a whimper to it, "Please, please don't do this." When push came to shove, she wasn't half as willing to die as she'd pretended. Humans never were.

Rachel gasped over something, then started hyperventilating. Water continued to leak out of her eyeholes in a very unattractive manner. Haltingly, she confessed, "I tried to stop her...oh God, the things she made me do, and I couldn't—I'm so sorry, Uncle Kevin, I didn't mean for any of this to happen," she said, taking a moment to suck in more air to fuel her tears, which were now so thick that Nix could barely see anything out of her eyes. Rachel crumpled in on herself, sobbing, and said, "I didn't mean to hurt anybody, I swear, I didn't...."

"I know you didn't, Rachel. I knew you could never...that it wasn't *you*," Kevin said, and Nix had to admit, there was more emotion in his voice now than she'd been able to provoke herself.

Rachel wasn't a bad pawn to have on her side.

Rachel looked up at him from beneath stringy, sweat-soaked bangs, and Nix hadn't even realized until then that she'd been sweating. "Then why...why are you doing this?"

Kevin seemed stumped for a moment, but offered the paltry explanation of, "I—I have to. It's the only way to kill it. Not just exorcise it, but get rid of it for good, forever. If I let it go now, it'll just keep hurting people. It'll come back for you, for everybody you love, now that it's got your scent. It'll never stop, don't you see?"

Rachel took a deep breath, sobbed a few more times for good measure, then asked, "Will...will it hurt?"

He looked away, his brow furrowing, and what might even have been tears built up in his eyes. "Yeah. Yeah, honey, it will. Just for a little while, and then it will be over and—"

In a fit of idiocy, Rachel said, "Okay."

"What?" Nix wasn't sure whether she or Kevin said it first, but she could certainly sympathize with his bewilderment.

Nix struggled to push herself back up to the surface, clawing at Rachel to draw her back down, but the exorcism had taken more out of her than she had first thought.

The scheming little martyr climbed back onto her cross, just like Nix should have expected her to. "I don't want to hurt anyone else," she stupidly mumbled. "Tell Danny and El...tell them I'm sorry. I wasn't strong enough to fight it. I should have tried harder. I let them down."

And there it was, she was hammering the nails in now, a full-on self-crucifixion if Nix had ever seen one. Just as Nix felt like she was making some progress getting back into the driver's seat, ready to slip into damage-control mode, something changed in Kevin's voice, something Nix hadn't expected to hear. Something that sounded an awful lot like defeat.

"No, Rachel," he said, real quiet, shaking his head. "You didn't. Your Pops would be proud of you. I *know* he's proud of you."

Kevin stared down at his hands for a long moment and said nothing. Nix held Rachel's breath for her until Rachel felt faint.

"This exorcism, it's different from most others. Real old magic. I uncovered it years ago, but even then I didn't realize how much power it held. It was only in the past few months that we figured out how to channel it, make it so the demons weren't just destroyed, but trapped, so we could use them. This right here," he said, holding up the vial so she could get a good look, "a little splash will immobilize a demon no matter what form it's in. Won't be able to get into or out of anybody on its own until you release it or it wears off. Just a splash, and you'll have it trapped long enough that you can exorcise it." He set the vial on the ground between them. "Your Pops will know how to perform the exorcism."

Kevin pulled his phone out of his vest, setting it next to the vial in a neat line. The gun followed.

Rachel sniffled, confused, and asked, "Why are you telling me this?"

Nix couldn't believe this was happening. Rachel was having a hard time following the matter, but Nix could see it in Kevin's eyes. He was giving up. More importantly, he was giving her a chance to escape. And this, this right here was why Nix had managed to survive as long as she had, even through all the madness hunters and fanatics brought to the world. Luck. Sheer, stupid, blind luck. And Nix had never been happier for it.

"Make this count, kid," he muttered, then his words slipped into Latin this time and Nix could feel herself coming undone. She had no control over it. The sound just wrapped around her, a familiar tune and far less painful than the other exorcism. The sensation was like an itch under skin she didn't have that swept through her like wildfire over grassy hills.

For a moment, she felt free and weightless, which would have been a more pleasant sensation if it were not accompanied by a sinking feeling of dread. Rachel went slack below her, briefly thrown by the shock of Nix's loss and no doubt sorry to see her go, but Nix knew she wouldn't be down for the count for very long. If nothing else, their little escapades throughout the day had acclimatized her host to the process.

Nix felt herself drawn forward, toward Kevin, and though she was a little offended by the prospect of being forced to possess someone against her will, Nix saw that this had the potential to work out well for her. Kevin breathed her in and Nix's perspective shifted from the detached ethereal state of looking down on the hazy gray world to the high definition and vibrant color of seeing it through Kevin's eyes.

She inhaled with him, falling into place, but the exhale was all her. The smell of sulfur overwhelmed the sweet reek of the perfumed oil.

Stupid little man thought he could beat her. No one beat Nix. Nix took in the room around her, but while she was working out the kinks in her new body, Rachel was already diving out of her chair, no longer bound by the same restraints that had held her immobile with Nix inside of her.

Rachel crashed to the floor in a fit of gracelessness that was altogether unsurprising, and she reached desperately for the little vial resting on the blue and white linoleum floor.

For one cold second, Nix was almost worried. Then the vial slipped out of Rachel's fingers as she scrambled to grab hold of the thing, and Nix remembered that this was *Rachel*. Nix had met trolls with more grace and competence than the pitiful little sapling rolling about on the floor.

To give credit where credit was due, though, Rachel did manage to get ahold of the vial, even to get the top twisted off and to raise her arm all menacingly in Nix's direction, but Nix wasn't concerned about the vial. Nix's focus was on the hunk of porcelain cow sitting innocently on the kitchen island right beside her.

In one smooth move, Nix grabbed the tacky ornament and Rachel took *Hefty* the cow right to the side of the head. True to its name, Hefty didn't even crack, but Rachel's skull certainly sounded like it did. She dropped to the ground in a heap, the vial tumbling from her grasp yet again.

Nix scooped it up before it could spill all over, and she set it on the counter for safekeeping. Rachel didn't stir or moan or give any indication that she'd be up and running anytime soon, but Nix didn't want to take any chances. She didn't have a lot of time with Kevin, and he needed to be properly punished.

Nix had once convinced a widow to drink lye, back in the 1600s, when things were simpler and people just did what you told them to without putting up a big fuss about it. She'd been wearing the widow's dead husband at the time.

Kevin resisted. He was still getting his bearings though, so his resistance was more of a disoriented yet rude barrage of slurs against her character—and her kind, and her sexual prowess, and her mother, and so forth. He didn't offer any particularly enlightening comments so Nix tuned him out.

What she really needed from the man before she could kill him was something she didn't require his participation or permission to find. Nix sunk her teeth into Kevin's memories, running through them with as much efficiency as she could manage, accidentally starting out too young—

"*Kevin Jeremy Rousoe, you put that cookie back in the jar this instant or you're gonna get a right leckin'.*"

Then too mundane—

"*Mr. Rousoe, care to share your insightful commentary with the class or would you prefer a visit to the principal's office?*"

Then too repulsively sappy—

"*Marybeth Janine O'Casey, do you take this man to be your lawfully wedded husband, to have and to hold until death do you part?*"

"I do."

Nix searched the kitchen, pulling open drawers and cabinets until she found what she was looking for. It wasn't a brand she recognized, but the ingredients listed sodium hydroxide along with a host of unprounceable chemicals that sounded like they'd be fun to test out.

Kevin wasn't as green as Rachel had been and though he had little control over Nix's access to his mind, he was still managing to jerk her around, dragging her through empty fields when all she needed was that one piece of information that would make all of this make sense. She tried to narrow her search, landing on a memory of Rachel as a little girl hiding in a closet.

Through Kevin's ears, Nix could hear her whimper, both here and in Kevin's memory. It was a soft, muffled sound that spoke of restraint and the loss of it. Rachel never was any good at self-control. In Kevin's memory, Nix followed the soft whimpering noise to an upstairs closet.

The house was dead silent, the air tinged with the sharp scents of smoke and burnt meat, the wall along the stairwell was black with soot, but underneath all the death and fear, Kevin could still hear that soft whimpering sound, a sound he would forever associate with hope when things felt hopeless.

His hands were wrapped with cloth and his t-shirt was pulled up over his mouth though the blaze itself had been brief. He reached out and grasped the door handle of the closet, a tiny screech coming from the ungreased springs, and the whimpering abruptly stopped. Kevin eased the door open, asking even before he could see her, *"Rachel?"*

Hers was the only body unaccounted for. Nix could remember the way his heart was pounding so loud that he wasn't sure if he heard her in the first place, if he was just making it all up out of desperation. Then he saw her, curled up in a ball, bright green eyes peeking out from the darkness.

Nix skipped ahead, fast-forwarding through years and years of aimless crap she didn't care about. She searched for Danny and found him.

"You don't have to do this," Danny was saying. He sat on a rock overlooking the grassy valley. He didn't look at Kevin. His hair was too long. He needed a cut. Kevin couldn't help but notice, nor could he help but notice the way Danny's t-shirt clung to him, or how those jeans looked like they were sewn on they were so tight.

"I made a commitment."

Danny nodded, turning to him. "Do you love her?"

Kevin paused, thinking it over. It was a different kind of love, but it was still love. "Yes."

Danny nodded again, looking away. Their trucks idled nearby. Kevin stood next to him, taking in the landscape below and knowing this would be the last time he came here, to their spot. Kevin unclasped the chain around his neck and grabbed Danny's hand.

"Here," Kevin said, pouring the amulet into Danny's palm. Danny's fist tightened around the still-warm metal. "To keep you safe."

Danny stood up, his lanky frame just beginning to fill out with muscle and maturity. He'd make a hell of a hunter someday, like his father. "I'd rather have you."

Kevin should have known Danny would only make this harder. "I know," he confessed. "I'm sorry."

Danny strode forward, grabbing Kevin's face between his hands, and kissed him hard. Kevin allowed himself a moment to linger over the feel of the other man's dry lips, warm and promising against his own, but that was all, only a moment.

Kevin pulled away. They didn't say anything for a long time, listening to the wind sweep through the valley. When the sun dipped below the horizon, Kevin got in his truck and drove away, future ahead of him, past behind, and this was the way it had to be.

That was...unexpected. Not exactly what she was looking for, but closer. Something a little more recent, perhaps. He'd mentioned that the whole trapping-demons thing came into play a few months ago, maybe she could start there. And then she hit it:

"Are you sure we can trust her?" Danny asked, his voice a low rumble in the empty barn.

Kevin wasn't sure. He didn't have to answer Danny for him to recognize his meaning. Danny nodded. They both knew the risks, and maybe it wasn't worth it, but they'd both lost too much to stop now.

The barn door creaked open and they both turned to look as Valerie slid in through the crack. She approached them without a word, coming to stand a foot away, looking them over, assessing. Finally, she asked, "You have the book?"

Kevin nodded and handed it to her. She took the thick tome, flipping through the pages, nodding to herself. Danny glanced at him.

Kevin asked, "And you have what we want?"

She looked up from the old, worn pages. "I do. It stays in my possession though, you agreed."

"Yes."

"Good."

"Where'd you find the sphere?" Kevin asked.

"Been looking for it for years. Ran into an old acquaintance of mine not long ago who specializes in the procurement of such rare and unique objects, and he just happened to have come into possession of it. And here we are."

"Can it really do what you say?" Danny spoke up, his tone uncharacteristically uncertain.

"That and more," Valerie said. She set the book down on an overturned crate and from her handbag she produced a strange blue sphere. It rested in the palm of her hand, just large enough for her fingers to envelop it. It was polished, lustrous. Kevin felt oddly drawn to it. "It'll contain the displaced spirits until it builds up enough energy to be used at its full capacity."

"But it'll get rid of the demons, all of them, for good?"
"Yes."
"How do you know?"
"I know."
"How do we use it?"
"You perform the spell, and I'll capture the spirits."
"Spell?"
"Exorcism. Semantics." Valerie waved a hand.

The evening light filtered in between the slats of wood that comprised the old barn, giving the dirt floor a golden hue.

"What are the risks?"

"Well, I think it's fair to speculate that soon as word gets out about this, we're going to have an awful lot of pissed off baddies on our asses."

Kevin nodded. "So we'll keep it quiet. Just between us. That should give us a little time, right?"

"Should do. But I wouldn't get my hopes up. An operation like this, word always gets out eventually. The good thing is, once the demons catch on to our plans and start coming for us, I reckon we'll find ourselves with an endless supply of them coming right to our doorsteps. They'll be looking to stop us, but if we're ready, I believe we can take advantage of such an opportunity. We'll need a lot of them to fuel this...mass exorcism, if you will. I brought a few more goodies with me to help you boys along."

She reached back into her bag, placing the sphere gently back inside and rooting around a bit until she pulled out a handful of glass vials. She handed two to each of them, saying, "This way, when we're apart, we can keep the demons bound to their hosts and immobilized until we release them."

She grinned, her red lips parting around her smile to show white teeth that seemed to go on forever. Neither he nor Danny looked directly at her face. Both pretended not to notice the scars, pink-tinged and still healing where they stretched across her cheeks. This woman had seen things, he knew. She was one of them, a hunter.

Kevin accepted the vials. He turned them over in his hands and they clinked together like wine glasses making a toast, the liquid sloshing around inside, and he thought, 'All this time, this is what I've been waiting for.' For once, the prospect of exorcising a demon wasn't tainted by the inescapable disappointment of impotency, of knowing that despite all of his good work, nothing was ever really finished, nothing was ever really fixed. This could change everything.

Danny asked, "How many demons do we need to make this happen?"

Valerie shrugged, her hair bouncing against her shoulders, the curls a strawberry blond in the golden light as opposed to her usual fiery red. It made her seem softer, more feminine. "As many as we can get. Maybe a hundred. Maybe more. Maybe less. The sphere will show us when it's ready."

Kevin hadn't known her for long, not the way he knew so many other hunters, the ones he trusted with his life, the ones like Danny, but Kevin knew that there were moments in life that required a leap of faith for anything truly worthwhile to happen. This was one of those moments. Kevin took the leap.

Perfect.

Nix unscrewed the child-proof cap and opened Kevin's mouth wide, stretching his lips around the neck of the bottle. The thick gel poured over his tongue and down his throat, smooth at first until the skin started to burn and blister as it slid slowly down.

Kevin gagged, his body instinctively trying to reject it, but Nix held the poison down, chugging more and more until Kevin's throat couldn't keep up with the demand and the excess gel poured out the corners of his mouth.

Bluish-black sludge dripped in thick lines down Kevin's neck, over the front of his shirt. His eyes stung from the chemicals, blurring Nix's vision. Nix kept drinking until the bottle was empty and she could feel the pain blossoming in Kevin's stomach, so sharp and powerful that it shot like an electric current through his body, right out his fingertips.

She could feel his struggle as she held him up. A cold searing heat burbled through his digestive tract, ripping at his sensitive insides, and it was glorious. She could feel his teeth loosening in his gums and his mouth caving in on itself.

It was like he was dissolving around her and oh, how he *hurt*. Nix didn't want to deprive him of the full experience, so after a minute, just long enough to make sure the damage was irreversible, Nix pried her way back out of his throat and into Rachel's.

Nix lifted Rachel up, the girl still floundering in unconsciousness, which was a shame, but she could still enjoy the end result.

His face was a mess of red blisters where the drain cleaner had leaked out. It still bubbled up in his throat. His fingers twitched at his sides, the movement sporadic and lacking direction.

His eyes were wide, but in spite of the horror written across his mutilated, melting features, he had a certain peaceful quality to him, like he'd been posed this way intentionally, an artistic statement—more Picasso than Rembrandt.

Chapter 26

Nix had been saving this up as an extra special treat for Rachel, but unfortunately, her host was a bit too out of sorts to fully enjoy the experience. Still, Nix dragged her around the house and out into the yard.

The whole time, Rachel didn't protest. Something about failing spectacularly to save Kevin and Joan and, well, pretty much everybody, really hit her hard. She was past the point of tears or screaming, seemingly even past the point of giving a fuck. Might've been shock, but Nix wasn't a doctor, so she couldn't say for sure.

It was a little disappointing, like Nix was riding around in an empty body. It wasn't as liberating having the place to herself as she thought it might be. Mostly, it was just quiet. She'd tried that before, the whole empty-body thing, but it just didn't suit her.

"Nice day, isn't it?" Nix tried, looking up at the sky. The breeze was warm against Rachel's skin and the air smelled clean. Sunlight splashed about on the grass in patches, but dark clouds were rolling in. Still, the weather was good. Pleasant.

Nix didn't see why Rachel wouldn't appreciate this. It was the small things in life, after all, that made it all worthwhile. "Looks like rain," Nix added when Rachel didn't respond. She turned in a slow circle, face angled toward the sky. "Yep, definitely a storm coming in."

Nix sighed. She hated the post-murder blues and could feel them inching toward her like always. Fantasy never measured up to the real thing, but once it was over, once that ultimate climax of ending a life had passed and the afterglow started to fade, everything else seemed so...mundane. The sun had a touch of gray to it. The grass wasn't quite as green anymore.

She remembered her first kills still, back when it was all shiny and new, back even before she'd been in her current not-quite-corporeal form—she'd had to *earn* this state of existence, after all. Back then the high seemed to last for months. One kill and she'd be floating on clouds, sated and full in a way that nothing else ever came close to.

But now, she could barely hold on to that feeling for more than a few heady moments afterward. Ah, well. Like any addiction, one always had to deal with an increase in tolerance, she supposed. At least Danny and Elliot were sure to be satisfying.

Nix padded across the grass to the little shack in the backyard next to a big lawnmower. Sympathetically, she said to Rachel, her silent host, "Listen, kid, I know today's been tough. And maybe more so for you than anybody else, but there's no reason we can't be civil to each other."

Nothing.

She rooted around inside the shed and found a couple big jugs. Probably not enough to bring the whole place down, but what mattered most were the bodies inside of it. There was bound to be physical evidence all over the place and Nix still needed this body for a little while longer, preferably without the hassle of humans chasing it and slowing her down.

This would buy a little time. Nix carried the plastic jugs to the backdoor, then through the kitchen, past the still-gurgling but most certainly deceased body of Kevin Rousoe, and into the garage.

Systematically, Nix poured the gasoline out in a circle around the car, splashing as much as she could onto the bodies. For obvious reasons, Joan got a better soaking than Jake, but thoroughness wasn't a big deal here. This was just biding time.

Rachel watched all of this disinterestedly. Her stomach flopped around a bit at the sight of the bodies, but other than that she seemed pretty dead inside. Her hands were even colder than usual, cold in spite of the warm day, in spite of the warm clothes. But that was okay, Nix was going to warm her right up.

She trailed the gasoline into the house, propping open the garage door with a wayward boot, and made quick work of prepping Kevin's swiftly decomposing skinsack. Bile burned in the back of her throat, a testament to Rachel's continued presence, weak though it may be.

The trail of gasoline ended on the front porch, the smell of it sharp and overpowering. Nix left the empty cans by the door. Rachel's interest piqued ever so slightly for a moment, but Nix just said, "Not done quite yet, doll."

Fifteen minutes later and Rachel was showered, all scrubbed clean and somewhat better-smelling with fresh clothes and no trace of gasoline, sulfur, or physical distress on her person. In the kitchen she gathered up the vials, thinking they might come in handy.

When she grabbed the gun, it was lighter than she expected it to be. Contemplating the polished wooden hilt and the elaborate string of sigils adorning the silver barrel, Nix popped open the cylinder to check the ammunition. There was none. It was completely empty this whole time.

Nix shot Kevin's corpse a dirty look. She hated feeling foolish. Snapping the cylinder closed again, she tucked it into Rachel's purse anyway. It may be functionally useless without the right ammo, but she couldn't exactly leave something this potentially dangerous just lying around, either.

She flung Rachel's bag over her shoulder and grabbed the keys to Joan's El Camino sitting in the driveway.

"All right," Nix told Rachel, snatching a book of matches from the coffee table, "you're going to love this part."

Chapter 27

Nix barely heard the ringtone over the jazz music blaring from the radio of Joan's immaculate 1970 El Camino. She reached out and turned the thing off begrudgingly, then dug around in Rachel's bag with one hand on the wheel, pulling out the cell phone after more hassle than it was worth. The screen flashed with Danny's smiling photo and the icons at the bottom alerted her to eight other missed calls and several text messages.

Nix sighed. She hated phone conversations—always had. Without being able to see people, they were a lot more difficult to read. She doubted he'd be as friendly as his grinning picture suggested after she'd repeatedly missed his calls, but she answered anyway.

"Rachel?" Danny's voice boomed. Oh yeah, definitely not smiling.

So he already knew. Word traveled fast among the hunter communities, but even Nix hadn't thought they'd find out this quickly. In all likelihood, they had informants placed strategically throughout all manner of public services—law enforcement, fire departments, who knew where else they had weaseled their way into. She'd be impressed, if they were actually as impressive as they seemed at first glance.

With cultivated tentativeness, Nix asked, "Pops? What's the matter?"

"I've been calling you for thirty goddamn minutes, that's the matter! Where were you?"

"Ah, I'm on the bus," Nix lied. Nix didn't do public transportation. At least, not when the alternative was an El Camino in perfect condition with an A/C that rivaled the arctic, genuine leather seats, and a sound system worth killing for—and she had. Killed for it, that was. "I'm just outside of Manteca, a few minutes away. I must have forgotten to turn my phone on."

"What the hell good is a phone if you don't turn it on, huh?"

He sounded distressed. Nix was no expert, certainly, but he did *sound* distressed.

Nix had witnessed humans respond to such situations many times before, so she decided to test out their go-to method and offered, "I'm...sorry?"

"No," he dismissed with a long sigh, his tone already softer, "I'm just...I'm just glad you're okay. Didn't you get Bill's mass alert? It came out a half hour ago—but no, no I guess you wouldn't've, what with your phone being off. Honestly, Rachel, turning off your goddamn phone when..." Danny degraded into mumbles.

The line went quiet for a moment. The soft hum of the lovingly maintained engine filled Joan's car. Prolonged phone silences usually meant that she was expected to respond. "What's going on, Pops?" Nix asked, trying to keep her tone somewhere between worried and confused—and nowhere in the vicinity of gleeful.

With a tremor in his voice, Danny confided, "There's been...there was a fire. At Joan's. When I heard, I thought...I thought you might have still been there."

Nix counted to three before speaking, in effort to verbally convey hesitancy and concern, then said, "Was anyone hurt?"

Danny also paused. Nix wondered if she might have overdone it, but then he said, "Yeah. We've got word of three bodies so far. No identifications yet, but I haven't been able to get ahold of Joan and Jake. And...Kev—Uncle Kevin, his...his vehicle was at the house."

Okay, this was the time to sell it. Nix put an extra dash of urgency into her words, and after a moment's thought decided that denial was usually a pretty safe bet, too. "You think it was their bodies? That can't be true, I only just saw them. Joan dropped me at the bus station. Everything was fine. They can't be—it can't be them, Pops. It *can't*."

"I thought Joan was going to drive you in?"

Nix hesitated. "She, uh, was...but, uh, she said something came up and she had to take care of it, so she just dropped me off at the closest bus station and left real quick—but I didn't think anything of it, she didn't seem worried, just a little stressed. You don't think something happened after she dropped me off, do you?"

"I don't know what to think," Danny said. "Joan's vehicle was gone, so maybe she wasn't there. Maybe she was dropping you off when it happened and just...hasn't contacted anyone yet. The fire damage is pretty bad. It's going to be a while before the police and fire department clear out. Bill was first on the scene, said the fire couldn't have started long before they got there. He's already saying it weren't no accident. I'm on my way to check it out right now."

Nix wondered if perhaps she ought to have left Joan's car and walked into town until she found another one she could commandeer, but she quickly dismissed the idea on account of the fact that she didn't actually care if she got caught.

All of this would be over tonight, anyway, one way or another. Though now there was some *Bill* character she had to kill, too. It was never-ending. How many hunters could there *be* in this area?

Danny didn't offer anything else, and Nix wondered at the protocol in a situation like this. Three close family friends were found dead in a burning house less than an hour ago...should she be baking somebody a casserole? But who? And what kind of casserole? No, that was too elaborate, too soon, a funeral thing not a just-got-the-bad-news thing. Something smaller then, to convey her sympathy long enough to keep Danny where she wanted him—in the dark.

"Should I...get off the bus and go back there?" Nix tried, hoping her offer would be taken as perfunctory since the drive so far had been tedious and she didn't feel like repeating it. She was just outside of the town they were hunting in and it had already taken an hour to get this far.

"*No.* Don't go there. You don't need to see that. But you'll have to change buses and turn around—we aren't in Manteca anymore. I sent Elliot home and Bill's sending in somebody to take over the succubus case. Elliot'll be waiting for you at the house while I...while I figure this out. Lock up tight when you get in and don't answer the door for nobody. And keep that phone *on*, you hear me?"

"I hear you. Be safe, Pops."

Nix breathed a sigh of relief at the prospect of their little phone call ending. He didn't seem to suspect her yet, didn't even seem to question her flimsy bus alibi. On top of that, she now knew Danny would be out for a while and Elliot, well...Elliot was fair game.

"You too. And, darlin'? Don't you ever scare me like that again, you hear? It's, ah...it's just good to hear your voice."

The line went dead. She ended the call and flipped through the text messages—five increasingly concerned texts from Danny, two from Elliot, and the aforementioned mass alert to hunters from a man named Bill Havensport with the fire department.

There were hunters *everywhere*. But she'd always known that. And with her own kind and all the others that had been attracted to the area by the foolhardy activities of these idiots, hunters were probably being drawn here in droves.

She couldn't possibly get rid of them all. She had to go to the source, get this dealt with, then get out.

But for now, all Nix could do was drive. Drive, and maybe stop in town before turning around to find a less conspicuous vehicle to take to Rachel's house, which led to the question..."Where *is* home, exactly?"

Rachel offered one of her patented internal glares and surprised Nix by actually answering. *"About two hours in the opposite direction. By the time you get there, they'll know what's happened. They'll see you for what you are and they'll stop you."*

Nix rolled Rachel's eyes. The snark was unnecessary, but not unexpected. The girl had clearly recovered from murdering her family's friends, and in record time, too.

Nix rooted around in Rachel's head, easily pulling up the big empty country house in her memories, both old and recent. The place was located way out toward Yosemite, not all that far from where Val lived—or stayed, or squatted, or whatever the Evil Hell-Bitch was doing there. She was getting awfully tired of rural California. Why couldn't they be somewhere fun, like LA or even San Francisco?

It was going to be a long drive.

Nix flicked the radio back on.

Chapter 28

Two and a half hours later, without any help whatsoever from her host, Nix found the old house in the middle of fucking nowhere and pulled up in a stolen SUV that she figured would be at least slightly easier to explain than Joan's El Camino, should she be questioned. She didn't plan on enduring any questioning, though.

Danny's latest texts suggested he'd be gone all night, and it had been a very long day. Nix needed a break. And what could be more relaxing than breaking someone?

Rachel started to squirm as they approached the house, walking past the old Ford parked in the driveway. Danny must have caught a ride with someone else and left Elliot with the truck. Rachel muttered angrily and thrashed about in her head. *"Leave him alone,"* the girl demanded, as if she had any right to be demanding things from Nix.

Still, Nix was feeling good. She had plans and she was getting back into her element. She finally had a chance to unwind from a stressful day of unexpected almost-exorcism and she'd been waiting for this moment since she'd first taken Rachel out for a joyride and met Elliot in that diner.

The anticipation, the excitement, it made everything look brighter even with rain speckling the ground and heavy clouds making the afternoon sky dark.

"Don't worry," Nix reassured her, "I'm only going to hurt him a little at first. And if he's a good boy, maybe I'll keep him."

Rachel was not reassured. Nix tuned her out, stuffing the muzzle back on, not wanting to dampen the moment with the girl's foul mood. Nix had earned this.

It had been ages since she'd had a pet. And Elliot was so very handsome, so painfully *good*. Why not draw it out and make the fun last? But it was an idle thought, a flight of fancy. She couldn't keep him, not really. There could be no loose ends in this now.

The house was ancient and looming, a remarkably compact two-story, considering how much land it could have been spread out over. In spite of its obvious age, it didn't look like it was falling apart. No, Danny took good care of it. Nix wasn't sure when he'd find the time to do so, what with all the running around butchering her kind and bringing about an end to civilization he was doing lately.

When she walked in, Elliot was sitting with his back to her at a wooden table in the small dining area off the entrance. A silent audience of empty beer bottles stood in front of him. She kicked off her muddy shoes and tossed Rachel's jacket onto an old coat rack.

The room was dark. The whole house seemed dark, save a soft glow drifting down the stairs adjacent to the foyer, its source unknown. Nix left the lights off, leaving only the thin rays of sunlight fighting through the clouds beyond the windows to guide her way.

Elliot slouched low in a chair, boneless and tired looking, his military posture shot to hell. The empty bottles weren't even arranged in a neat line, which was perhaps the most disconcerting thing of all. The curtains covering the bay window were closed.

Elliot didn't look up when she entered. Nix closed the French glass doors between the dining area and the foyer harder than necessary, but she didn't get a rise out of him. She nearly tripped over the shoes he'd left scattered haphazardly on the hardwood.

His feet were propped up on one of the chairs across from him as he tipped his beer bottle back. His throat worked as he swallowed, drawing her attention to the way the muscles shifted under his skin.

He continued to ignore her presence, staring intently at the bottle in his hand.

Nix didn't like being ignored.

Crossing the room in two long strides, Nix stood over him, took the bottle from his hands and set it on the table. He offered no resistance, no indication that he even noticed. She ran the back of Rachel's hand over his cheek, her thumb brushing lightly over his bottom lip.

He turned away from her. "You heard what happened?" he asked, voice cold, flat. "They're all dead. Joan, Jake, Uncle Kevin. All of them. Dead."

"You don't know that," she challenged, because Rachel would have and they couldn't possibly know for sure, not mere hours after finding the bodies.

Elliot looked at her like she was terribly naïve. "I don't...I don't *know?* Three bodies, Rachel. Three missing people. Kevin's car was there. It's Jake and Joan's *house* for God's sake. It's not that hard to put it together. So don't tell me I don't *know*. They're *dead.*"

All right, so he was past the denial stage, probably closer to anger judging by his tone. It wasn't ideal timing, but each human dealt with grief a little differently. Anger wasn't a bad place to be. Anger could be...fun.

She just needed to direct it, catch his attention long enough to draw him away from those bottles to where she wanted him.

"They're dead," he repeated in a whisper.

Nix unbuttoned the first button on Rachel's clean red blouse, then the second, the third, until her shirt was open enough to reveal the black bra underneath, the same one she'd worn that night with Rodney, and Elliot was finally looking at her.

Nix reminded him softly, "We aren't."

She reached for him again, pressing her palms against his chest, intending to divest him of his shirt, but he pushed out of his chair abruptly and grabbed both of her hands.

"Don't!" he said. "Why are you acting like this?"

He squinted at her and swayed for a moment, the alcohol seeming to hit him harder when he stood up. She mustered all of Rachel's suppressed vulnerability to transform her countenance into that of a helpless little sister in need of guidance. Eyes wide and brimming with manufactured tears, Nix told him, "I need you, El. Please don't shut me out. Not now."

He licked his lips, staring at her, his hands tight around her wrists. He said, "It's just...I'm not thinking clearly right now. I'm so *angry* and I can't—I don't want to hurt you, Rachel. Please."

She fisted the soft, cottony fabric of his shirt and confided, "But I want you to. Come on, El. Hurt me. Make me scream for you. I know you want to."

His brow furrowed in confusion. She could see the war raging in his eyes, always raging. He shook his head vehemently. "No! *No, I—*"

Nix didn't give him the chance to protest further. She lifted herself up, standing on tiptoes to reach his mouth, and kissed him forcefully. She could taste the alcohol on his lips.

After a tense moment, his hands slid down her body, cupping her ass, then he bent just enough to get a good grip on her and lift her onto the table. Her legs hung over the edge and he insinuated himself between them. He palmed her breasts over her bra, rubbing hard enough that she could feel it through the fabric.

Elliot's tongue clashed with her own, and for a minute all he did was explore her mouth with the same desperate intensity with which she explored his.

Abruptly, Elliot pulled back. His hands fell to his sides, flexing as if in restraint. Breathing hard, his eyes closed tightly, Elliot rested his forehead against hers and sang his old refrain, "We shouldn't be doing this, Rachel. Not right now. Not like this. I...before...it was a mistake, I shouldn't have...."

Rachel's stomach clenched at his words, his admission of his error in judgment, the regret in his voice.

"Shut up," Nix told him, recapturing his lips. "Just kiss me, El. Touch me. I need you to touch me. Please, Elli, I need you."

She took one of his hands in her own and moved it back to its earlier position on her breast. She arched into his touch, then let go, just to see if he would follow her lead. He did. Elliot was not so overcome by regret to seriously reject her advances, and the tendril of hope twisting around Rachel's heart eased the fear there, giving the rest of her body the will to respond.

Nix wanted him. Rachel wanted him. Elliot's hands were moving on their own. The combined arousal in the room was overwhelming and they were both wearing far too many clothes. Rachel wanted to make love slowly, intimately, but Nix knew that the gratification of making the boy fuck her hard and fast would outweigh anything slow intimacy could provide.

His touch was gentle, his anger already seeming to dissipate just from her presence here. That wouldn't do.

She slid off her perch, bunching her fists in his shirt and guiding him, pushing him away from the table and accidentally backing him into the French doors. Elliot reached behind himself and twisted the handle, his lips never straying from hers, then he was the one pulling her across the foyer, tripping over carpet and stumbling into railings, leading her into a bedroom up the stairs.

An oval-shaped lamp on the table next to the bed cast a weak yellow light across beige walls, beige sheets, beige carpeting. Nix pushed Elliot to the bed, spreading the boy out on the sheets like she owned him, and Elliot wasn't complaining. Instead, he was whispering to her, confiding, "Thought I'd lost you, Rach, when we couldn't get ahold of you today...thought you were one of the bodies in that house...never been so scared in my life...."

He reached for her, pulled her closer, caught her lips with his own and kissed her like it was their last night on earth. And maybe he knew that it was. Not really, not explicitly, but somewhere deep down maybe he could sense that this was where his story would end. He was trying to make every second count.

Even as he lavished tiny butterfly-soft kisses over her cheeks and jaw and brow, she pulled at his belt roughly, tugging it loose, trying to provoke him and draw all that beautiful dark pain back to the surface so she could play in it.

Elliot sucked at her neck, his lips on her pulse point as he drew involuntary shivers from her. She pushed him back, hard enough to surprise him and leave him looking up at her with wide, innocent eyes as her fingers worked at the final few buttons of her shirt and she pulled it down her arms in a slow, tantalizing glide. She tossed it over the edge of the bed, then brushed the straps from her shoulders and held his eyes as she unclasped her bra and let it fall.

Elliot just watched, stared really, eyes dark with lust. Nix could work with that.

The mattress sank under her weight as she leaned forward, knees making indentations in the soft, beige sheets on either side of his hips.

Her hands slipped beneath his shirt and Elliot jolted. "Christ, your hands are freezing, Rach," he mumbled, covering them with his own but not hindering her. He was so warm, she couldn't stop touching him.

Rachel, on the other hand, was cold. Unpleasantly so. This wasn't as much of a problem with the younger ones, the kids, usually they lasted a few months before the warmth drained out of them—longer, if she was careful.

Rachel wasn't holding up as well as Nix had hoped. Her muscles were getting tighter, harder to maneuver, and her skin was cool to the touch. Even the air in her lungs seemed to be frosty by the time it hit the air. Nix was just so tired of being cold.

She ran her hands over the firm muscles of Elliot's abdomen and his chest, bunching up the fabric on her way until he propped himself up slightly and helped her pull it off.

His hands landed on her hips, holding her in place. Her thighs tightened around him and she rolled her hips, eliciting just a spark of friction, a promise of things to come. He fell back onto the sheets again, bucked against her and moaned.

She wanted him inside her. She wanted to ride him in this body until his eyes rolled back in his skull and his brain short-circuited. Or until hers did.

She ran her fingers over the corded muscles in his arms, enjoying the texture of his skin and wishing that she could keep him for a little while longer—a few days, maybe, just until she'd truly worn him out.

"Rach," he rasped, voice ragged and deep.

Rachel shivered like she had that time in the diner, like icy fingers were tracing up and down her spine. Nix found the sensation surprisingly pleasant, didn't really want it to stop, so she leaned down close and whispered against his lips, "Say it again."

The boy didn't require further instruction, just tilted his head up and mumbled her name, Rachel's name, before kissing her.

The shivers continued like electric sparks through Rachel's body and distantly Nix wondered if it would feel this good to hear him saying her own name, her real name, and not the string of syllables tied to the body she was riding in. But this, too, was an idle thought, something she'd never be able to have while hiding in a human's body, so she nipped at his lip a little harder than necessary.

Elliot grunted, grabbed her by the arms, and suddenly she was on her back, pinned to the mattress with Elliot hovering over her. The change in perspective left her with a view of the ceiling, which Nix wasn't overly fond of, but the weight of Elliot's body pressing her down had a certain unanticipated appeal to it.

His hands found Rachel's bared curves and he wasted no time lavishing her breasts with soft, fleeting kisses, trailing his tongue down her body in a way that was almost reverent. His lips stumbled over the scars written along her ribcage, the sigils Nix had carved there to keep from being seen. He moved his hand from her waist and Nix felt the warm tips of his fingers trace the marks. Against her skin, he asked, "Where'd these come from?"

His tongue darted out to follow the lines his fingers had traced and Nix fumbled for a lie, finally offering, "Hunting. While you were gone. Supposed to keep me safe from possession."

He hummed, his breath hot against her skin but cool where his tongue had been. "They don't look very old."

"I don't want to talk about that now. Just don't...don't stop touching me, El."

For a second she didn't think he'd let it go, but the moment passed and his mouth moved up her ribcage, ghosting over her breasts and along her collarbone, then back down again.

Rachel sighed blissfully at the sensations, but Nix wasn't content with Elliot's gentle ministrations. She squirmed impatiently, trying to push him to action, but his hands just slid down to her waist, holding her in place. She groaned in frustration and could feel the soft rumble of his laughter where his chest pressed against her stomach.

He shifted lower, Rachel's flesh so sensitive under his touch that his skin seemed to scrape over hers as his body moved. Elliot's tongue dipped into her belly button on his descent as his fingers worked at her jeans, flicking the button open and gliding the zipper down. He edged them past her hips, pulling away only long enough to strip her down, and then himself.

Nix propped herself up to get a good look at him. Either the dim light was exceptionally flattering or Elliot really did have that cut-from-stone physique under all those clothes. He lowered himself back onto the bed, easing her legs apart with tender hands and pressing her into the mattress.

He kissed the soft skin of Rachel's inner thighs with such delicate intensity that for a brief, searing moment, Nix hated him.

Something stirred in her and whatever it was saw anger close behind.

She didn't know what he was playing at here, being so gentle, so...soft. Like he was fooling her—fooling *Rachel*. Some fucking big brother he was, screwing his baby sister and acting like it was anything more than what it was. She hated them all, this whole freak show of a family.

"Stop," Nix said. Her voice sounded too loud in the little beige room, like shattered glass.

Both Rachel and Elliot seemed to snap free of a daze and take notice of her. And it was about goddamn time. She was the one running this show. Nix sat up, pulled him by his shoulders, hooked her legs around his waist, and twisted until Elliot's surprised face was staring up at her.

Nix leaned over him, predator over prey, then bent down and pressed her lips—*Rachel's* lips—to his. "Not tonight," she breathed in explanation. Then, "I won't break. I need more."

He didn't fight her. Elliot stared into her eyes, kissed her, and didn't question, didn't ask for clarification, like he finally understood what she needed. His hands returned to her waist, tentative, but lacking the excessive gentleness he'd shown before.

He gripped her hips hard when she ground against him, his head tilting back and a moan escaping the fine column of his throat.

Fuck, that throat. She couldn't stop her hand from raising up, couldn't stop her fingers from tracing the lines of his neck and pressing just a little as her other hand drifted down and wrapped around him.

Elliot reached for the hand encircling his throat and drew it away, sucking two of her fingers into his mouth and looping his tongue around them like she'd done to him the night before. He released her fingers, pressing a kiss to the palm of her hand as he rocked into her other palm slowly, a staccato rhythm, like he didn't even realize he was doing it.

Rachel's body hummed, her pulse so high it fluttered like the wings of a hummingbird. In her head, even with the gag on, Nix could *feel* her chanting his name on every breath. When she listened, she could hear Elliot doing the same, whispering, the noise almost lost beneath ragged breaths, shifting bodies, twisted sheets.

Nix swept her hand along his length just once more before abruptly lowering herself onto him. This time Elliot's moan was the shattered glass, loud and sudden in the small room.

The stretch of Rachel's virgin body was painful enough to take the edge off Nix's irritation and she took a moment to enjoy the connection between them, to savor the precipice of disaster before she brought them crashing down.

Rachel's body couldn't take the tension any longer—she had to move. It was a slow friction at first, but her thrusts quickly grew violent and though Elliot seemed to be trying to keep up with her, he was always just slightly behind the rhythm she set. But it was better this way, wild and frenetic, unrestrained.

Elliot thrashed beneath her, his head lolling side to side as he held on to her, his lips wet and parted and enticing. Nix leaned down to swipe her tongue across them as Rachel's delicate hands tightened around Elliot's neck, her fingers pressing into the cartilage, compressing the veins, tighter and tighter until Elliot started gasping. He pulsed inside her with a soundless, surprised expression, and his fingers dug hard into her hips as he came.

His hands lifted to hers, trying to pull her away, but she didn't budge. She was stronger than he was, even in a body much smaller than his own. Nix could not be moved.

The sobering edge of panic started to cut through the haze in Rachel's head as she finally caught on to Nix's intentions, the sweat of cold fear dripping between her bare breasts, frightened terror making her heart thrum.

Elliot struggled, choking as his air supply gradually cut off and all those lovely veins and arteries and capillaries started to swell. His eyes widened, lips parting and gaping like a beached fish.

Nix loved this part. The sensations throbbing through Rachel's body felt sublime, but they were nothing compared to the gratification Nix could feel brewing inside of her, even stronger and more overpowering with the climax building in her host body.

Elliot's movements became erratic, hands reaching for purchase, clawing against the sheets and then clawing at Rachel's skin. He tried to bat her away, tried to buck her off of him, but his movements were increasingly feeble and disoriented.

His hands landed at her wrists, twisting ineffectually, nails piecing her skin in an instinctual attempt to save himself. The unexpected jolts of pain threw her over the edge.

Rachel's vision sparked with stars, like the roof had been torn open and there was nothing left above them but the vast, endless night sky. Elliot's eyes rolled up, blue to white in an instant as she rode out the pleasure.

She gasped, or maybe shouted, maybe screamed, she couldn't be sure with all the noise in her head. And somewhere in the bliss-streaked turmoil, something slipped.

A strange pulling sensation overcame her and all of the sudden Nix was floating. The rest of the world seemed distant, foggy, and she was stuck in some sort of invisible mud. She could feel it weighing her down even as it kept her buoyant.

For a moment she didn't understand what was happening, and then it hit her. This was Rachel's doing.

Somehow she'd wrangled control from Nix and managed to stage a coup, the little vixen. Nix pulled at her invisible restraints, feeling them stretch and snap and reform just as quickly as she could shed them.

Nix didn't know what the girl thought she could accomplish with this. But then again, somehow, inexplicably, Rachel had managed to trap her here.

Outrage stirred in Nix, splashing and burning, boiling over. But in spite of her anger, Nix couldn't help but be a tiny bit impressed. This girl, the wallflower, the one who wanted and craved and dreamed but could never bring herself to *take*, to fight. This girl. She was a woman now. A tiny bubble of pride filled Nix at the thought, but it quickly passed and the urgency of the situation dawned on her.

In a panic, Nix tried to jump, channeling her energy in an attempt to leave Rachel's body behind, but she couldn't seem to gain any traction.

Rachel, however, was moving now on her own, no strings to guide her, and she was doing a shitty job of it.

Rachel clambered off Elliot, falling over the edge of the bed and hitting the floor hard. Nix watched, distant and removed, seeing only the floor and Rachel's legs twisted up in the sheet. Rachel gasped, disoriented and kicking at the sheet, trying to free herself.

The gasp was echoed above her and everything stilled. Silence followed, then they could hear Elliot choking and coughing with every sharp intake of breath.

Nix scrambled to pull herself up and drag Rachel back down, but the girl resisted more effectively than Nix had anticipated. A loud bang sounded on the other side of the bed, something hitting the floor, probably Elliot, then drawers were being pulled open and small objects were clattering against each other. Nix found her footing, grabbing onto the darkness hidden deep in Rachel's mind and using it to propel herself back into place.

Nix slammed Rachel out, pushing her deep into the dark borderlands of her mind and, finally, Nix regained control.

Nix pulled her body up, breathing hard as she moved Rachel's limbs again and stretched her muscles as she pleased. The sheet pooled on the floor at her feet.

At first glance, Elliot was nowhere to be seen. Then she felt him, a wave of radiant warmth against Rachel's cold spine.

Nix turned toward the heat at her back and found herself facing the sharp end of a hunting knife. Its thick silver blade shone in the lamplight, intimidating but for the shaking hand that held it.

Nix let fear fill Rachel's eyes, let her lower lip tremble as she slowly met his gaze. "El?" she said, laying it on thick with Rachel's frightened voice. "Elliot, you're scaring me."

In a measured tone at odds with his shaking hand, Elliot said, "You aren't Rachel."

Well, he had her there, she supposed.

Nix smirked, twisting Rachel's countenance into something dark and sinister, offering him a tiny glimpse of what he was dealing with as a reward for his long-awaited tenacity. She always knew he had it in him. It was nice to finally see that revelation in his eyes, that *fear*.

"What are you going to do with that?" she asked, motioning to the knife in his hand. "Stab little sister? Doubt it."

The boy hesitated, still gasping to catch his breath, standing there in front of her, completely bare, glancing nervously at the knife, then back at her.

She tsked, stepping closer as Elliot stepped back. Her irritation at having been temporarily thrown by her host quickly dissipated into delight at the prospect of the conversation she'd been so hoping for.

Nix grinned. "Don't you think you've been inside her enough for one day? Just can't help yourself, can you?"

A look of horror crossed the boy's face and Nix cherished it. The way his eyes widened and his chest stopped rising and falling with air as everything fell into place inside his pathetic little human brain, this was the purest form of satisfaction.

All the nonsense leading up to this, the ridiculous war, the research, the tedium, all of that was very nearly worth it just to see the look on his face right now. Nearly. The tedium had been pretty goddamn awful, but she could put that aside to enjoy the moment.

A storm raged outside, unnoticed until now. Wind lashed at the windows, and Elliot just stood there, free hand rubbing his neck absently.

"Hmm," Nix said, enjoying the pleasant tingle of the sound in Rachel's throat, particularly the way she was entirely in control of it. "You see it now, don't you?"

Elliot caught her eyes, narrowed his own. Oh yeah, he saw. But there was one question, one very, very pertinent question that he hadn't asked yet and Nix was positively dying to hear it from him.

"Well," she prodded, "aren't you going to ask?"

In a flat, suspicious voice, Elliot said, "Ask what?"

Nix smiled softly, kindly, because with these hunters, Nix had always felt especially kind. "How *long* have I been in your sister?"

Tensely, the boy played along. She could tell he didn't really want to know the answer, they never did, but he *needed* to know and that was what made it such sweet torture. "How long?" he said, his voice cracking between words.

"How long, *indeed*," Nix answered. She grinned with Rachel's mouth, nearly giggling.

Elliot frowned as the rain chimed against the window panes.

He took a breath then let the air slip out between his teeth in a hiss. He lowered the knife. "What do you want?"

"What does anyone want? A billion dollars, a fancy car, immortality, you know the drill."

His frown deepened. "I'm serious."

Nix rolled Rachel's eyes, took a step back from him, and shrugged.

Rachel had done the bargaining thing, too, but it was hard to bargain when they had nothing to bargain with. "What I want, kid, you can't offer."

"Try me," he challenged, and Nix had to give the boy credit, he *did* sound sincere. But then again, Cirrik always did, too.

Nix was tired. It hit her unexpectedly just how tired she was. Tired of these hunters, their messes, this whole game they had her playing.

She raised an eyebrow. "All I wanted was to be left the fuck alone. And don't get me wrong," she told him, "under other circumstances, I'd ask for that. But we both know that's never going to happen. And now, *now* I'm caught up in some insane end-of-the-world ploy with your pals that I never wanted anything to do with—but of course I don't get a choice because the whole lot of you are so unrelentingly stupid that I'm the only one that could clean up the mess you've gotten yourselves into. So what I *want*? A fucking vacation. Think you can provide that for me, lover-boy?"

Elliot stared stupidly at her, as though she'd been speaking Greek, which she was pretty certain she hadn't been, but it was all Greek to him, apparently. Eventually he managed, "What...what are you talking about?"

Nix huffed. "Of course you don't know. You don't know *anything*. The both of you are completely fucking worthless." Oddly, he was probably the smartest of the bunch, and the least annoying. That wasn't saying much, but still.

He raised his hands in a gesture of surrender, holding the knife delicately between two fingers. "Please, just...just leave Rachel out of this. Just let her go."

Nix pretended to consider this, then shook her head. "Mm, I don't think so," she said. "It's nice in here...well, you would know, I suppose," Nix added with a chuckle.

Elliot didn't take her bait. "Whatever you're involved in, if you let her go, maybe we can help."

Aw, and said with such honest intention. He was adorable with his little knife and bare ass and the bruises just beginning to form around his throat.

Adorable...but not quite broken, and what was the point, really, if she didn't follow through with her goals? What would that say about her character? Rachel was floundering in her own mind, lost and confused, so Nix threw her a rope to drag her back a little closer, close enough to join the party.

Nix strode toward Elliot and he instinctively moved away from her until she'd backed him against the wall.

"You're going to help me? Are you kidding? You can't even help yourself. You sure as hell couldn't help Rachel."

Elliot cringed away from her words and she could feel Rachel watching them now.

Nix leaned her weight into him, her face close to his, but he refused to look at her. She glanced down to see his hands clenching tightly at his side, his knuckles white around the hilt of the knife. She wondered if he'd stab her, and hoped he would, just to see what would happen.

"You should have heard her screaming for you, begging for you to save her." Nix chuckled and added, "But you didn't even notice, did you?" When he didn't answer her, she demanded, "*Did you?*"

"No!" he said, eyes tightly closed. And softer, "No."

"It's not like you weren't looking at her," Nix pointed out. "I mean, you were looking at her all the time, right? Fucking her with your eyes, biding time until you could fuck her for real."

"No, that's not—I wasn't...I—I thought—"

"Shh, it's okay. You don't have to pretend. The way your body responds to hers, that's something you can't deny. She's still all sticky inside from you, you know." Nix sucked his earlobe into her mouth. Elliot tried to jerk away, but there was nowhere for him to go. He panted and groaned in what could only be distress. Nix smiled against his neck. "I understand. You just needed a release. She was convenient."

"*No.* You're wrong, it wasn't like that."

Nix pushed her tongue flat against his pulse point, tasting his heartbeats, counting one, counting twenty, counting fifty...she pulled away and said, "Oh, I'm sure it wasn't. Don't worry, between you and me, she isn't even mad," Nix confided. "She's disgusted. With herself, mostly." Nix grabbed his hand and coaxed it open, pressing it against her chest so he could feel her heart beating as wildly as his own.

With his palm over Rachel's heart, he met her eyes.

Nix smiled. "Oh, you should feel how much she hates herself for what you've done to her. She's begged me to kill her. She's begging *you* to kill her right now."

"*Stop this,*" Rachel pleaded.

Nix took Elliot's other hand, lifting the knife to Rachel's throat. When she let go, his hand hovered there, shaking so hard she was half convinced he'd slit her throat by accident. Rachel's stomach churned as she looked on. And it was true that she wanted it. She was watching to see if he'd do it, if he'd set her free.

Elliot's eyes were wide as he stared at her, the beginnings of some rather unmanly tears brimming up in them. The knife pressed into her throat, deeper, harder, until Nix felt the skin split.

Elliot's mouth fell open. A thin line of blood dripped down her neck and in a rush Elliot tossed the knife away. He dropped to the floor in front of her, leaning on an old radiator and gasping for breath.

Pitiful. Nix went to move away from him, but his arms wrapped around her bare legs. "I'm sorry, I'm so sorry, Rachel—God, I'm so fucking sorry," he mumbled, over and over and over again.

She sneered. "She doesn't forgive you," Nix informed him.

He shook his head adamantly, soft hair brushing against Rachel's thighs. "She will. She'll understand. I'll make her understand."

"That's an awfully bold assertion coming from a sister-fucker like yourself."

"I love my sister."

"Clearly."

"She loves me."

"I'll give you that. Fucked up family if I've ever seen one. And I've got some wild stories, let me tell you."

She grasped his chin and stared down at him, wondering what to do now that she'd had her fun. She'd have to kill him, she supposed. She'd spent too much valuable time here already. She couldn't justify spending anymore.

A phone rang. Nix glanced toward the sound, then tried to pry Elliot away from her. When he wouldn't let go, she grabbed the knife from the floor and bashed him in the skull with the hilt of it. He collapsed against the wall. Nix walked over to the pile of clothes the noise was coming from, digging the cell phone out of Elliot's discarded jeans.

Just a text from Danny, checking in. *Hunting with Val, don't wait up.*

Nix replied, *Stay safe* to keep the man from getting suspicious if no one answered him. She tossed the phone onto the bed, gathering up what she could find of Rachel's clothes and pulling them on. She needed to deal with Elliot.

"No, you don't."

Nix sighed. Rachel was in denial. Great. "You know I do."

"You said yourself that you've wasted too much time here already. Danny and Val are going to be out hunting all night. You can't miss this opportunity."

Frowning, Nix asked, *"What opportunity?"*

Rachel huffed, like Nix was the dense one. *"You want that blue sphere, right?"*

Obviously, but it wasn't that simple. *"Yeah, but Val has it."*

"If they're out hunting right now, Val would be crazy to take the thing with her. You saw how delicate it looked, how careful she was with it. If it's the same as that marble your boyfriend had—"

"*Cirrik was not my boyfriend.*"

"*Whatever! The marble was glass, the sphere's probably glass, and glass is breakable.*"

Nix wasn't sure what the poor girl was getting at with all of this. Nix wasn't going to be dissuaded from killing Elliot. Was this some sort of ploy? *"What's your point?"*

"*My point is that they are both out hunting together and there's no way they would've taken a delicate glass sphere with them. Meaning: it's probably unattended right now at Val's place. We could get to it. We could destroy it.*"

Nix considered this. Rachel wasn't wrong, her logic was sound, but... "*They wouldn't just leave it unprotected. There would be traps in place to keep the thing safe, or else any demon looking for it could walk right in and take it.*"

"So what?"

"*So, how would we get past them? It's no use bothering if we can't get to it.*"

Rachel said calmly, "*Leave that to me. I'm the walking grimoire, remember? I may not have much field experience, but I know magical traps and protections. I can break them.*"

Nix had no idea where Rachel's confidence was coming from, let alone her calm, reasonable tone. That temporary coup she staged back there must have inflated her ego. But Nix could see the tomes of spells and incantations looping through Rachel's mind.

It would take Nix ages to sort through them all and find the right ones, and that was time they didn't have. It would be easier to do all of this with Rachel working with her and not against her. "*And why would you help me?*"

"*I don't want the world to end any more than you do,*" Rachel said.

Nix glanced down at Elliot where he lay crumpled and naked on the floor next to the radiator. "*I still have to deal with him.*"

"*Later. We don't have time to waste right now.*"

"*Nonsense, it'll only take a moment to kill the boy.*"

"Kill him, and you're on your own. If you want my help, we leave him here and go deal with this thing together, once and for all."

After a moment's thought, Nix agreed. "All right. It's you and me, then, kid. We'll finish this."

Unable to relocate her shirt, Nix spotted Elliot's bag in the corner and dug around inside, finding a mixture of clothes and weapons. She pulled out a black long-sleeved shirt several sizes too big and pulled it over her head. Nix caught sight of something shiny as it shifted in the bag and she reached in, pulling out a pair of handcuffs.

A thought struck her. She couldn't very well just leave the boy here, but Rachel was right. She didn't have to kill him right now, either. She'd deal with him when this was over. Until then, she'd just have to make sure he couldn't leave.

Nix grinned, snapping one cuff onto his wrist and the other to the cast-iron radiator beside him. She grabbed his cellphone to take with her, and the knife to cut any other phone lines before she left. After that, she'd leave the knife buried in the tires of the Ford in the driveway. It wouldn't be a permanent fix, but it would buy her some time to deal with the things she had to take care of, and if everything went smoothly, well, they could finish this later.

Elliot didn't even stir, so Nix figured she'd give the boy a little incentive to pep him back up for when she returned. Nix cranked the heat, ignoring Rachel's protests. She'd only hurt him a little, like she promised. The radiator clanked and hissed as it started up.

Turning to Elliot, she said, "Stay warm while I'm gone. It's a chilly night tonight."

She liked them so much better when they were warm.

Chapter 29

Nix pulled up to Val's dilapidated farmhouse just after sunset. The clouds overhead were black and heavy with rain. Drops splattered against her cheeks as she got out of the borrowed SUV in her borrowed body and looked up at the sky.

The buzzard was gone, frightened away by the storm, but it would be back. She slammed the car door, leaving Rachel's bag on the passenger seat, full of cell phones and keys and various bullshit for safe keeping. She was so ready for this to end.

Nix dug out the marble from her pocket. It glowed dimly in her palm.

Lightning flashed in the distance and thunder followed quickly after. It seemed fitting. A touch melodramatic, but fitting nonetheless. Val's car wasn't in the driveway, but there were tire marks squished into the mud, fresh and already accumulating pools of rain. The air smelled fresh and clean.

Rachel's body was chilled. The girl was still reeling from the events of the day, alternately disoriented and hyperfocused, but rarely throwing any comments or attention Nix's way. Elliot had been granted a reprieve, and Rachel wasn't fighting her. It was quiet.

Nix pocketed the marble and tried the door, prepared to break in if she had to, but it was unlocked. Cautiously, Nix wandered in. If Val wasn't here, she probably hadn't been gone long. If she *was* here, this might be a trap. The lights were off all over the house. She moved slowly through the foyer.

A sound caught her attention, coming from the back of the house. Nix stepped into the kitchen. She stopped in the doorway.

Danny sat at the kitchen table. He glanced up at her, surprise evident in the furrow of his brow.

"Rachel?" he asked.

Fuck. "Pops?" she said, keeping her voice as unreadable as possible.

Danny sat at Val's kitchen table. In the dark. Alone. A plate of food sat untouched beside him, the steak knife and fork still clean and resting together on one side. She wondered if he knew—if he was waiting for her. Rachel's interest was miraculously renewed.

Danny glanced away from her, his focus locked on the flask in his hands.

Whiskey, Rachel supplied subconsciously. *Cutty Black.*

"Valerie tell you to come here?" he asked the flask.

Nix went with it as Rachel watched the two converse, her attention decidedly rapt if her breathless silence was anything to go by. "Uh...yeah. Yes, she did." She flicked the switch next to the door, flooding the room with light.

Danny cringed. "I thought as much. You shouldn't be here. You should be home with Elliot. He didn't let you come here alone, did he?"

"I...told him I'd bring you home."

Now that she had Danny alone, Nix would have to take care of him before Val showed up. Taking on the two of them at once would be too risky. She'd hoped to deal with Val first, take out the crazy before the big guns and all, but she'd have to reconsider that plan. It was a shame, but business was business, and Danny had always been part of her endgame. She expected a little more resistance from Rachel at that admission, but the girl seemed all tongue-tied.

"The ME all but confirmed it," Danny started. "They recovered Joanie...Joanie's *body* with Jake's in the garage. They say she was pinned under her old car. I don't..." he trailed off, shaking his head. "I didn't think I'd manage to outlive the pair of them, honestly. Gotta find a way to contact Joanie's sister who she hasn't spoken to for years. And Kevin." He took a drink. Danny worried at his bottom lip, nodding and staring at the table. "*Kevin.* They found him in the kitchen all...all burned up. I just don't know where to start with it all."

Quietly and with the detached air of a traumatized soldier, Rachel said to Nix, *"You killed them all. This has to stop."*

Feeling generous, Nix reminded her, *"Don't give me all the credit. Couldn't have done it without you. Besides, we're a team now, remember?"*

Nix walked to the table, standing over Danny as he slumped in his chair. "So you started with whiskey?" Like son, like father.

"Don't. Just don't. Not right now." Defeat. It was a beautiful sound. Nix wanted to hear more of it.

Nix glanced around the sparsely decorated kitchen. A roll of paper towel and a striped cloth hanging from the stove were the only indications that anyone even lived here. She watched Danny stare at the table, and she listened to the quiet sounds of the house.

The rain pattered outside, splashing against the windows and the tin eaves troughs. The furnace rumbled below the floor, a low and steady hum, but the house was still cold. She listened for signs of movement, indications that they weren't alone in this house, but she found none.

"Don't hurt him. Please," Rachel was saying, blathering really. Nix got bored quickly of the same refrains. *"We still have a plan. I won't help you if you hurt him."*

Nix crossed Rachel's arms. Things were different now. Danny was here, and Nix was wondering if maybe she didn't need Rachel's help after all. "Where's Val?"

"Out."

"Out where?" Nix persisted.

"Didn't she tell you? The two of you are conspiring against me now, isn't that right?"

"No," Nix said. "She didn't say."

Danny grunted, frustration clouding his voice, but he still answered her, "Couldn't get ahold of that Rodney kid. Worried something might've happened to him, too, so she's out looking for him."

"Oh." Well, she'd be at it for a while, then.

Water dripped from the faucet into the kitchen sink, an even counter-rhythm to the rain. Nix dragged one of the cheap metal chairs out from the table with a prolonged screech. She dropped into it, sitting across from Danny, and stretched her right arm out across the Formica tabletop, palm up: an invitation. Elliot's shirt barely covered the scratches adorning her arms.

After a moment of Danny hesitating and Nix thinking that she couldn't *possibly* have blood under her fingernails, Danny rested his hand on top of hers. He squeezed Rachel's hand lightly and sighed, looking away.

"Pops..." Rachel whispered.

"Pops..." Nix mimicked, voice an octave lower than the splatter of rain against the roof, nearly lost in it, "you don't think the fire was an accident, either, do you? Someone...or *something* did this to them."

His tone was soft and unreadable as he said, "I don't know what to think right now."

She paused, then added, "Are we in danger?"

Danny glanced up at her, held her hand firmly and said, "No. No, darlin'. I'll *never* let anyone or any*thing* hurt you. I promise."

Nix smiled tenderly as something tightened painfully in Rachel's chest. It was cute how much she cared. "I know that."

He nodded to himself and pulled his hand away.

Nix continued, careful to maintain her ignorant façade, "But what do you think it was, then, a hit? Another hellhound, maybe?"

"I don't know. Maybe," he said, not meeting her eyes. He was lying. He did know. Or at least, he thought he did. With the amount of demons he and his moronic little pals had been attracting with their ambitious world-destroying plans, it didn't take a genius to narrow down the list of candidates. But he still wasn't acting any different around his dear immaculate daughter, so Nix wasn't too worried just yet.

"Do you know when Val's coming back?" Nix asked. She glanced at the clock above the kitchen door, but it wasn't ticking. She could see the dust on it from across the room.

"No."

Nix pressed, "But not for a while?"

Danny huffed. "I don't know. What do you care? I thought you didn't like Valerie."

Nix shrugged. "Just asking. I mean, she's got that demon-sphere thingy, right?" What she wanted to ask was its exact and current location. Val could tote the thing around with her everywhere for all Nix knew, even if Rachel argued otherwise. Or it could be right here in this house, right now, totally unattended like they'd suspected.

The marble was dim, but Nix wasn't sure how much stock she was willing to put in a marble. If it had protective magic around it when Val didn't have it on her, that could affect the brightness. How the fuck would Nix know? Anything was possible at this point.

Nix wasn't a professional world-saving hero by any means, but in her estimation, the only good demon-catching sphere-thingy was a broken demon-catching sphere-thingy. Get that out of the way and at least her worries would shrink from a global scale to only having to deal with the whole demon-killing exorcism—they didn't even try to hide their disdain for her kind, there were never any demon-pleasing spells or demon-cuddling spells, no, it was always the exorcisms with these people.

His eyes narrowed slightly. "What makes you think that?"

"Well...I just assumed, I guess. Am I wrong?" She threw in her best naïve teenage-girl expression.

"You don't need to concern yourself over that right now, Rachel. I don't want you any more involved than you have to be."

Of course. She should have seen that one coming. If the man could wrap his daughter up in bubble wrap and keep her locked in a house the rest of her life, it would be a dream come true for him. She tried to reason with him gently, "But I'm already involved, Pops. Don't you think I deserve to know about something that affects me?"

"No." No hesitation. No room for logical arguments. Just as obstinate as usual. He lifted his fork absently, poking at a piece of meat for a second before setting it back down across the plate. No steam rose from the food. It had gone cold long before she'd arrived and it looked as though it had come from a take-out container.

She pursed Rachel's lips and frowned. "That isn't fair."

"Kevin knew, and that might be what got them all killed."

Well, there was that. He wasn't *wrong* about that. Nix tried not to let her frustration get the best of her. Val almost certainly had the sphere. Slow and steady wins the race, after all.

Out of nowhere, Danny threw in, "You and Elliot are going to Flagstaff. First thing in the morning."

"But I thought—"

He slapped his hand against the table, resting his palm flat on its surface. "No arguments, Rachel. I told you I'd keep you safe, and that is exactly what I'm going to do. I already made the arrangements. You'll stay with Aunty Caroline. Then...then, we'll go from there. Long as you don't stay in any one place too long, nothing should be able to track you."

Interesting tactic. Might have been more effective if she hadn't already been riding his daughter around for the last few weeks. Hard to keep evil out when it's already worked its way inside. "You mean you're not coming?"

He shook his head. "I have work to do here. And I can't do that work if I'm worrying about the two of you. Elliot will protect you."

Wow. He'd regressed completely from his previous declarations of respecting her autonomy. Must've been the stress of the situation. "I thought we were going to stay home for a while after the succubus case?"

"The case doesn't matter anymore. We have bigger problems. We're into something real dangerous here, darlin', more than anything we've dealt with before. I don't know what's responsible for killing the others, but it will be coming for us soon enough. We can't go home, Rachel. Not anymore. You shouldn't have left your brother to come get me. You have to stay together."

"Okay, sure, got it. You're just going to stay here then? With Val?" Nix asked. Danny shot her a strange look and she pulled back a little. "I mean, not that there's anything wrong with that, of course, but are...are you *sure* you can trust her? I mean, don't you find her a bit...odd, Pops?"

"What is it with you and Val today?"

"I'm just saying, how well do you really know this woman? You've known her since, what..." Nix mentally reviewed Kevin's memory, "a few months ago?"

"Well, I—"

"That's not a very long time to know a person before you start making these huge world-altering plans with her."

"But—"

"Listen, I know she's told you that this spell of hers will cleanse the earth of demons, but how can you be sure what she's telling you is the truth? What's her agenda in all of this? Has she told you her plans?"

"She—"

"This woman comes out of nowhere a few months ago and you don't even question her motives? Since when have you ever met a hunter in the field whose reputation *didn't* precede them? How do you know she's even a real hunter at all?"

"Rachel," Danny said, holding up a hand. "Stop."

Nix stopped.

Danny rubbed his chin and stared at her.

"I just—" Nix started, but the hand came back up.

The clock on the wall continued not to tick. The rain continued to patter against the windows. Time seemed to stretch on and on.

Danny watched her. She'd pushed this too far. This whole charade. Danny didn't seem to know anything more useful than Kevin did—or at least nothing he was willing to share. This was a waste of time. Val could be back any moment, Nix had to make her move.

It was clear that he didn't have the sphere on him, and in the time they'd spent together, Nix had never seen anything of the supernatural caliber of Kevin's weapons in Danny's possession. Presumably he'd have those vials hidden somewhere on his person, so she'd have to be careful not to give him an opportunity to use them.

But Nix wasn't convinced that Danny had nothing left to give. He was tightlipped to the extreme, even with his kids. He was a man with secrets and Nix wanted in on them.

Danny cracked his jaw, narrowed his eyes. "What has gotten into you lately?" Danny paused with his lips still stuck on the last syllable of 'lately' and something in his gaze shifted.

Nix saw the change the moment it happened.

Danny locked up, movements stiff with forced nonchalance as he placed his thirsty flask on the kitchen table. His mouth formed something approximating a smile, but it didn't reach his eyes. She slipped a hand behind her back.

He reached forward, grabbing for the steak knife on the kitchen table next to his untouched meal, he but stilled when Nix pulled out Kevin's gun from the back of Rachel's jeans. She took aim.

"I wouldn't," she warned.

She heard Rachel gasp. It wouldn't take long before the girl was in a full-on panic now. What a bother.

"That gun..." he mumbled, then his eyes hardened. "That gun's outta bullets. Has been for years."

"Mm, yes and no," Nix corrected. "It doesn't have any of your 'special' bullets, the kind that would hurt me, but it seems to take regular bullets just fine. So don't test me, old man."

For a moment she thought he'd go quietly—how very foolish—but his hand darted forward and grabbed the hilt of the knife.

Knife versus gun. There was no question as to which would prevail, yet the poor man seemed dead set on trying his luck anyway. Nix didn't know what he thought he could accomplish here.

He waved his knife at her, looking as fierce and determined as ever. His muscles tensed in preparation to lunge. "It was you. You killed them, Demon. Well yoasu've messed with the wrong folks this time."

Nix sighed. "I did warn you." Instead of tightening her finger on the trigger, Nix turned the gun on herself.

His eyes went wide in fear or surprise, maybe both. She pressed the barrel of the revolver to Rachel's temple and cocked the hammer pointedly. Beneath the steady beat of the rain, she could hear the sound of his breathing, measured but shallow. Relief spread through Rachel's veins when Nix didn't automatically shoot the man, but Rachel was getting ahead of herself.

The knife fell from his fingers and clattered to the table. He raised his hands up in a gesture of surrender, knocking over his flask, and Nix was actually a little let down. The mostly empty flask dripped whiskey on the tabletop in slow, rhythmic drops. Rain pounded on the roof, sluicing down the closed kitchen windows and obscuring the night.

They stood there for a moment in utter silence in the empty house. Danny's voice was soft and controlled as he said, "Just let her go," like it was a command when they both heard it for what it really was.

Nix smirked and pretended to consider this poorly veiled plea of his. "I don't think so, Pops. I kind of like it in here. Might just keep this one for a while, until it's worn out."

"She's just a girl. She's of no value to you. You...you could take anyone." He paused before continuing cautiously with the proposal, "You could take me."

Nix laughed, the sound thunderous and jarring in the quiet room, but she just couldn't help herself. "How noble of you," she said. "I might just take that into consideration. Now sit back down, *Pops*."

She nodded toward the chair he'd vacated, and without protest, Danny complied. "What do you want?" he asked, leaning forward across the table with the expression of a diplomat willing to concede but not overwhelmingly happy about it.

Always the same question, layered and heavier than it should have been. What did she *want*? As if that was easy. As if she knew. "What makes you think I want anything?" Nix said.

His eyes bored into her as though he could see her clearly now and wasn't willing to let her out of his sights. Carefully, he pointed out, "If you wanted to kill either of us, you would have done it already."

"Hmm. Can't argue with that, I suppose." She stared at the pendant around his neck. Danny followed her gaze.

"You want it?" he asked tentatively. "It's yours. Just leave the girl alone. This is between you and me."

Nix shook her head. "Hmm, now that's where you're wrong, see. You've already brought Rachel and your boy into it. You recruited them into a war you can't win. What did you expect would happen? You'd just be one big happy family skipping through fields of puppies and rainbows all day, slaughtering my kind and getting away with it?"

He ground his teeth together, so hard she could hear it from across the table. "You want the amulet, or not?"

"Take it off," she proposed reasonably. It wasn't the amulet she wanted, it was the lack of it.

He kept his hands on the table where she could see them. His fingers didn't fidget. His legs didn't twitch under the tabletop. He wasn't new to hostage situations or tense standoffs. This was all old hat to him, except that his daughter was involved now. That was where Nix's advantage was. Danny said, "Not until I know Rachel is safe."

"Fine. I won't hurt her." Nix set the gun on the table, raising her hands away from it, as though the gun was the real problem here.

"And why should I believe that? You clearly have no trouble hurting people."

"Ah, you've got me there." Her body count had climbed pretty fast over the past couple days. She'd been doing so well, too. Old habits were just so easy to fall back into. Her fingers brushed over the hilt of the gun as she watched his eyes. "Fine then, if you don't want to play nice, I'll just blow the sweet little thing's brains out."

He didn't even blink. "Kill her and you've lost your leverage."

Nix narrowed Rachel's eyes. "You drive a hard bargain. But I could just beat the hell out of you, rip that thing off, and take what I want."

"You could," he conceded, his right hand coming up to rest on the chain as if by habit, the first example of self-comforting behavior she'd seen from him yet. "But if you thought it was that easy, you could've done it five minutes ago. You know you can't touch this, not a foul creature like yourself. It'll suck the life right outta you, burn you like you've never felt before. It ain't no ordinary hunk of silver. It protects me from things like you and it ain't coming off until I take it off. You don't get into my head without my permission."

Nix watched him carefully, taking note of the slight twitch of the left corner of his mouth, the tightness in his jaw. She'd been watching him for weeks, but still hadn't figured out the man's tell. Elliot got nervous when he lied, like he expected the Lord to come down and personally smite him. His ears reddened at the tips and his speech became stilted. But Danny...it was harder to tell with him. He was a closed book. He could be fucking with her...he probably was.

"You're lying," she said.

"If you're so sure, take it."

"What about Rachel? Aren't you worried about her precious life being sucked outta her?"

"Far as I can tell, she's already got a parasite living in her and doing just that. No, you're the only one here who needs to be concerned."

Nix plucked through Rachel's thoughts, looking for additional information about the amulet, but all Rachel knew was that he'd had it forever and never took it off. She hadn't even known it was from Kevin. Nix huffed.

"All right," Nix said. "Take it off and we'll make a trade."

"Fine. But you let her go first."

Nix frowned, annoyed. "And how am I supposed to do that? Far as *I* can tell," she said, "you and your darling girl are the only warm bodies around here for miles. Where do you expect me to go?"

"I already told you," he said, tone none too patient, "you could take me. So here you go." Danny raised his hands in invitation. "I'll remove the pendant and you can hop on in, Demon. Then you can read my mind and whatever it is you things do, but once you have me, Rachel walks away."

Nix watched him inquisitively. Danny was a lot of things, but he wasn't stupid. He had to be playing an angle here. "That...sounds like a bargain. And I'll be true to my word," she lied, "but I've got to ask: what is there to stop me from killing her anyway once I've got you? Hypothetically."

"Hypothetically," Danny said, "you'll be true to your word, or I will spend the rest of my time here on earth making yours the worst kind of hell you can imagine. See, sweetheart, you may think you've got it all worked out, taking advantage of a young girl without much experience, but I'm no teenager. I've been doing this job since I was old enough to hold a shotgun. If you don't think I've got my own arsenal of tricks, you're dead wrong. And besides, I don't see you've got much choice in the matter. Agreeing to my terms is the only way you're going to get inside my head."

"I don't know about that. I have all manner of tactics to make men like yourself come around to my way of thinking."

A spike of fear flashed through Rachel's mind, and for a moment Nix was lost as to its cause. Then she realized. She almost laughed aloud at the fact that it hadn't occurred to her before. Was she losing her touch? Well, this kind of oversight simply could not stand. If anyone were to find out about such an uncharacteristically overlooked opportunity, she'd never live it down.

"You in or ain't ya?" Danny demanded.

Nix smirked. "Oh, I'm in."

Danny nodded and reached around, unclasping the necklace and pouring it into the palm of his hand. Pointedly, he dropped the amulet in the center of the table and waited.

Nix took a good look at the man sitting across from her. He was all muscle, tall and toned and tanned. He lacked Elliot's boyish charm and thinner frame, but in his day Nix was willing to bet the man had been quite the looker. Kevin seemed to think so, at least.

She tried to remember any time that his hands had been on Rachel's body, but couldn't quite recall anything but the weight of them, solid and heavy. She wondered if his hands were gun-callused or softer than they looked, and of course there was only one way to find out as far as Nix was concerned. And to think, if Rachel's mind hadn't been even dirtier than Nix's, it may never have occurred to her to bring them to this point.

Nix stood from her chair, her movements easy and slow so as not to startle her prey. He watched her carefully, eyes tracking her every minuscule movement, weighing the risk. Elliot was a lot like his Pops with that intensity in his gaze.

Rachel, sensing where Nix's intentions had shifted, started to panic. This wasn't the same overblown, histrionic little outburst she'd exhibited back at the lion's den when the three hapless hunters had met their untimely demises. No, this was something different. Nix gently twisted Rachel's head from side to side, trying to lessen the tension there but not even making a dent. It was just as well, really.

Nix slipped into the space between Danny and the table, Rachel's lithe frame just the right fit, and lowered herself onto Danny's lap.

His hands lifted away from her, just hovering in the air a few inches from her hips like he had no idea what to do with them. That was preposterous, of course. Nix was confident he knew exactly what to do with his hands, given enough incentive.

She let the weight of Rachel's body rest on his thighs as she wrapped her arms around his shoulders and leaned in close.

Danny was still. The kind of stillness of a caged animal with its door left ajar, frozen in a state of tense hesitation, knowing this was a trap but not how to react to it.

She brushed Rachel's lips against his earlobe and asked, "Isn't there anything else *you* want? Negotiation goes both ways, you know. I feel like you're getting the shorter end of the deal here, and that just isn't fair, is it?"

Nix ground Rachel's hips against him. Danny made a strangled sound and jerked his head away from her, trying to insinuate distance between them where there was none.

Rachel shuddered and mentally turned away. Nix couldn't have that, of course, not now, not when things were just about to get fun again. Nix had promised Rachel they'd have fun together, and she was determined to hold up her end of the bargain. Nix paused just long enough to lock Rachel's focus to the present, to make sure she couldn't tune this out.

Danny didn't move at all, barely breathed.

"Stop this," he demanded. The horror on his face was priceless. Suddenly her whole day was looking up. His wide eyes, tensed jaw, the way his brow furrowed in confused anger and his lip trembled just the slightest bit at the corner—this shit was poetry. She could hear his teeth grinding together and it made her smile.

She liked him when he was demanding—much better than when he was a sappy old lump of sentimentality. She knew there was a man in there somewhere, hiding behind the fatherly façade. Nix shifted a bit closer, enough to press her breasts against his chest, then ran a hand down his side. She stopped at his belt, ran Rachel's fingertips along the edge of it.

"Rachel doesn't want to stop," she lied.

Danny cringed away from her words like she'd spat on him and he grabbed her biceps to push her back.

Nix hummed, then confided, "This is Elliot's shirt, you know. Not exactly form-fitting, but it smells like him. We had a little fun of our own before I came here."

Danny glanced up at her but said nothing.

"Our father who art in heaven," Rachel started, *"hallowed be thy name..."*

Poor girl, resorting to such trivialities in a misplaced effort to dull the moment. Prayer was like cigarettes, drugs, alcohol, all just the grown-up versions of a wailing baby's attempts to self-sooth in the face of its crippling dependence, its own inability to save itself. An escape. Normally the words might annoy her, but tonight Nix was really feeling the Lord's Prayer. Rachel's distress was too beautiful to interrupt, so Nix let her have it.

She could feel Danny's muscles straining to move her, but Nix didn't want to be pushed away and Nix never did anything she didn't want to do.

Nix made a whining noise in the back of her throat, pouting. "Now, don't be like that," she warned, licking her lips. She undulated her hips, writhing wantonly against him. She tossed her hair over her shoulder with a flick of her head. "Shh," she soothed him, "it's okay. It's okay. Just do this one little thing for me and I'll let her go."

"Thy kingdom come..."

Nix pressed her moist lips against his jaw, flicking out her tongue to taste the dark shadow of stubble there. His attempts to push her away had lost some of their direction and the force he'd been trying to exert had transformed into a bruising grip on Rachel's arms. He was shaking.

She was a pretty young girl, all blossomed and ripe. Sure he had a thing for Kevin and maybe she ought to have worn Elliot here instead, but there was no reason for him to resist her advances, not really. Nix would teach him to play nice.

Nix bit down on Rachel's lip. "Please, Pops?" she whispered on a sigh, pushing one hand between them and pressing the heel of her palm against him. He still wasn't interested, which was frustrating, but Nix persisted. *"Please.* Touch me."

"Thy will be done..."

"Rachel..." he begged, voice deliciously pained. The sound made Nix want to hurt him more.

Nix caught a glimpse of tears forming in his eyes, and she gasped at the shot of arousal. Her thigh suddenly felt warm. She rolled her hips against his and moaned softly into his ear.

He shuddered.

"Get off him."

Chapter 30

Nix glanced up to see a tall Amazon-warrior Hell-Bitch standing in the doorway, shotgun in hand. Hunters and their guns.

"Busted," Nix muttered, rolling Rachel's eyes disdainfully as she dismounted, careful to place Danny between Val and herself.

Danny panted with relief, hanging his head and mumbling disjointedly, "Thank God...gotta help me...gotta get it out of her...I—I didn't know, I—" but neither Nix nor Val were really listening. Nix was sizing the woman up and Val appeared to be doing the same.

"A gun isn't going to hurt me," Nix reminded her. "It might hurt sweet little Rachel though. Don't think Danny-Boy here would be too pleased about that, do you?"

Val's aim didn't waver. She stepped closer, nearly within splashing-distance if she had that vial on her like Kevin had. Nix lunged for the abandoned steak knife and pressed it up against Danny's neck.

"Any closer and I'll slit his throat," Nix threatened.

Val offered a calculating look, glancing disinterestedly at Danny. Nix pressed the knife down, the blade sinking deep enough to draw blood and provoke an irritated noise from Danny.

Val lowered the gun a few inches.

She pulled the trigger.

The shot rang clear and booming over the storm, so loud and so sudden that Nix was taken aback. It took a second for her to realize that Rachel's body wasn't experiencing any pain. It took another second for Nix to notice that Danny had slouched forward against the knife.

Nix dropped the knife and Danny fell out of the chair, collapsing on the floor and hitting the table on the way down, shoving it forward with a screech.

Rachel gasped.

"Looks like you're out of leverage," Val pointed out.

Nix stared at her. "Fuck," she said after a long moment. "That was cold. I'm impressed."

A numbness swept through Rachel's body. Her hands trembled, skin pallid and chilled. It was all Nix could do to try and suppress Rachel's reaction, make it less obvious that this body was seconds away from crumbling without Nix to hold it up. Now was not the time for her host body to fall apart.

"She shot him," Rachel whispered.

Nix clenched her jaw. *"Not now, kid."*

"She...she shot him."

Val arched one eyebrow, not even bothering to glance at Danny's crumpled form. The table was obstructing the back door now. It would take too long to maneuver it out of the way. She needed an escape route, but Val was blocking her access to the front of the house. Thunder clapped. The lights flickered out.

While Nix was skimming through strategies in the darkness, Val was moving forward and reaching into her jacket pocket. Nix heard the clink, wine glasses toasting, and she couldn't wait any longer. Nix sidestepped Danny's body and bolted before Val could bind her.

She got as far as the living room, the solid oak door slamming shut behind her, before she was soaring unexpectedly through the air and crashing into an empty bookcase. The shelves snapped and groaned as Nix smashed into them and slid slowly to the ground.

"Wrong way," Val's voice told her from the other side of the room where she'd headed Nix off at the entrance.

Nix scrambled to stand.

The woman had power. She wasn't just some hunter. A witch, maybe—but no, stronger than a witch. Or she was using something to make it seem like she had power. Either way, Nix was woefully unprepared for this development and had every intention of getting the fuck outta Dodge until she could come up with a new strategy.

Just as she got her legs back under her, Val raised a hand and with a flick of her wrist, Nix was free-falling down the basement stairs, missing the steps altogether and slamming against the far wall.

She hit the workbench on her way down, rolled gracelessly off it, and smacked Rachel's head against the concrete floor. Her vision blurred. Pain shot through Rachel's right shoulder—dislocated. Her left leg felt like it was on fire.

Slow footsteps sounded from upstairs. A door closed. A lock clicked into place. The heavy thump of boots on old, creaking wood moved down the stairs.

From the ground, Nix could just barely see Val's boots as she emerged from the shadows. Concrete, stained rust-red, stretched between them. An empty chair sat in the center. Nix could still smell the blood, the sulfur, the charred flesh. This was the last place she'd seen Cirrik. This was where they'd killed him. This was where they'd kill her, too.

Val strode toward her as Nix pulled herself up with Rachel's left hand. Nix jerked the dislocated shoulder back into place to make it easier to work with.

Rachel was hyperventilating. Nix wasn't stopping her.

"Ah," Nix muttered as a jolt of pain spread up Rachel's left thigh. Nix hastily dug the marble free. It seared the palm of her hand, so bright it burned. Nix dropped it. The marble rolled across the floor, coming to a stop in front of Val.

Rolling her eyes, Val said, "Where do they keep finding these damn things?" The glass ball crunched under her boot. The glow ceased.

This wasn't working out as well as she'd planned...but the situation wasn't *unsalvageable*. No, this was just a minor hiccup, nothing she couldn't work around.

"Wait," Nix said, raising her hands and moving to place the chair between her and Val, "hold on—maybe...maybe we can work something out here, you and I?"

Val stopped. "I don't negotiate with demons."

"No," Nix agreed, "I can see that. It's probably a good policy. But, uh, I think you might want to reconsider, just this once. See—and trust me, I know how this is going to sound, but I swear it's true—the only reason I'm doing this is to stop you from destroying your entire species. Well, I mean, that's one of the *primary* reasons. I might have gotten a little carried away.

"But the point is: your spell is wrong. You think its purpose is to destroy demons—which is kind of offensive, by the way—but it doesn't work like that. If you go through with it, we're talking full-scale apocalypse here, a blow-out sale—everything must go. Humans included.

"Now, it's an easy enough mistake to make, so it's not like anybody's blaming you here, but I've gotta say, it'd be pretty fucking stupid to eliminate the entire human species over some ridiculous crusade to destroy demons," Nix said, pausing to catch her breath. "Am I right? It'd be in everybody's best interest for you to just stop while you're ahead. You see where I'm coming from here, don't you?"

Val snickered. "You always were an odd one, Nix."

Nix stilled at the use of her name.

"But consorting with humans? Trying to *save* their species? Don't you think you're going a little far to keep your closet full?"

The sky rumbled and a flash of light filled the basement, not long enough for Nix to get a better look at the woman, but long enough to make her wonder what she'd missed.

Water trickled in along the edges of the tiny basement windows.

"Who *are* you?" Nix finally asked.

"I didn't recognize you at first, either," Val admitted, "but I *see you* now." Val stepped closer.

Nix stepped back, circling the chair. "You didn't answer my question."

"Oh, I'm sorry," Val mocked, "in case you've forgotten, I am the one whose vessel you *stole* and then drove off a *cliff*."

Oh, shit.

"Oh shit," Nix muttered.

Oh shit, oh shit, oh *shit*.

Val grinned. Or at least, her host body did. 'Val' probably didn't even exist, she was just a cover, but Nix had never met her in person like this before, didn't even know her real name.

"Indeed. I've had my sights on you for a while since that stunt you pulled. Who would have thought you'd end up coming to me? Small world."

It couldn't be. How could this have happened? No, she'd been so careful to go undetected, how could she have ended up *here*? It wasn't fair. Maybe...maybe if she just explained the situation—it wasn't like they couldn't be civil about this. "That...that whole cliff thing was an accident," Nix said. "I...I didn't even know she was yours, I mean, I just needed a ride and she happened to be headed in the same direction as me and I thought, you know, what's one more body—"

"I'm not interested in your excuses." Val closed in on her, but Nix kept backing up.

"But come on! What's one little vessel to you anyway? Successful archdemon like yourself, I'm sure you've got vessels lined up all over the place," Nix tried to reason.

"This vessel was pregnant," Val spat.

"Oh," Nix said. Then, "*Oh*. I didn't—I mean, was it...yours?"

"What? No! It wasn't mine—well, it was *going to be* mine. Don't you get it? Haven't you ever wanted one perfect form, something that fit you so flawlessly, so impeccably, that it was just *yours*?"

Her words struck a chord with Nix. She'd blown through so many bodies, they barely even registered anymore. Still, she understood that longing. She understood the perpetual sense of being out of place.

Even the bodies that fit better than others, they never lasted. A few months at most, and they start to feel chilled and worn. The life would drain out of them all eventually, no matter how careful she was about maintaining them. That was usually why she didn't stay. The human souls inside with her would start to fade until they were gone completely, and all that was left was silence and a gradual disintegration.

So yeah, Nix had wanted a form that was *hers*. But didn't everyone? It didn't mean anything.

"Of course," Nix admitted dismissively.

"The right vessel, the perfect vessel, it's impossible to find." The archdemon gestured to her Amazon-warrior, decked out in combat-boots and a leather duster, living undercover as a hunter. "This one's a realtor from Ohio," she said. She ran one hand thoughtfully over her scarred cheeks. "She can barely hold me. Got all torn up on my way in and it was such a fucking mess, but what other option did I have? So I'd figured, if you can't *find* a perfect vessel, why not *make* one?" Her tone communicated a peculiar sort of intimacy and it took Nix a moment to realize that she was appealing to Nix's sense of camaraderie. And for that moment, it was working.

Somehow, it had never occurred to Nix before. The idea was intriguing, but already Nix could see the flaws in it. A baby might last longer than a child, certainly longer than an adult, but to create a perfectly suited body, that was just..."Impossible." Wasn't it?

Then Val's tone slipped back into disdain and she leaned over the chair and said, "Maybe not. But we'll never know since you came along and fucked it all up. It must be hard, Nix. Being such a fuck up, that is."

Nix bristled. "I'm not—"

"Nonsense," Val interrupted, waving a hand in Nix's direction, "your reputation precedes you. Everybody knows what a fuck up you are. Thing is, your real mistake, out of your whole laundry list of mistakes, Nix, was getting in my way. And yet, here you are, *again*. Doing what, exactly? Some sort of human-saving crusade? As if. Humankind doesn't want any more to do with you than Demonkind does. What's next? Going to rescue of box of puppies?"

Val withdrew a vial from her jacket, and Nix was running out of options.

"Well, I mean, who doesn't like puppies?" Nix joked.

Val did not find this amusing. She raised an eyebrow. "Truly, I have no idea how you've managed to survive as long as you have. Creatures like you are no better than scavengers. You disgust me."

Something scraped across the floor above them. Nix glanced up to see dust motes fall from the rafters.

Val's hand shot out, and though she was five feet away and out of reach, Nix found herself trapped in place.

Nix struggled, digging her heels into the ground as Val pulled her forward. The chair jerked, then swept under her, screeching as they were both repositioned at Val's whim. The chair stopped in front of Val.

Nix looked up at her. She wasn't panicking. She would not panic. "How...how is this whole cleansing-the-earth business possibly going to help you get a better vessel? Maybe I can help, you know, I—"

The handle of the basement door twisted. They both glanced up at it.

Val turned back to her. "I'm over the vessel," she said, voice lowered. "Why bother hiding in humans when I could be ruling them in my true form? And thanks to you, Nix, I think I'll finally have enough power to pull it off."

The door banged.

"Thanks to me?"

"Our destinies have been intertwined for a long time now, Nix—just took me a while to figure it out. Because of your reckless stupidity, I ended up meeting with an old friend while putting a price on your head and trying to track you down. He sold me the Soul Catcher I'd been searching for so many years, and warned me about a bunch of hunters who'd uncovered an old spell and were using it as an exorcism. And here we are. Then, like I said, demons just started showing up on my doorstep after a while. And here you are. Just in time for the finale. You see? Fate." The pungent perfume smell hit the air and Nix was doubly trapped. "Now stay." Val walked over to the workbench, returning with a foul-smelling strip of cloth stained with all manner of shit Nix didn't care to analyze. "And hush."

Val shoved the cloth between her teeth, pulling it tight behind her head and tying it. Rachel gagged. Nix tried to gnaw herself free.

The banging came again and again until Val sauntered up the steps and unlocked the door. It swung open. Danny stood at the top of the stairs.

For the span of a breath, Nix entertained some elaborate and disturbing notions involving zombies—a breed of creatures that Nix found especially distasteful and messy and had no desire to deal with at all—before it occurred to her it had been a trick. Rock salt, most likely. Or he was wearing a vest. Bastards. She should've known.

"*Oh, thank God.*" Rachel melted with relief. Tears leaked out her eyes and down her face. Nix growled. The last thing she fucking needed was to look like she'd been moved to tears. This girl was getting on her last nerve.

"You could've warned me," Danny said, rubbing his chest roughly with one hand and sounding pissed off. The pendant was back in place around his neck.

"Would've spoiled the surprise," Val returned.

Danny glanced down the steps, catching Nix's eyes. "You didn't hurt her, did you? Is she bleeding? Why's she bleeding?"

Val turned around, walking back down the stairs with Danny trying to push by her. "She fell down some steps. She's fine. Not like it's going to matter for long, anyway."

"Rachel?" Danny lumbered up to her, reaching for Rachel's face where Nix could feel the drops of blood sluicing down from her hairline, but Val stilled his hand.

"Fuck, Daniel, don't touch her! That's still a demon inside."

Danny pulled back, but didn't stop looking at Rachel. Nix tried to convey with her eyes the sentiment of *"She's fucking batshit crazy, get me out of here!"* but probably only succeeded in looking a little batshit herself. Danny's brow furrowed. His fists clenched at his sides.

"Go light some candles," Val said. "It's too dark down here to work."

Danny nodded, then disappeared behind her, rooting around noisily in the workbench.

They left the door open. If she could get out of the chair, she could make a break for it. *If* she could get out of the chair.

A spark of light penetrated the darkness, accompanied by the click of a lighter. Another joined, and another, until the room was dimly lit.

"You got a bible around here?" Danny said behind her.

Val glanced down at Nix with a scowl. "Don't be silly, we don't need that."

"How are we going to do an exorcism without a bible?"

Val rolled her eyes, her arms crossed. "We aren't going to do *an* exorcism, we're going to do *the* exorcism. Now stop fucking around over there and start chanting."

Danny moved back into Nix's line of sight, brow perpetually furrowed. He rubbed the back of his neck, looking to Val. Water dripped down the walls. The storm shook the windows. Danny's breathing was the only thing Nix could hear clearly above it all.

"You...you're trying to say..." Danny trailed off. His voice rose as he finally reached the startlingly obvious conclusion, "That would *kill* her."

Val shrugged. "Yes, well."

Looking appropriately appalled, Danny said, "I'm not killing my kid."

A sigh. "Daniel, you're looking at this all wrong."

"Oh, I'm sorry, is there a right way to look at killing my daughter?"

Val threw her hands up. "You're killing the *demon*. Honestly, how many times must we have this conversation? You think this filthy demon is simply going to disappear after you exorcise it and never return?"

Nix nodded her head exuberantly but neither of them looked in her direction. Disappearing, never returning, those sounded fucking fantastic. She could do that. She'd lied about these things in the past, sure, but this time Nix was really feeling the commitment.

The gag muffled her sounds of agreement. Danny's eyes flicked to her for an instant, then he was right back to staring at Val. It was annoying being spoken about like she wasn't even in the room.

Danny's jaw twitched. "I'm not—"

"You agreed to this."

"No. Not to *this*."

Val huffed. She was really pushing this, for an archdemon who clearly didn't take shit from anyone. But maybe she needed Danny, maybe the whole soul-relocation spell thing really was just close enough to an exorcism that she couldn't perform it herself. "Suddenly you care that people are dying here? People *die*. That's what they do. At least we're giving them a chance for a noble death, a chance for their death to mean something."

Danny shook his head, looking at Nix and seeing Rachel. His eyes softened. "No. No, we'll find someone else—we'll take the next one, we...."

"We can't stop now," Val said, snapping Danny's attention back to her. "Not when we're *this* close! This is it, Daniel, everything we've been working toward, everything centuries of hunters have been trying to achieve...it can all end here, tonight. She's the last one we'll need. I promise."

"Not her." His lips flattened.

The candles flickered, and shadows crept across the walls. "Sacrifices must be made for the greater good. You knew this going in. Rochelle would *want* you to go through with this."

"Her name is *Rachel*."

"Why are you making this so difficult?"

"Are you *insane*?" Danny spat, and neither Rachel nor Nix had ever heard him quite so outraged before. "This is my daughter!"

"Oh come on, she's not even really your daughter! She's just some goddamn stray you took in. We'll get you another one—a better one, it'll be fine, you'll see."

Danny stilled, his demeanor shifting from agitated to a deadly, focused calm. He glared at Val. Rachel shivered.

Slowly, with obvious restraint, Danny ground out, "Don't...don't ever talk about my kid like that again."

And there he was. Finally. The Daniel Whipsaw of Rachel's bedtime stories. The man born with a shotgun in his hands and a bitter scowl on his lips. Nix found herself pleased to see him.

Val didn't seem to see the change. "Fine," she said loudly, "what are you going to do, huh? Drag her out of here and exorcise her yourself? 'Cause I'm sure as hell not helping you and you can't do it here—and oh, maybe you've forgotten, your precious little princess over there has a hell-spawn up inside of her that isn't going to cooperate with any ludicrous relocation plans, I can tell you that!"

Danny shook off the calm, slipping right back into the agitation, rocking back and forth on his heels and scrubbing a hand down his face. "I'll figure this out myself, I'll—"

Val returned his glare, eyes hard. "I'm getting real tired of arguing about this. Do it now."

The demanding tone of her voice seemed to pull Danny back toward that deadly calm. He wasn't backing down. Nix liked him more than ever before.

Danny straightened. "No."

Val's jaw cracked as she ground her teeth together. "Last chance."

"I said no."

Val raised her hand and Danny flew into the wall adjacent the workbench. The force knocked the wind out of him and he hit with a thud, eyes wide, and if Nix hadn't been certain before, she knew now that he hadn't had any idea what kind of shit he'd gotten himself into.

Val lifted her hand higher. Danny rose up the wall, feet dangling. With her free hand, she pulled the glass sphere out of her jacket and held it up, its blue glow casting eerie shadows around the room. "Start chanting."

He had the good grace to look shocked. "You...you're..." he muttered, voice an even cadence belying the surprise written on his features.

"I said, *chant*."

Val's fist tightened and Danny's hands flew to his chest, movements fluttery and uncoordinated like he was trying to hold his insides inside and not doing a super job of it. He groaned, cringing in pain. Her fingers tightened further as the seconds extended between them. Danny's feet smacked against the wall as he struggled to free himself, making no progress to show for it, and damn if Nix didn't know *that* feeling of futility.

Gasping, Danny choked, "Never."

Val stomped her feet like a child, face a canvas of red overlaid by pink scars. The muscles in her neck strained. "Now!"

"Put him down."

Nix startled at the sound of Elliot's voice. Rachel's fear tripled even as hope spread warm and light through her chest.

He stood at the base of the stairs, Kevin's gun in one hand and a bulging rucksack in the other. Elliot strode a few feet across the room, dropping the bag on the ground with a clatter. It popped open, and Nix didn't have to see inside it to make out the shape of a cross and a bottle and a book and she knew this tune all too well.

Apparently the handcuffs hadn't been enough to hold him, nor the lack of a functioning vehicle or line of communication enough to slow him down. He was more resourceful than she'd anticipated. Nix would be irritated if she wasn't so thrilled.

Val didn't even turn. "Boy, did you walk into the wrong house."

Elliot reached down and pulled a little baggy from the rucksack, never taking his eyes off his target. Nix wondered at its contents—could be anything, maybe some super-secret archdemon-defeating powder or something that would bind her power or maybe a huge monstrous creature that shrunk to fit into tiny bags for easy storage but would blow the lid off this joint once released.

Slowly, Val turned a raised eyebrow on him.

Elliot flicked his wrist and white powder burst free from the bag, landing on Val's jacket and scattering on the floor.

Val blinked.

Salt. Fucking salt—against an archdemon! His stupidity was astounding.

Elliot dropped the empty bag and braced both hands on the gun. The useless fucking gun. Oh, if only he wasn't such a moron, the arrival of the cavalry would have been so much sweeter.

"You—you let him go and...and my sister...right, uh...now. And don't try anything! This whole place is about to be swarming with hunters!"

It was like watching a train wreck. A really shitty, embarrassing train wreck—not the fun kind with the explosions.

Nix tried to make a case for his usefulness. He'd brought an exorcism kit with him, which under normal circumstances would be quite distressing but was actually looking pretty good right about now. And sure, he had the aforementioned useless fucking gun, which would have been pretty fucking useless at the best of times but was now pointed at an irritated archdemon and so was actually *spectacularly* useless in this instance. That wasn't a point in his favor. But Elliot was a reasonably smart boy most of the time and if he was to be trusted at his word, he hadn't come without some backup.

Val looked him up and down then glanced back to Danny. "This is Junior, I take it?"

Danny didn't answer.

Val shrugged. "Well, okay then. Maybe this will be better incentive for you." Her focus snapped to Elliot and with only a look, Elliot dropped to his knees. The gun clattered to the floor. His hands rose to his already-bruised neck as he choked.

"Stop!" Danny's hands mirrored Elliot's, reaching up to rip the pendant off. He started muttering Kevin's little spell to pull Nix into himself, but Val glanced at Danny, easily pinning his arms to the wall, pendant still securely in place just like Nix.

"Chant."

Danny struggled. "Please! Stop! I—I don't remember the exorcism, I—"

"Bullshit," Val countered over Elliot's screams. "Chant. And do it nicely this time."

Elliot flailed, shouting incoherently, fingers clawing at his eyes as he writhed on the ground. The scream that came out of him was so piercing, Rachel instinctively cringed.

Nix and Rachel looked on as blood caked under Elliot's fingernails, leaking down his cheeks like tears. Wisps of smoke rose from his face and when his hands fell away Nix could see nothing but black holes where his pretty blue eyes should have been.

"All right! I'll chant, just stop, oh God, please stop this!"

Val shot Danny a glare. "I'm not hearing any chanting."

A string of Italian erupted from Danny.

Elliot crumpled to the ground, twitching.

The pull started immediately this time, Danny's words rushed and frantic, and the pain followed like a wave, crashing into her unexpectedly.

Nix tried to hold back any sounds that would betray her discomfort, but stopped bothering as soon as it occurred to her that Danny had just sacrificed his daughter for his son because of Elliot's carrying on. If humiliating herself in front of an archnemesis would turn the tables here in her favor, Nix was going to do it. The words slipped under her skin like a brand, tearing and burning.

Nix screamed against the gag.

Danny stopped to stare at her, meeting her eyes before Val demanded he continue.

Danny stuttered, slowing his words and taking the pain down a notch with them. Nix struggled in the chair, digging her fingers into the steel armrests until Rachel's nails started cracking down the center and piercing her fingertips.

Heat surged through her body, escaping in puffs of black smoke around the gag, and all she could taste was ash, all she could smell was her own flesh burning. The heat spread through her, invisible tongue licking up her forearms and neck. Rachel's skin curdled in its wake, melting, dripping, bubbling and bursting, leaving nothing but raw, oozing flesh beneath. Rachel and Nix were both screaming.

Distantly, she heard Elliot still writhing and groaning on the floor, and Danny's words had degraded into slurred sobs. Every time he stopped, Val got him started again, probably by hurting Elliot, but Nix was finding the whole thing increasingly hard to follow.

It was her second brush with exorcism in one day. It was getting tiring. Dull, really. Terminally boring. She'd always suspected boredom could be fatal, and look, she was right. After this, Nix was going to take a long fucking vacation...to Fiji, maybe...and she'd have some of those frou-frou coconut drinks with the little umbrellas in them...and...and Cirrik would probably be there because he always was when she least wanted him to be and she'd have to kick his ass for showing up on her vacation uninvited but she'd probably relent and share a drink or two with the asshole and they'd laugh about this whole thing and maybe she'd just never go back...and—

A particularly nasty jolt of pain in her skull sent her head snapping back and Nix tried to like it, tried to own it, but it was different than human pain, deeper, scaring, and she couldn't escape.

She was being ripped apart, unseen hellhounds tearing at her from the inside out. She choked on the ash in her mouth, struggles weakening and lacking direction as her vision, already distorted by Rachel's tears, dimmed.

Centuries of not-quite-living and not-quite-being-dead and she'd finally found a new experience, something she could say she'd never felt before. Nix supposed that was something, at least. Centuries of the same old songs repeated, of feasts that ended only to begin again, of one life bleeding into the next with no real progression. Centuries of nothing ever really changing...and maybe this was it. Maybe she could stop now.

Nix still felt the instinct of survival as acutely as she ever had as a human, and the thought was contrary to everything in her being begging for another day as if she hadn't seen a hundred thousand of them already.

Nix wondered if this was what Cirrik had been thinking in his final moments as she watched him burn. Knowing him, he'd say it was romantic. If she was lying to herself, it almost was.

The room went dark and everything shifted in Rachel's perception.

The glow of the blue sphere and the candlelight disappeared and they were falling, the dark borderlands of Rachel's mind pulling them both down until there was nothing else.

Silence permeated the room but for a soft sniffling.

Nix glanced up, but she couldn't see anything. She looked down at her hands, but they were small, so small, and it was so chokingly dark she could barely make them out. Something brushed against her forehead when she moved. She reached up, tiny hand brushing over fabric. An old, musty smell wrapped around her.

It was so quiet, she could hear her breath hitching. Her cheeks were wet, eyes tight and slightly swollen. Under her breath she was whispering, "Mommy, Mommy, Mommy..." over and over and over. Her arms wrapped around her knees. What was this? *Where* was this?

She was breathing so fast her cheeks were numb and her chest ached. Her heart raced with fear. It was so dark. So very, very dark. And with her eyes open in that blackness, she could see monsters staring back at her, shifting through the shadows. She knew they were waiting for her in the dark, and here everything was darkness.

Nix couldn't hear Rachel anymore but she could still *feel* her. Nix didn't recognize their body. She was small and she felt even smaller. She was lost in here, in a corner, walls closing in all around her.

Something moved above her, she was sure of it, and Rachel gasped, clinging tighter to her knees. She was locked in. Nix didn't know how she knew this, but she knew it was true. Locked in and waiting to be let out, knowing it wouldn't be until morning or later and not knowing how much time had passed. Here, there was no time, only black and cold, and Nix recognized it now, this place, this feeling—the darkness she'd been scratching at in Rachel's mind had finally broken open, sucked them both in.

Rachel was bad and bad girls deserved punishment, but she was so scared she couldn't stop shaking. She wanted light so badly that she cried. She couldn't control the tears. It was too dark, too cold. All she wanted was light, light, *light*, just a little, just a flicker of it to frighten off the monsters.

She imagined the fireplace downstairs where a fire would be burning, concentrating on the image until she could feel the glow of warmth on her face. The longer she thought about it, the warmer she got, until she was so hot that sweat poured off her.

She coughed, opening her eyes without having noticed she'd closed them, and now she could make out a sliver of flickering light underneath the closet door.

Her fingertips tingled and she coughed again.

Smoke slipped in through the cracks and she wished she was like the smoke, able to sneak in and out if she pleased.

Then Mommy and Daddy screamed and screamed and screamed, and Rachel had never felt so light and warm and safe.

The basement snapped back into focus, and with it, the agony. Underneath the searing pain and the screams torn from Rachel's raw throat, Nix felt something change.

The darkness of Rachel's fear slipped away like smoke, and in its place was another kind of darkness, one that belonged to her, one that she belonged to.

Rachel's fingertips tingled, and all that beautiful pain Nix had so lovingly tended during their time together burst free. It was in that moment Nix realized why Rachel had brought with her a stirring of familiarity in Nix when they met. *Abyssus Abyssum Invocat.*

The candles on the workbench exploded.

Val jumped back, concentration faltering in favor of extinguishing the fire burning her left leg. Danny collapsed.

Flames leapt like ravenous wolves up the walls, across the floor, over the roof, spreading, swelling, *consuming*. The fire erupted so quickly, the smoke came like an afterthought.

"There was darkness in you long before I got here," Nix acknowledged fondly.

It wasn't the whole world Danny had been trying to protect Rachel from after all. What he'd tried to protect her from was the one thing he couldn't: herself.

She heard Danny's voice, words lost in the chaos, but with the last snapping syllable Nix felt the invisible straps binding her abruptly fall away.

Nix fell out of the chair, ripping out the gag and stumbling toward the basement steps.

Her coordination was lacking and so was her speed, but she pushed herself forward, closing in on the stairs. If she could just make it out of the basement, a little farther, just—

The stairs jerked out of view and she felt her back hit the concrete wall.

Val walked toward her, not stopping until her face was mere inches away. Her hand wrapped tight around Rachel's neck.

The blue glow leaked through Val's jacket pocket. The fire raged. In her peripheral vision, Nix could see Danny crawling toward Elliot, wrapping an arm around him.

Val leaned in, blocking Nix's view of the charming family scene. The smoke stung Rachel's eyes and obscured Val's face and a jolt of recognition hit Nix as she remembered watching a priest burn at a spring festival so long ago. Nix had looked through the smoke and met the eyes of an old woman humming under her breath, watching Nix through the flames. The same darkness resided behind the old woman's eyes as those now staring into hers. Val was right. Their fates had been intertwined much longer than Nix had imagined.

Val's breath reeked of stale cigarettes and sulfur as she asked with narrowed eyes, "What *are* you?"

Calmly, Rachel said, *"We need to kill her."*

Nix couldn't agree more.

Val's grip loosened as the bright blue light of the sphere splashed across her face. Nix held the liberated object tightly in Rachel's hand, then they threw it to the ground.

The glass shattered.

Val gasped, stumbling back as smoke burst from the broken orb. Thick black and white plumes spiraled at their feet, chaining Val into the center of a maelstrom.

"No!" Val commanded as it climbed up her calves, its form shifting and malleable, thicker than the smoke from the fire. "No, stop!"

Nix and Rachel stared as the smoke twisted up Val's host body like a rope before suddenly wrenching in different directions.

Val howled as her bones cracked. Her spine snapped sideways, twisting her torso one way and the rest of her another.

The smoke pushed down her throat, piercing into her through her ears and nostrils, until her eyes rolled back in her skull and her screams turned to choking gargles.

Nix wasn't even breathing.

The smoke pulled back abruptly and Val crumpled to the ground.

The plumes of smoke rose up, bursting through the small windows of the basement. A rush of air followed as the fire sucked it in.

Just as she was wondering if it was over, a single wisp of black smoke wrapped around her legs. Nix tensed, waiting to be ripped apart, but the smoke passed like a gentle caress and followed the others out the window. Its touch had been familiar.

Nix smiled, dizzy with exhaustion. She collapsed against the wall, vision shifting in and out of focus. The near-exorcism had taken a lot out of Nix, but Rachel felt strong, powerful, unrestrained.

Rachel whispered with her own lips, and Nix almost didn't recognize the Latin that Kevin had used before.

A sharp pain hit her stomach and Nix fell forward, gagging, choking, spitting up blood. She gasped for air, but none came.

Rachel's palms hit the gritty floor and the sensation was distant. Her stringy, sweat-soaked hair hung in her eyes, but it wasn't Nix's hair anymore. Her stomach clenched painfully as she heaved, and it was Rachel's stomach now. Her eyes stung from the smoke, but they were Rachel's eyes, and suddenly Nix was spiraling.

The world blurred. Sounds culminated into a mass of indistinct white noise.

When she slid between slack, wet lips, she felt the damage—broken tibia, shattered collarbone, fractured skull, severed spine. Nix dizzily tried to orient herself, eyes open but unblinking.

Everything was above her. She was below everything. On the ground. Lying on the ground in an empty, broken body.

The fire gnawed at her legs, crawling up and licking at her flesh, but she could barely twitch a finger.

Three blurs stood over her.

Danny held Elliot up with one arm. Elliot's shirt was pulled over his mouth, his eyes, if he still had any, too dark to see.

Rachel stood tall beside them, disheveled but unbothered by the smoke or the heat or the flames that closed in around them.

"We've gotta get outta here before the whole goddamn place burns down!" Danny shouted.

Rasping, Elliot said, "What about...the demon?"

Rachel's skin was peeling off, her body wrecked and oozing. She probably wouldn't last the week in this state, but she glanced down at Nix with a look of disdain that Nix knew well, a predator standing over her prey. "Let it burn."

Rachel turned away, her broken little family close behind her, the flames and smoke bending around them curiously.

Nix's new eyes fell shut, and as the fire burned, Nix burned with it.

Chapter 31

People were staring. Not the subtle, pretending-not-to-stare kind of staring, either. No, this was full-on gawking. It was actually rather rude, in Nix's opinion, but it wasn't unexpected. And she was also technically naked and walking down Main Street, so there was that.

With every step, every movement of every joint, bits of her were flaking off and fluttering to the ground. The flesh was red and raw and throbbing where the charred pieces fell away. Behind her, a long trail of ash marked her progress.

A middle-aged man dropped a bagful of groceries to the sidewalk, a glass jar inside shattering on the concrete, apples rolling into the gutters as the man stood perfectly still and watched her walk by him. Shop doors slammed all down the street, little bells chiming cheerfully as their owners huddled together behind the panes of glass, as if a locked door could keep them safe.

She'd considered commandeering one of these impolite gawkers for a brief reprieve to speed the process up a bit, but it wouldn't make a difference now. Her destination was only steps away. And even torn to shreds, like the former realtor from Ohio, most humans were still wearable.

The light touch of the January sun felt like searing flames, but there was nothing left of her to burn. Nix kept moving, slow and steady, almost there.

She walked through the wrought iron trellis leading into the park. A nice day like this, the place was packed with families and tourists, but even the yappy-looking dogs on leashes cowered behind their silent masters. It was so quiet, she could hear the wind rustle through the half-dead bushes and old oak trees; the calm before the storm.

And then the world kicked back into gear. Shock turned to panic. Little kiddies scattered. A young mother screamed, pulling her son tight to her chest and abandoning the stroller as she bolted.

In seconds, the place was empty.

Almost empty.

Nix's singed Glasgow smile split wide open as she made her way to the swing set. As she sat, her legs and back cracked and oozed. Her broken spine shifted, bone piercing through the skin in sharp white contrast to the charred black and ash gray.

A single cloud eclipsed the sun, casting a shadow over them. Buzzards circled quietly overhead.

Working her jaw and wetting her torn lips as best she could with a dessert-dry tongue, Nix turned her attention to her sweet little hostess sitting on the adjacent swing. Her flaxen hair hung in twin braids, pinned in place with pink Minnie Mouse barrettes.

"I'm home," Nix announced, the words little more than a breath of stirred air between them, what with her trachea and face mostly burnt up.

Baby blues open wide and knowing, Callie stared up at her and smiled. Kid was a natural, a real charmer.

Nix held out her hand and Callie took it, like she'd been waiting here this whole time, and maybe she had been. It wasn't a perfect fit—it never was—but it was close enough.

ABOUT THE AUTHOR

J.J. Reichenbach lives in California with two affectionate hellhounds and bookcases full of nightmares. To keep up with future releases from J.J. Reichenbach, follow the author on Twitter @jjreichenbach. To give feedback to the author, please leave a review or feel free to contact the author personally at j.j.reichenbach@gmail.com.

Dedication

To Stephen and Pamela. Love you to the moon and back.

Acknowledgments

Special thanks to Mags, AprilVolition, and V. Reed for their endless encouragement, support, and friendship.

COPYRIGHT AND LICENSING

COPYRIGHT 2014 BY BROKEN LEVEE PUBLISHING

All rights reserved. This book or any portion thereof may not be reproduced or used in any manner without the express permission of the author or publisher. Requirement of author or publisher consent is not, however, necessary for the use of brief quotations in critical articles or reviews.

DISCLAIMER

This is a work of fiction. Names, places, characters, and events are either fictitious or used in a fictitious manner. Any resemblance to actual persons, living or dead, is purely coincidental.

LICENSE NOTES

This book is licensed for your personal enjoyment only. It may not be resold or given away. If you enjoyed this author's work and would like to share this book with friends, please encourage them to purchase an additional copy for their own use. Thank you for respecting the hard work of this author.

Made in the USA
Charleston, SC
07 May 2014